Sixty - Six

Broadway Books
New York

Sixty-Six

A NOVEL

BARRY LEVINSON

PRINTED IN THE UNITED STATES OF AMERICA

BROADWAY BOOKS and its logo, a letter B bisected on the diagonal, are trademarks of Random House, Inc.

Visit our website at www.broadwaybooks.com

First edition published 2003

This book is a work of fiction. Names, characters, businesses, organizations, places, events, and incidents either are the product of the author's imagination or are used fictitiously. Any resemblance to actual persons, living or dead, events, or locales is entirely coincidental.

Grateful acknowledgment is made to the following for permission to reprint previously published material: *The Crack-up* by F. Scott Fitzgerald, copyright ©1945 by New Directions Publishing Corp. Reprinted by permission of New Directions Publishing Corp.

"Anything Goes," by Cole Porter, copyright © 1934 (Renewed) Warner Bros. Inc. All Rights Reserved. Used by Permission, Warner Bros. Publications U.S. Inc., Miami, FL 33014.

"Eve of Destruction," by P. F. Sloan, copyright © 1965 Universal-MCA Music Publishing, Inc. All Rights Reserved. Used by permission.

"Ballad of a Thin Man," by Bob Dylan, copyright © 1965 by Warner Bros. Inc. Copyright renewed 1993 by Special Rider Music. All Rights Reserved. International copyright secured. Reprinted by permission.

Library of Congress Cataloging-in-Publication Data
Levinson, Barry.
Sixty-six : a novel / Barry Levinson.—1st ed.
p. cm.
1. Young men—Fiction. 2. Male friendship—Fiction. 3. Baltimore (Md.)—Fiction. 4. Vietnamese Conflict, 1961–1975—Maryland—Fiction. I. Title: 66. II. Title.

PS3562.E9213S59 2003
813'.6—dc21
2003049600

ISBN 0-7679-1533-X

10 9 8 7 6 5 4 3 2 1

In memory of Vi and Irv

A C K N O W L E D G M E N T S

To the Baltimore guys
who have provided friendship and inspiration.

Sixty-Six

"If I knew things would no longer be, I would have tried to remember better."

My grandfather said that. I was young, maybe five or six at the time, and I thought, What's to remember? At that age, memories are quickly recalled, always at your fingertips.

Now, years later, I realize that what he was saying is that it's not just that we forget, but that fragments live in our minds—our lives are turned into disconnected bits and pieces. We desperately want more, but there's no way to fill in the blanks . . . the gaps. Our past is not unlike the ruins of some ancient civilization: a piece of pottery, a pattern, something written on a wall. But there are no archaeologists of the mind—not that we are necessarily important enough to explore. We are just people passing through here for a moment, then gone.

The strange thing is, it seems to be the insignificant moments that stand out. Of course we remember marriages and births and deaths—they're stored and recalled, laughed and cried over. But more often than not, the moments that remain—the very ones you think you should forget—have little consequence and no revelatory insights. These are frivolous moments, stand-alone moments that have no beginning, middle, or end. Moments that you can't explore. They're the ones that haunt you.

I have one that comes back to me constantly: I am eleven years old, sitting on a sidewalk early one summer's eve. A car starts down the street. I close my eyes and listen very carefully to the sound of the engine. From that sound alone I try to guess what type of car it is. I can hear it to this day, the gentle chugging, the smooth rhythm, the ever so harsh grinding as the gears shift. I am about to guess the name of the car and then there is a gap. I can't remember what the guess was. I can recall the fading light behind my neighbor's house as the sun was beginning to set, but the object of that game—naming the car with my eyes closed—remains elusive. Nothing I will ever do for the rest of my lifetime will help me recall that mystery car. Nothing. And, of course, it's insignificant anyway. Selective memory for no apparent reason. Sometimes I think my memory bank is determined by someone sitting somewhere hitting the erase button periodically saying: "This is not important . . . This is . . . This is not important . . . This is . . ." My very existence is being edited. And the worst part about it is that the editor is wrong most of the time. So the times that should have shaped my life have nearly ceased to exist.

Replaced by gaps.

And moments.

Another moment: I was thirteen years old, coming back from the auto show with my friend Neil. We sat on the streetcar and talked about the new 1955 Chrysler Imperial. For taillights, it had these little bulbs, surrounded by chrome that stuck up on the rear fenders. We'd never seen anything like it and were very impressed.

"You think they added the lamps on the fenders or you think that was the original idea?" Neil was definitely thinking this concept through as we continued our ride through the streets of Baltimore.

I recall noticing a sign on the crowded streetcar which read *KEEP ARMS INSIDE AND NO SPITTING*. I could understand the need to keep your arms inside, that would certainly make sense, but I'm not sure why the need for the "no spitting" part of the sign. I'd never seen anyone ever spit on a streetcar or even wanting to spit but stopping because of the "no spitting" reminder. I never heard anyone say, "I'm in such a mood to spit, it's a shame they have that sign."

Neil continued to stare out the streetcar window as we headed up Liberty Heights. Then I said, "They came up with the design and they liked the way it looked. You know, kind of sleek and all. But they made one mistake. They forgot there was no room to put the taillights—"

Neil interrupted, "What do you mean there was no room for the taillights?"

"They added them on the top. They came up with that idea because they couldn't figure out how to put them into that sleek look."

Neil thought about my theory. Squinting, he shook his head. "How can it be a last-minute addition?" he asked.

"Because you can see that they just added it on. You've never seen any other car that just had bulbs sticking up at the back."

I remember, as I said that, the whole streetcar began to shake, because we were crossing one of those junctions with the tracks going four different ways. And I remember it was getting dark outside—it was sometime during the late fall. Then, nothing. It doesn't go anywhere else from there.

There are no dark secrets, no great revelations to be made from this. That much I know. I won't wake up one night in a cold sweat and remember that a Chrysler Imperial had run over my bike, destroying my childhood innocence. There are no great answers forthcoming—it's not a riddle to be solved or a message to be decoded. There is no reason for the Chrysler conversation to still exist in my mind. I never knew anyone who had a Chrysler Imperial. I never even wanted a Chrysler Imperial. Nothing eventful happened on that streetcar ride. It was not an important auto show. But I can recall it all as if it happened yesterday. I can't, however, remember getting off the streetcar. I don't remember where I went. I have no memories of any other conversations that may have taken place during that day. There's only that one brief moment. What I wouldn't give to be able to start that moment in my life again, then get off the streetcar and continue the conversation, so I could make some sense out of it. But maybe there is no sense to be made from such moments. Maybe memories are just random and the question of why that Chrysler remains in my mind can never be explained.

A recent revelation occurred; frightening at first, but then logical and ultimately satisfying. The reality is, some of my memories aren't even mine. They've become intertwined with the memories of people close to me, and so my life isn't a singular recollection but rather that of a collective; a group memory. As stories are passed back and forth and built upon, events and experiences are caught in a blender of time, diced and chopped and fragmented into moments—and my search to clarify those moments, to give them meaning, has become endless.

Only one thing is for certain: it's all just life. For better or worse, that's it.

And always there are gaps.

One

Neil lived up the street from me, from the time we used to live in the old neighborhood—with row houses that went on for miles, to the end of the horizon—and then even after we moved to the new neighborhood, where there were three-story wood homes covered in shingle, and front lawns with hedges, and big trees that seemed to stretch on forever.

My first awareness—my first memory of Neil—was somewhere around the age of three. I had cut the index finger on my left hand very badly, and it was taped up in an elaborate bandage. Neil had cut the index finger on his right hand, and it too was taped in a very large bandage. My cut was vertical and ran the length of my finger. His was horizontal and cut into the bone. We were lucky in one respect—I was right-handed and he was left-handed. So there we were, two three-year-olds who liked to duel, using our bandaged fingers as swords. On occasion, if I blocked Neil's finger thrusts too strenuously, I felt a little bit of a stinging sensation that ran down the whole length of my arm and straight up to my brain.

We moved to suburbia when I was six. There, we lived almost parallel to one another, separated by one block. I would run out my front door, down the steps, across the front walkway, jump across the evergreen bush, across the street through the neighbor's front yard, zigzag around the back of their garage, watching out for the clothesline, through the alley, through the back of another house, around the front, across Main Avenue, up Neil's walk and then finally his brick steps. It was about a minute and thirty seconds, depending on ground conditions. Sometimes, if it rained, the little puddles that I had to sidestep slowed me down.

Neil was six weeks older than me. Those weeks separated us the most in our early lives—he was able to start the first grade in February, and I had to wait until the following September. Because of that, we never attended the same class. He started junior high and high school before I did, and then, because of those six weeks, ultimately he was drafted for Vietnam and I was not. Six little weeks.

Neil and I saw each other almost every day for at least sixteen years. Even when we were sick, we still found a way to play together. We both came down with the flu one time and played tic-tac-toe over the telephone. We each had a tic-tac-toe grid with numbered boxes—upper left was a 1, upper middle a 2, upper right a 3, middle left a 4, and so on.

As soon as our mothers were out the door, we got on the phone and the games began.

"O on 6."

"X on 3."

"O on 9."

My mother had a fit when she came home later that day. She was trying to call the house and couldn't get through for four hours.

"How could you tie up the line like that?"

Logic was on my side. "It's free, Ma. They don't charge to call a block."

"Someone could have been run over or something and I'd never have got through. Tic-tac-toe on the phone! How high is your fever?"

"I don't know. I'm winning 138 games to 96."

"Get the thermometer."

Then there's a gap.

I can't remember how long the flu lasted; I don't know whether we ever played tic-tac-toe on the phone again.

I do remember that, in school, I always wanted to write "5/5/55" at the top of my paper. The entire spring, I looked forward to May 5, 1955, and writing "5/5/55." But I never did. I got sick and missed school that day. I actually tried to hide the fact that I was sick. I got dressed, thinking 5/5/55 the whole time. I came down to have breakfast, and knew I had a fever. I even started shaking at the table the way you do when your temperature gets high. I tried to make as if I was just cold, but my grandmother immediately knew something was wrong. I saw the hand reaching out to feel my forehead. I tried to block her, but I couldn't. Then I heard the words, those terrible words: "Oh my God, he's burning up." She looked at my mother. "He's burning up."

I could see 5/5/55 slipping away. I put my own hand to my forehead and said, "No, your hands are cold," but I could see my mother wasn't buying it.

She stared at me across the table. "His eyes look glassy."

That's when you know you're in trouble, when they talk about you in the third person. "His eyes." Goodbye 5/5/55.

Freddie Krauss got blown up at the gas station after school on 5/5/55. Freddie was three years younger than me. What happened was, some gas main exploded up at the Texaco station, which was almost three blocks from my house, and Freddie was the first to go and investigate. He quickly wormed his way through the confused spectators and went right up to the scene of the blast. There was a secondary explosion, and Freddie was blown into the air and suffered a fractured skull. He survived, with just a little scar by his temple where they put in a metal plate. The explosion was so powerful that the shock waves shook my house three blocks away, on 5/5/55.

They say it was a miracle that Freddie survived the blast. Some people said he was actually blown as high as the Texaco station sign. He came down over twenty feet from the actual spot of the explosion. There'll always be a point of contention whether he was blown as high as that sign or not. You couldn't see him clearly, they said, because there was so much dust in the air. But the pages from his notebook came floating down all over the street.

He was just a little crazy after that, but always lucky. He got a Corvette when he was in high school and went racing on Route 29, at over 120 miles an hour, when he lost control of the car. There was nothing left of his Corvette, just little fiberglass pieces sprinkled across the countryside. Paramedic trucks were all over the highway, lights flashing. A low fog hung over the wooded area where the car disintegrated. It looked like the scene of a tragedy. But Freddie stepped out of the night mist with nothing more than a broken finger. His pinkie finger. He held it up to show everyone. Freddie immediately became a legend. He was the Evel Knievel of our neighborhood, the Houdini of disaster.

There was always a sense of awe when you spoke about Freddie. When I heard the story of him being blown up, I tried to visualize it in my mind. Was it like someone being shot out of a cannon? The image I always had was Freddie just floating over the Texaco station sign like some kind of kite. Maybe that's because they said he had a red windbreaker on. Then I wondered how long he was in the air. How long can you *stay* in the air? Of course, I had a high temperature, and when you have that kind of fever, you have a tendency to hallucinate anyway. I remember those youthful fevers and that dreamlike feeling that went along

with them. And I remember that when you had high tempera-
tures back then, for some reason you were always getting baths in
alcohol. Not that you actually got into a bathtub, but alcohol was
applied to your body . . . or was it vinegar?

So those are my memories of my childhood with Neil and
Freddie Krauss . . . and 5/5/55. Most of all, I remember that
5/5/55 was an extremely depressing day, because I knew that on
6/6/66 I would no longer be in school, and therefore that date
wouldn't have nearly the same significance.

Two

When 6/6/66 came along, I *was* still in school—in my next to last year at the University of Baltimore. We didn't have an exam, so there was no need to write "6/6/66" on a piece of paper for any reason. But while the date passed without being documented, I couldn't have been more wrong about its lack of significance. It was, in fact, the most influential day in my first twenty-four years of life. It was on that day that I decided I wasn't going to complete law school. I was not going to be a lawyer.

The evening of 6/6/66 I talked about my decision with the guys at the Hilltop Diner. Ben leaned in when I told him the news, his eyes wide open, checking to see if I was bullshitting him.

I was waiting for him to start a riff on me, put me down, give me some hard knocks—Ben Kallin was famous for that. When you opened yourself up to Ben you always had to take your life in your hands. He'd find whatever weakness was there and belittle you unmercifully. And yet he was a great friend. He would say the most offensive things and somehow you could never get mad at him. He'd flash that smile, pull on his lower eyelid, and say, "You're me." None of us knew where the phrase came from. He'd made it up. But we all knew what it meant. It was a reference to the fact that he was the best. And he was right. For much of my youth he was the coolest, the most hip, the guy we most admired. He was *the* guy.

From ages fourteen to twenty, his glory years, Ben ruled. Girls found him incredibly attractive. He was voted best-looking in a high school fraternity contest. He was a good athlete and there was always talk that he was getting a scholarship to the University of Maryland in lacrosse, although that never happened. Ben was all about confidence and sarcasm, and during those glory years he was, without question, proclaimed "King of the Teenagers."

As he sat across from me in the booth, he was telling me some of the details of his upcoming wedding plans. At the end of the summer he was getting married to Janet Rawlings, a fairly attractive redhead who was in my senior year at Forest Park High School. I never knew her that well. She was very big in the drama department, turning up in all the school plays. I'm not sure if she was any good or not because she always seemed to be stuck with the role of playing a seventy-five-year-old woman. She would wear a fake gray wig and totter around with a cane, speaking with some kind of screechy voice: "Nooooow boooys . . ." This much I know to be true, no teenager can play a seventy-five-year-old woman. None. Ever. And now Janet was about to play the part of Mrs. Ben Kallin.

No matter how many times Ben had talked about "the big day," it was hard to get used to the idea that he was about to become a married man.

"Not a minute too soon, Bobby," he told me right after he'd announced his engagement. "Two years from now I'm gonna be bald and fat. My fucking grandfather. I saw a picture of him—he was bald at seventeen, I think. Fucking hereditary . . . you can't beat it."

Then he gave me his secret for finding a prospective wife.

"Watch the mother, look at her—if she's fat, that's what you're going to end up with, no matter what the hell she looks like now, no matter how cute, how sexy. Mother's fat, daughter will be fat. Marsha Cohn, sell your soul for her, a goddess—die for her—but here's the warning: Look at the mother."

The night drifted on at the Diner, that summer night of 1966, as it always did. The place was our home. More of a sanctuary really, although none of us recognized it at the time. To us, it was just somewhere to hang out, to relax and bullshit the nights away. The neon sign—lonely, still, but always inviting—was a constant. Neither rain nor sleet . . . it was always open.

Turko and Eggy—the Abbott and Costello of our group—joined us. Turko, upon hearing the news that I'd dropped out of law school, said, "One year to go. Don't be an asshole."

"I can't go on. It's bullshit."

Eggy jumped in with, "Then why did you go? Why did you go in the first place?"

"Because I saw Paul Newman in *The Young Philadelphians*. He had great suits, got the girl, seemed hip—he was an income tax lawyer in the movie. I figured I could be him."

The realization that I was trying to be a character in a film was frightening to me. My fantasy was that I would walk into my law office, sit at my desk, and be a lawyer. But then what? What was the next moment after that? What would I be doing all day long? The movie didn't have any scenes where Paul Newman was actually working on income tax law in his office. But I was going to spend the rest of my life behind that desk, doing what? Saying what?

I didn't really like the fact that I was so impressionable, too caught up in images that weren't mine. But I think I had always been that way, since childhood.

When I was three years old, I used to stare at the pictures in

Look magazine. I once turned to a page and saw a man and a woman sitting on a park bench on a nice sunny day. They were both smiling. I would stare at that picture for the longest time until I could make the man and woman come alive. Then I would see them actually get up and walk away from the bench; leave the park. But once they left, I couldn't visualize it any further. My young imagination couldn't take it beyond that. Where the couple went, why they were smiling, why they came to the park in the first place, all bewildered me. Too many unanswered questions. But to me photos were never just frozen images on the pages of *Look* or *Life* or *Collier's* magazines—they were all part of a game I was beginning to play. Little stories I was beginning to invent.

Unfortunately, I didn't ask any of those questions about being an income tax lawyer. I simply took Paul Newman's occupation at face value. It never even occurred to me that I needed to study accounting, so the first time I walked into that class I realized I was in trouble. There were little boxes where you had to write the debits and credits. Every student had sharp pencils and liked math. Paul Newman never did any math in *The Young Philadelphians*. I was in shock—the foundation of my so-called reality was shaken to the very core. I was heading for a future I had no interest in. I was living a lie from my first day at law school—I was trying to be an actor in a movie, but all the scenes were different. My life wasn't like that.

It was on 6/6/66 that I finally took stock of myself—a moment of introspection in a short life without purpose. I knew that I needed to do something. I was willing to move on, but to what?

Ben said, "First time Eggy saw Howdy Doody, he wanted to be a fucking puppet." Then in the next breath added, "You could always go to work in your father's carpet store."

"Yeah, talk about the features of wool versus synthetic fibers," I replied.

Turko laughed, and of course that meant that Eggy laughed as well. The two of them seemed to be joined at the hip, ever since the third grade at Liberty School 64. Turko saw Eggy racing on the playground and quickly recognized the potential in this fleet-footed runner. He began making bets and bringing Eggy in for a cut of the profits. Turko acted as agent/manager, and race after race, Eggy took on challengers. The money would pour in—fifty to sixty cents in a good week—and the duo's good fortune continued until they started the seventh grade at Garrison Junior High. At this time, Eggy's reputation was wildly known: the Albino Speedster . . . the Eldorado Avenue Rocket. Turko was Colonel Parker to his same-age phenom.

However, the streak of fifty-three consecutive wins came crashing to a halt in a humiliating loss against Dale Laws on the lawn of the junior high school.

No one knew of Laws. He was an unassuming, quiet, studious kid and wore wire-rimmed glasses. Turko thought this was the perfect warm-up race before the big one he had planned. Eggy was going to run against four eighth graders. A victory by Eggy could generate as much as ten dollars. It was the buzz throughout the school. Many of the upper-class boys had heard of Eggy's reputation but few had seen him run, so Turko had planned this tune-up race against Dale Laws just to whet their appetites . . . to generate some betting action.

He brought Eggy out of the school building as if he had Man o' War in tow. Eggy was cocky. His white, albino-looking hair seemed to match his skin as he did a dance around the starting line, showing off a little bit for the girls, reveling in the fame he had held since the third grade. He put on a pair of purple and yellow wool gloves that his mother had knitted, sliding them over his fingers as if they were made of the finest silk.

Dale Laws looked over at Eggy as if afraid to join in the race.

Laws wore baggy corduroy pants, the kind where one leg rubbed against the other. The waist was too big for him so he tied it up with a leather belt pulled tight, his sweater tucked into his pants to add some bulk.

Turko worked the crowd like a hotshot promoter, picking up extra nickels and dimes. He even bought a ten-cent ring at Ben Franklin's five-and-dime and wore it on his pinkie to give him a little more class.

Eggy kneeled into a running stance. Dale Laws stood upright and looked at the crowd nervously as Turko confidently yelled out: "Three, two, one . . . go!" Then, as soon as the race began, it was clear that it was over. Dale Laws pulled away so quickly from Eggy that the crowd was shocked. And just like that, Eggy stopped running. He knew he was beat, and he gave up. He was embarrassed. The surprise of someone pulling away from him was such a jolt to his system, he just stopped, lost and confused. He had never seen a runner in front of him before, never mind one who was leaving him in the dust. He stood on the school grounds long after the crowd had left, Turko by his side. The only one by his side.

That was the day Eggy's running years came to an end. The Albino Speedster would no longer be heard from again. It was also the last of the heady days for Turko. They both receded into the crowd as the school year continued, but in spite of this big setback in their lives, the two remained inseparable. They were one another's best company and they were great company for me and Neil and Ben, too. There was never any situation in which the two of them didn't find the humor. And it was impossible to slip a joke through without one or the other knowing the punch line.

They complemented each other as night did day. As white as Eggy's hair was, that's how dark Turko's was; he also contrasted Eggy's fair complexion with a very dark olive skin. Eggy was thin and Turko was stocky. They seemed to have the same taste and agreed on almost everything . . . except girls. The idea of making a commitment to a girl was unheard of as far as Eggy was concerned, but Turko could fall in love at the drop of a hat. Although he seldom found a hat that fit.

Ben continued to put me down about my future prospects. "Work in the carpet store, marry Annie, have a vacation once a year, get old, and just before you drop dead, think of Marsha Cohn in those blue shorts, her hair blowing in that light breeze . . . and die."

"Thanks," I said. "That's extremely helpful."

Then, out of nowhere, Eggy asked, "You ever ball Annie when she's wearing that nurse's uniform? Is that hot or what?"

"Yes, it is, and I can't tell you how thrilled I am that you're jerking off to my girlfriend," I said.

A night at the Diner could go on for four or five hours and cover every subject imaginable. The discussion of Annie's nurse's uniform went on for only ten minutes more. And that's about all I remember. I was at the crossroads of my life, but nothing else stands out in my mind about that night. I'm sure it was like every other night, which meant that we talked into the early morning hours and the topics tumbled out, one after another— our words laced with humor and sarcasm. We were constantly searching for the absurdity in our lives—in life in general—but seldom with much clarity, and never with any vision or sense of the future.

The future held little interest for us back then. It was the past that appealed to us. It was the past that defined us. We were arrogant enough to ignore the future. And young enough to be certain that the present was something that would never change.

Three

I stood in front of a mirror putting on my cuff links, dressed in a tuxedo for Ben and Janet's wedding. I danced to the music that was playing and stared at myself in the mirror. Then I heard that voice.

"Well, aren't you taken with yourself?"

Annie stood in the doorway to my bedroom, dressed in her formal gown. I danced toward her, full of excitement, about to spring the news—revealing the direction my life was about to take. I had done it in secrecy, without any real thought or much soul-searching, but it was the most substantial idea I had ever had. Moving as fluidly and rhythmically as any bad dancer could move, my words flowed.

"Got a job at the TV station, WMAR, training program, fifty bucks a week. Slave wages."

Annie was visibly shaken. "Oh God. You didn't?"

I continued to dance and did a spin. "TV."

"You gave up law school for a fifty-dollar-a-week training program?"

I danced around her. "TV," I said again, as if that explained everything. And I guess, in my mind, it did.

I was inches from her mouth, "T . . . V . . ." I said it as slowly as possible and as seductively as I could manage.

She quietly replied, "You're an F . . . O . . . O . . . L." She was much, much sexier in her use of the letters than I was.

I was almost to her lips. "Give me a little more tongue on the L."

I held her and danced around the room as the music continued to play.

"I hate you," she said, "or I want to."

"Your problem is, you don't say it with enough conviction."

She studied my face with those big brown eyes, still only inches away from me, and said very quietly once again, "I hate you." I felt as strongly for her then as the time I tried to see her through the haze of anesthesia in a recovery room.

I had been in and out of the hospital with intestinal problems since I was a kid. Stomach pains, the type that double you up, were common and a part of my daily life. So were vomiting and diarrhea—all the unattractive words.

"How are your stools?" the doctor would ask.

"Stools?"

"Watery? Firm?"

These were things I did not want to discuss. With anyone. Ever.

I missed half of the fifth grade, half of the sixth grade, half of the seventh grade, and half of the ninth grade because of spells in the hospital. Then the illness suddenly stopped.

In the hospital I faced my first experience with death. Admitted late one evening by my parents, who were concerned by the severity of my stomach pains, I found out that I would have to spend the night in a general ward—no semiprivate rooms were available until the following morning. My parents didn't want to leave me in the ward overnight, but reluctantly, at the urging of an admitting nurse, they agreed.

So I spent the night there, three cotton curtains separating me from the rest of the patients. As the curtains were being drawn,

I got a glimpse of a sickly, pale old man in the next bed who was being administered to by several nurses and a doctor. I didn't sleep much that night, listening to the man's moans and groans, his heavy breathing and his quiet calls for the nurse. At some point, I did doze off, and when I awoke, all was quiet. I peeked through the curtain to see the old man, but his bed was empty. An attendant was washing down his plastic-covered mattress, and then quickly and efficiently the bed was remade. The man was gone. He had died while I was asleep. Twenty minutes after the bed was remade, a new patient lay there. I remember thinking that in the short time I had slept, a man had lived, then died and was replaced. But it didn't frighten me. It just seemed . . . curious.

We had to write a school paper about what we had planned for our summer vacation. From my hospital bed I wrote only this: "Immaturity protects the young from the old. Senility protects the old from the truth." I failed the paper.

Years later, I was back in the hospital with a recurrence of stomach problems that required surgery. As I lay in the recovery room, a nurse was putting a cool towel to my forehead and feeding me ice chips. Her face was a blur. I could only make out the shape of a nurse's cap, but I was deeply affected and felt an overwhelming sense of joy—a feeling of closeness I had never experienced with any female before.

"Do you know your name?" she asked.

"Bobby Shine," I mumbled.

"Do you know where you are?"

"Memorial Hospital."

I desperately tried to focus, but she remained a blur. Then, proving the theory that when one sense fails another becomes more acute, suddenly I could smell her perfume. It was intoxicating, irresistible, and before I could ask her name, I fell back into a cold deep sleep. In the days that followed, whenever a nurse entered my room, I tried to smell her, searching for my Florence Nightingale, but no such luck.

As I was leaving the hospital, I was wheeled down a hallway (they wouldn't let me walk out of the hospital even though I could), and as we passed a room, I smelled that fragrance. I told the transporter, or whatever they're called, to stop and back up. Then I looked into a patient's room and there was a nurse making the bed. It was definitely the scent that I remembered. The nurse turned to me. "How are you, Bobby?"

I was stunned to see Neil's sister. My best friend's sister, Annie Tilden. I had seen her a thousand times before. How could this be? She was two years younger and I had never paid the slightest bit of attention to her. She was Neil's little sister. Now she was also the girl of my dreams.

"I hate you," Annie said quietly as I danced with her, holding her close. Then we fell on the bed.

"You wrinkle me, you die."

"I work my way up the ladder of the TV station," I answered, "we get married . . . T . . . V . . ."

"Married?"

She was as shocked as I was. It just came out of my mouth. I couldn't stop it, not that I would have tried. Then we kissed and we wrinkled each other, and we didn't care. This was the girl I loved, and I was making decisions, taking control of my life, and it felt good.

I whispered, "Say 'fool' again. Give me that F . . . O . . . O . . . L one more time."

"If I do, we might not make it to Ben and Janet's wedding."

"I'll risk it."

She kissed me seductively and said, "I'll give you an F for now. You can't handle the whole word."

Four

"Horror and waste, waste and horror. What I might have been and done, that's lost, spent, gone, dissipated, unrecapturable . . ."

Neil's best man's speech at Ben and Janet's wedding was one for the books. Actually it was one *from* a book. It wasn't a speech at all. He recited a passage—a *long* passage—from F. Scott Fitzgerald's *The Crack-Up*. No one seemed to understand what Neil was talking about, and the murmurs began to spread through the room about ten seconds after he began speaking. It didn't take long for Janet's father to become apoplectic, and his wife seemed to be having heart palpitations, but Neil continued to recite blissfully.

". . . I need not have hurt her, nor broken myself trying to break what was unbreakable. The horror has come now, like a storm . . ."

I sat with Annie, Turko, and Eggy listening to Neil rattle on, all of us beginning to wonder if he would ever stop. Eggy was holding back his laughter, choking on it, trying desperately to keep it together.

Annie whispered to me, and suddenly everything made sense. "He started taking LSD at Ocean City this summer."

Then I saw something that for some reason I hadn't been aware of earlier. "Does it also make your brother forget his shoes?"

"What?"

I nodded for her to look at Neil's feet. As elegantly dressed as he was in his tux, he was barefoot. Sort of Huckleberry Finn by way of Dean Martin.

Neil Tilden was a warm, caring kind of guy, but even though I'd known him all my life, he always seemed to be holding back a secret. Not that he was trying to, not that he wanted to, it was just part of his demeanor. No matter how much time you spent with him, you could always spend more. He was extremely well informed—very well read—but had been thrown out of more schools than any of us could remember. He dated frequently, and no matter what girl he went with, whenever he broke up with her, they would always remain friends. Neil had no enemies, no matter how bizarre his behavior might sometimes be.

I leaned over to Turko. "No shoes."

"He didn't wear them in Ocean City. Says he doesn't need them anymore."

Eggy wasn't impressed. "Nice decision . . . carefully thought out."

Neil's voice floated over the quiet grounds of the country club. *"What if this night prefigured the night after death? What if all there-after was an eternal quiver on the edge of an abyss . . . ?"*

Suddenly, Ben was on his feet and approached Neil at the microphone.

"Let's speed this up."

Neil nodded as if he knew what that meant. Ben headed back to his chair and Neil continued.

"No choice, no road, no hope. Only the endless repetition of the sordid and the sacred, the tragic . . ."

The wedding crowd was about to turn on him, so I quickly moved to the podium.

"I'm a ghost now as the clock strikes four . . ."

I approached Neil and he nodded again, but I felt I had to go one step further, so I grabbed the microphone.

"Neil feels he would like to continue this later."

Then I handed the microphone back to him.

"Thank you, and love and peace, Ben and Janet."

The entire room burst into applause. Neil took it as a sign that they loved his recital, and none of us mentioned that it was not so, thinking: Why burst his bubble?

A bunch of us guys gathered on the terrace overlooking the pool area.

"Do you think he's on LSD now?" I asked.

We knew little of drugs at this point in our lives. Acid was just coming onto our radar screens. Our biggest exposure to the world of drugs was the astoundingly crazy old film called *Reefer Madness*, which was made sometime in the late thirties, I think. We went downtown to the Century Theatre on Lexington Street to see it. Word was getting around that it was the worst piece of shit anyone had ever seen, and because of its serious drug message it was outrageously funny. One of the film's cautionary scenes was when a guy smoked a joint, looked in the mirror, and saw that he'd turned into a werewolf. It caused the entire theater to erupt in cheers.

Later that night we took the movie apart scene by scene—a bunch of brutal critics. We knew little about "pot" and less about werewolves, but the film did provide some great Diner talk that lasted well into the night.

Turko watched as Neil headed down the steps of the terrace with a few girls in tow. "That LSD lasts seventy-two hours, something like that."

This startled Eggy. "Seventy-two hours? What the hell kind of drug is that? I'd rather take cough syrup—a couple of hours with a buzz, boom, done."

"You're a connoisseur, having made the upscale switch from sniffing glue," said Turko.

Neil moved toward the pool area. The girls were laughing as he entertained.

"I don't like hallucinatory drugs," offered Turko.

"Meaning what?" Eggy asked.

"You see things."

"What things?"

I jumped in. "Fear, anxiety, stuff like that." I'd just read an article about it in *Time* magazine.

Ben walked over as the band played a feeble version of "Moonglow." He didn't seem to be enjoying himself. I wondered if he was secretly afraid that he had made the wrong decision or if the new responsibilities of being a husband scared him in some way. But he said nothing. He just held his drink up in an imaginary toast. "The first to bite the dust."

"Well, I'll be joining you in June," I smiled.

"No."

"Yep. Next June."

All the guys were stunned, and there was a long silence, then I got a loud chorus of congrats. Eggy said something about how he liked the idea of getting laid every night, but not the rest of the crap. He then went into a dissertation on the pros and cons of marriage. Then the pros and cons of a wife versus a prostitute. In Eggy's mind, a prostitute was a better way to go. He had it all worked out. "It's cheaper in the long run, and if you find a prostitute you really like, you can keep seeing her until the passion passes. Then you move on to a new one. You can't do that with a wife without getting into some very expensive divorce settlements."

I wasn't in the mood for Eggy's twisted logic, I was feeling too caught up in my romantic future, so I turned to watch Neil, who was now in the pool swimming laps in his tuxedo. He hadn't even bothered to take off the jacket.

A crowd was gathering to watch him, so we wandered down there. Turko yelled, "The rental place needs the tux back. They didn't waterproof it." It got a mild chuckle. Then Neil came to a complete stop in the middle of the pool. He floated on the top of the water, facedown, not moving. Like a dead man. Suddenly, everyone became quiet, wondering what he was up to. Was he playing a game? Was something really wrong? Seconds passed and concern swept over the crowd.

One of the girls said, "Oh my God, I think he's dead."

Turko reassured her, "No, he's just being dramatic," but the Turk was getting nervous, just like the rest of us.

"Are you sure?" the girl said.

Turko stared at the absolutely still Neil floating on the water. "With Neil you can never be sure."

I think we were all thinking the same thing. If we jumped in wearing our tuxes and he was faking it, he would have pulled off one of the great cons. On the other hand, if he was dead, we would have watched and done nothing. The seconds passed.

"Come on, Neil," Turko mumbled under his breath.

"Do we go in with these tuxes and get him?" asked a nervous Eggy.

There were looks back and forth—a ticking clock. The ultimate prank, or did he die from some kind of overdose? This was the showdown.

One of the girls screamed, "Oh my God, he's dead." And with that, the Egg man jumped into the pool. As his body splashed water, Neil stood up.

"Ta-da!"

The girls laughed. Neil had won.

Eggy was beside himself. He grabbed Neil by the neck and

mocked strangling him to death. "You got me, you fuck . . . you son of a bitch."

"Very impressive," said Turko. "Maybe you can join the Olympic team. They need someone to do the dead man's float."

Neil swam toward the edge of the pool. "There's nothing as refreshing as a midnight swim."

"It's one thing for Eggy to go in," Turko said as he moved toward him, "but if I had jumped with this monkey suit on, you'd be doing the real dead man's float."

"Turko, you care," Neil said. Then he looked at an attractive girl who was kneeling by the edge of the pool. "You can come in, the water's just right," and with that he pulled her into the water. She screamed and was flustered for a moment, but Neil flashed that smile. "May I have the next dance?"

"I'm Gail."

"Nice meeting you, Gail."

"I liked your speech."

"I'm the voice of F. Scott Fitzgerald." Then he began to dance with her in water up to their waists. The scene should have looked absurd, ridiculous, but as was always the case with Neil, it seemed to possess some strange dignity—a certain elegance. No matter how preposterous the situation, Neil brought that kind of formality to it. It was in his bones. It seeped through his most outrageous behavior.

Eggy was intrigued by the way Gail's breasts were accentuated by the wetness of her gown. He could not get enough of it. Her gown ballooned up and she had the appearance of half girl, half jellyfish. Eggy went under the water for a more careful look at her torso. Afterward, he reported back that she had nice thighs.

Later, as the wedding reception was winding down, Ben approached me. He still seemed quiet and pensive. I finally asked if he was nervous about anything. "You kidding? This is a smile. A complete smile." And then, to show he was cool, that nobody was as cool as he was, he said, "You're me."

I fed his ego. "You're the one, Ben."

"I was royalty, don't forget that. Voted best-looking guy of all the high school fraternities. All of them. Don't forget that."

I didn't realize it at the time, but Baltimore was one of the few cities that had high school fraternities, with such names as Upsilon Lamda Phi, Mu Sigma, and Sigma Eta Delta. Ben belonged to Upsilon Lamda Phi, which was more commonly referred to as ULP.

Each year there was a big dance where the fraternities voted on the best-looking male and female, and when Ben was sixteen years old, he was crowned king. He loved the attention. He relished that crown and played the "royalty" card for all it was worth. As time passed, that night became even more important to him. We also shared in his glory. After all, the guy who was royalty was a member of our group. That meant we were cool too. The following year a guy named Alan Sklar won the crown. Ben's run was over, and we gave up the bragging rights. We seldom mentioned it anymore, we had all moved on, but for Ben it was the event of his life, and nothing since then had nearly as much meaning. Nothing topped that triumph.

One night, when we were all out in the Diner parking lot, Neil got on Ben about his royalty fixation and jokingly said, "It's a little like Halloween—when the night's over, it's time to stop wearing the costume."

Ben did not like the joke one bit. His anger erupted and he punched Neil, hitting him in the nose. Blood poured out of Neil's nostrils onto his white shirt. We expected a big fight, but before any of us could react, Neil just looked at his bloody shirt and started to laugh. He and Ben exchanged looks for a long beat, and then in the most matter-of-fact tone of voice Neil said, "You wanna get some coffee?"

"Yeah," said Ben. And that was the end of that.

If Ben had just been good-looking, he might have constantly gotten the shit kicked out of him. But his sense of humor, his ability to put guys down, his sarcastic sensibility, made him the true unchallenged "King of the Teenagers." And so his vanity was permitted.

His problem was that he wasn't a teenager anymore.

"Fuck, I'm twenty-three and fading fast . . . losing my hair, getting heavy. It's gonna be hard to knock on the ugly guys when I'm turning into a bald, fat fuck."

Ben was back to his tirade about heredity, something that was becoming more and more a part of his repertoire. "That's what Neil was talking about in that fucked-up speech."

Then he offered up that marrying Janet gave him a nice apartment, a job at her father's Cadillac dealership, and a new Caddie each year. "Furnished pad, car . . . she's a penny." Which was Ben's way of saying her family had money, and for the first time in his life he was secure.

He pulled on his lower eyelid, the signature Ben move. "You're me," he said again. No one was better than he was, he was telling me. It seemed out of place, the wrong moment, but I didn't give it that much thought. I should have, but instead I just let it go.

Later on, after the band had gone and almost everyone had left, Annie and I danced to a melody in our heads. I loved her. I said it, believed it, and for a moment in life all things were perfect.

That was on a warm evening in late September 1966. Everything was about to change.

Five

The Diner was packed late into the night of Ben's wedding—the parking lot filled with all the familiar cars. As I walked across the lot, I heard jazz coming from Berger's car. Nobody knew too much about Berger, even though he'd been hanging around in the parking lot for seven years. Turko was Alan Turk, Eggy was Edgar Steinberg, but no one really knew what Berger's full name was. He was just Berger. No one ever went to school with him, so no one knew where he lived. He was just a guy in a car in the Diner parking lot. He had a phonograph wired up in some way so he didn't have to listen to the radio and could play his favorite music, jazz. His car was littered with albums, from Miles Davis, Thelonius Monk, and John Coltrane to the more obscure Yusef Lateef.

Berger had all the attitude of a jazz musician without any of the talent. All through the night he played his jazz collection, sipped Robitussin cough medicine, and sold grass, uppers, and downers. He said little, never actually ventured inside the Diner, and seldom got out of the car. He had a slight twitch in his eye except when he was really into a piece of music.

Sitting with the guys at our regular booth, I started the night with a rehash of the Donald Crowley story.

"The best . . . the best . . . was Donald Crowley."

"You saw this? Because I know this story," Eggy jumped in.

"Donald starts the eighth grade with a hearing aid in his ear, like he'd gone deaf during the summer or something. Tells all his teachers he needs his hearing aid—having a lot of trouble hearing. But what they don't know is, he had the wire hooked up to a transistor radio."

"To do what?" Turko asked. Somehow he had never heard the tale.

"Teacher thinks he's gone deaf, but come October and the World Series is on, he's listening to the games."

The guys all laughed.

"He establishes the hearing aid from the start of the school year."

"Teachers don't have a clue he's listening to the series," added Eggy.

"So it works like a charm until, I don't remember the whole thing, but somebody hits a home run for the Yankees. It's real quiet in the classroom as we're studying something, then suddenly Donald yells, 'Okay, way to go!' "

The guys cracked up at this.

"Teacher's looking over like, What the hell's going on?"

"And that's how he got caught?" asked Turko.

"No, no, no. He didn't get caught! He bullshitted himself out of it—said he was just excited about the problem he was working on."

They laughed again. The guys always loved that story. There is a value in the retelling of some stories, I'm not sure why, but at the right time it just works—maybe like an old movie that you've seen over and over again, or a comedian's routine you've heard a thousand times. Some things just work.

Shade wandered over, all six feet four inches of him. We called him Shade because he was tall like a tree. Years ago we were out in the school playground on a hot sunny day and Ben called him over and told him to stand next to him. Shade was called Larry then, but since he provided a relief from the sun for Ben, Larry became Shade.

Now he stood before us looking like a tree wearing a Nehru jacket.

"Sure, go ahead and laugh," said Shade, having heard the guys reacting to the Crowley story. "I'm a dead man," he said. "A dead man."

I asked what was up. Shade just mumbled, "Dead man . . . I'm a dead man."

Neil added, "Death is an abstraction."

Shade came out with, "Fuck you! I got drafted. You know what I'm talking about?"

We were confused. He had a student deferment. What happened?

"Failed out this past summer," Shade admitted.

"I saw your father at the gas station," I told him. "Shade this, Shade that . . . all about you and medical school. You know, the whole puffery."

"I didn't tell him I failed out. I've been wondering what to do this whole summer, trying to figure something out, and now I've got this fucking draft notice."

"I'm glad I'm not in your shoes," Eggy offered up.

"Danny's got a doctor who can write a note to the draft board for five hundred dollars. It's a sure thing," imparted Turko.

Shade didn't believe him. He'd heard the story and said it was a bullshit number, but Turko pressed on. "He got Barts out."

He tried to make a case for it, but Shade wasn't buying into it. Eggy wanted to know what could possibly be in a note like that, but Turko said it didn't matter as long as it got you out.

"It's a bullshit note. What kind of a note can get you out of the army?" Shade asked.

The note debate went on for quite a while. At one point Neil offered up, "Maybe the note says you're dead."

Shade's face got red. "What the fuck is with you? I'm going to take a note to the draft board saying I'm dead?"

Neil smiled. "I just wanted to make sure you were paying attention."

This was typical of Neil. He seldom ever participated in the discussion, he was always outside of it. Then suddenly he would come in with some crazy line from left field.

I was looking out the window when I saw Ben crossing the parking lot, surprised that he was coming in. It was his wedding night. Later on, he told us that he just wanted to stop by and put Berger down. Berger had the hots for Janet ever since Ben once showed him a photograph of her poolside at Carlin's Park. As Ben passed his car, Berger said, "How did Janet look all dressed up in her wedding gown?" Ben smiled. "Beautiful, you would have had a hard-on." Then Berger gave Ben the ultimate twisted compliment. "You were royalty, Ben. Try not to forget that."

A few days later, while Ben was on his honeymoon, I happened to run into Berger. In our conversation, it came up that Ben had wanted to buy some grass that night. I was surprised. Ben had never done any drugs as far as I knew. But I didn't give it much thought—maybe it was a honeymoon experiment—and the conversation moved on to other topics.

When Ben came into the Diner on that wedding night, he immediately did a run on Shade—attacking his appearance. Upon hearing that what Shade was wearing was called a Nehru jacket, Ben said, "Since when was Nehru a fashion plate? Why don't you dress like Gandhi—walk around in a diaper?"

"Fuck you!" Shade said as he left, trying to figure out what to do about his draft problem.

Ben continued his riff. "Shade in a Nehru jacket. Since when does India have great taste? They still don't know you can eat a cow."

"They believe the cow is sacred," offered Neil.

"Sacred? With all due respect, all they do is piss and shit. In fact, the asshole on a cow is up too high. When they take a dump, it gets all over them."

We laughed. Ben was on a roll.

"God put that thing on earth so we could eat it, no other reason. It's worthless otherwise."

At some point I asked what the hell Ben was doing out with the guys. He answered that he and Janet didn't leave until eight o'clock in the morning and he needed a little Diner before the honeymoon.

"Very romantic," said Neil.

Ben immediately launched into an attack on Neil about his crazy speech and how he almost destroyed the whole night, but Ben seldom really got angry with Neil (except for the Diner parking lot punch) because Neil was always amused. That smile took all the bite out of Ben's comments.

After a while, he took one last sip out of Neil's coffee cup and said, "I'm off on my honeymoon."

"You make it sound as if it's some kind of a chore," I said.

There was a moment when I could see real conflict in his eyes, genuine sadness. I think everyone saw it. Then Ben said, "All that we've ever done is history. I'm married and now suddenly things are expected. I'm a husband. You know what that means?"

"We'll look it up in the dictionary," Neil joked.

"Fuck you! I'm serious. This is my first night as a husband."

I didn't say anything, thinking that Ben was going to explain more clearly what he had on his mind. But he didn't, he just repeated, "I'm a husband."

Then Neil said, "An awesome revelation . . . you're a husband. Thanks for clarifying that."

"I feel older, like I'm an adult or something, you know, like I lost something. You just wonder . . . you wonder . . . where do you go from here? You know?" But none of us really knew, and no one wanted to think that through. We were not in the wonder mode.

I broke the awkward silence and said that I knew where we were going from here. I was going to start working at a television station. Neil was going to finish law school. Turko was happy in the bail bonds business, and Eggy was perfectly content to work at Sol Kirk's selling clothes. At some point in the conversation, Ben pulled on his eyelid and said, "Too bad. You're me." He was trying to convince us that everything in his life was just the way he wanted it to be, but this time it didn't have the conviction. For the very first time, we didn't believe him.

We all split up around dawn. Neil started to recite some more F. Scott Fitzgerald, *"Silence, silence and suddenly I'm asleep—sleep, real sleep, the dear, the cherished one, the lullaby. So deep and warm the bed . . ."*

As Ben drove off with Neil, Neil continued to recite, until Ben got so pissed off he told him if he didn't stop that shit, he was going to throw him out of the car. Of course, Neil made the only choice Neil ever made, he got out of the car and continued to recite. Ben drove away and Neil walked the streets, in his bare feet and his wrinkled tux, reciting F. Scott Fitzgerald as the sun came up.

"Life was like that after all. My spirit soars in the moment of its oblivion—then down, down, deep into the pillow."

Six

It seems odd to me that when we're young we understand so little about what we are, how we are perceived, and what we really want. So few of us ever see the shape our lives will take. Some things are accidents, there's no control. Things come out of nowhere, inflict their pain; we suffer, survive, or die—the tree that meets the car on that fateful night. But it is the ordinary nature of life that surprises the most. It sneaks up on us and we never seem to see it coming. The signposts are all there but we seem illiterate, unable to read.

I certainly didn't see what that little war in Southeast Asia would mean to all of us. Never realized it would reshape the American landscape politically, socially, and economically. Never realized that my generation would be caught in the seams of change, having to make a decision either to align ourselves with our parents' generation or to join a new one, a generation that was still evolving and still undefined.

The evening news told the Vietnam story, but back then it didn't have a beginning, middle, or an end. Well, it had a beginning, but we weren't paying attention. Just like Ben buying drugs from Berger, it had a beginning. The end just never occurred to us.

University of California students seized the administration building . . . Auto safety crusader Ralph Nader

called the Rolls-Royce overpriced and overrated and said
the doors pop open in crash tests . . . Senator Fulbright
insists the U.S. has succumbed to the arrogance of power
in Vietnam . . . plus John Delman's commentary. These
stories, weather, and sports in just two minutes.

It was my first day at WMAR-TV working as an intern on the
news. Things were fast-paced and frenetic and it seemed impossible to be able to learn all that went on. John Delman, an on-air
reporter, arrived late for his segment, and Mickey Kolgin, another intern, one who had much more experience than I did, told
me to get Delman made up quickly. I said I had no experience and
he just said:

"Powder him and get him on the set. Fast."

Then he walked away as the anchorman, Tony Crane, told me
something about wanting to drop a story and needing to make
some changes on the TelePrompTer. I was left with Delman sitting in a chair waiting for his makeup.

John Delman was a short, stocky man with a dark complexion
and deep-set eyes. I stared at the makeup kit on the counter for a
long beat, and then thought: What the hell, this can't be that
complicated.

"Sorry I'm late," said Delman. "For some reason I had a dick-
ens of a time writing this Vietnam piece."

I started to powder Delman's face.

"You're new here."

"Yes, sir. Bobby Shine."

I continued to powder away and Delman's face began to look
very white.

"Isn't that a little heavy?"

"Not when I'm finished," I lied as I put more powder on, trying to avoid his eyes. This simple task was a lot harder than I

thought. Then they were calling for him. I'm not sure how much time I had spent on him, but I did the best I could without any supervision. He didn't look that bad actually. Well, in person. On the air was another matter.

As I watched Delman on the monitor, my heart sank. My artistic creation was a disaster. His face was absolutely white, with dark holes where his eyes should be. I had my headset on, and I heard the director, Duke Sellars, say, "Oh my God, he looks like he's dead."

I didn't see them up there in the control booth, but I heard later that the entire crew was in complete shock. Duke was screaming now, "A dead man! A ghost! Holy shit!" Duke was the star director of the station and, as I was to learn, loved the sound of his own voice.

I could hear the assistant director, Richard Towers: "He looks like a snowman—no eyes, just big holes in his head."

Then Duke asked, "Who did this?"

I moved the mouthpiece closer to my lips and spoke.

"I did."

He asked who was speaking, and I told him:

"Bobby Shine."

Some of the crew tried to hold back their laughter as they watched Delman on the monitor, this shocking powdery white figure. Duke screamed through the headset, "Look at him, Mr. Shine. Look what you did to him, for Christ's sake. A ghost. A fucking ghost!"

He kept screaming at me, saying, "Listen to me, Mr. Shine, you shape up real quick or you'll have no future in television! None, you hear me? I will personally throw your ass out of the building!"

I tried to explain my problem, that no one told me what to do, but he was not having any of it.

"No excuses! None! You are a trainee! No excuses."

He was screaming so loud it was actually hurting my ears, and I had to move the headset.

Through it all, Delman continued his commentary, blissfully unaware of his appearance, and I watched him on the monitor.

> . . . Mr. U Thant has even addressed the UN, saying that force alone cannot solve Vietnam's problems. It seems that this would be a good time to reappraise our policies, both militarily and politically, in Southeast Asia . . .

On the monitor he looked almost surreal—a ghost commenting on the Vietnam War. In retrospect, it was appropriate.

After the broadcast, a few of the guys were having coffee and cigarettes in the directors' lounge when Duke quickly entered the room. I'd never seen him before, only heard that screaming voice, and suddenly the real-life version was standing before me. He was big—over six feet four inches tall—and reminded me of that cartoon character Baby Huey.

"You know how many calls we got? Thirty-eight. Thirty-eight calls. Some of the viewers were so concerned they thought Delman was going to die."

The guys standing behind Duke were amused, but I could do nothing but listen to his tirade and look repentant. He was really getting wound up as he continued.

"John Haynes called. The GM. He wanted to know how I could have let this happen. He called *me!*"

"I'm sorry. No one explained—"

"You spoke. You *spoke* to me." He was starting to foam at the corners of his mouth now. "Never, *never* speak back to me when we're face to face. Never!"

As he continued his diatribe, a very strange thing happened. I actually calmed down. The more he screamed, the more out of control he got, the calmer I became.

"You're off this ship, mister! You don't get on my team again until you earn it! I'm going to see that you're put on *The Ranger Al Show*! Let you work with the fucking puppets!"

Spittle was flying out of his mouth now as he continued.

"Thirty-eight! Thirty-eight fucking calls."

Then he was gone. The other guys immediately started laughing. Mickey smiled at me and said, "That went well."

Richard Towers offered, "Far be it from me to make an assessment, but I would say you're on his shit list."

"Ranger Al?" I said. Then Mickey did an impersonation of two of the puppets on the kids' show—Doctor Fox and Oswald Rabbit—using stupid voices. I was being sent to the station's version of Siberia. Banished to *The Ranger Al Show*. The lowest of the low in the trainee world. It was day one and I'd already been demoted. It was almost impossible—in less than two hours I had managed to work my way down the ladder.

As I sat there, I was overcome by a revelation about my life. I had never worked . . . never *really* worked before. Sure, I was a busboy in Atlantic City, delivered newspapers for a three-week period, and even caddied at the Forest Park golf course. But the caddying only lasted seven holes because I put the golf bag down on the green.

"How can you put a golf bag on the green? It's on the green! Are you out of your mind?" the guy I was caddying for screamed. He called what I had done "sacrilegious."

No one had ever told me this: You can't put a golf bag on the putting green; it just isn't done. Of course, there are probably fifty other things I didn't know about golf. The one thing I did know was there was a lot of walking and the bag was heavy. When the golfers made the turn at the ninth hole, I was gone, realizing that my future wasn't in the golf profession. I had no interest in playing the game, and the golfing attire was definitely much too bright and cheerful for my taste. So when I walked away from those links, never to return, there was no sense of remorse or regret.

But at WMAR there were real stakes on the line. I had quit law school, I was the low man on the totem pole with this trainee job, and now I was getting my ass fried. I was scared. I had nothing to fall back on. Nothing else even interested me. I began to laugh quietly to myself. The absurdity of it all. What was I doing? On the precipice of adulthood, I was suddenly forced back to a child's world—Ranger Al. I was so embarrassed, I never mentioned it to the guys. Or even to Annie.

The station received another fifty calls on Delman's sad state of health, as well as twenty-five get-well cards, over the next few days. Normally Delman's segments were replayed on the eleven o'clock news. They dropped this one, though, not wanting to frighten any more viewers. The guys downstairs in Telecine, where the films and tapes were run, made a videotape copy of the Delman "ghost" commentary and I heard that every so often, in the years that went by, they would pull it out for some laughs. It became a classic. And I had accomplished that feat in only one day.

Seven

It's hard to live in a city and suddenly discover that a whole part of it is missing. It didn't happen overnight, of course, but it seemed that way to me. Lexington Street was where all the movie palaces were—the RKO Keith's, the Century (where we saw *Reefer Madness*), the Valencia, which was upstairs. I used to love going to the Valencia. Its ceiling was painted like a dark sky, with clouds and twinkling stars. I felt like I was watching the movie outdoors, and on a few occasions when I found a movie boring, I could always do some stargazing.

The whole movie district was squeezed into that narrow part of Lexington Street—one theater after another. And smack right in the middle of the block was the Planters peanut shop with Mr. Peanut standing on the street welcoming everyone inside. They were simpler days—nothing could be more exciting for a kid than the smell of fresh-roasted peanuts filling the air on a cold winter day.

The urban renewal projects of the mid-sixties put an end to all of that. City planners looking to the future of downtown Baltimore tore down every building on that narrow part of Lexington Street and erected a high-rise office building. They killed a major artery, and the downtown went into a fast decline—a downward spiral that turned that part of the city into a no-man's-land.

Not six blocks from the now forgotten movie district was the University of Baltimore School of Law, my former alma mater, which Neil still attended and where he was beginning his own downward spiral.

As the fall semester began, Dean Allen spotted Neil in the hall, books in hand, impeccably dressed . . . and barefoot. The dean sent him home to get shoes. Neil came back the next day, well dressed but still shoeless.

Neil told us the sequence of events as he puffed on a cigarette and sipped coffee in the Diner.

"So the dean says to me:

" 'Have you got your shoes today?'

" 'Yes, sir.'

" 'Where are they? They're not on your feet.'

" 'They're in my closet.'

" 'Your closet?'

" 'Yes, sir.'

" 'I don't seem to be getting through to you.'

" 'Yes you are.'

" 'Good. The shoes tomorrow. And let me make this a little clearer, Neil—the shoes tomorrow . . . on your feet.' "

I asked Neil, "When was that?"

He said, "Two days ago."

We all looked at one another. Were we missing something? He didn't bother to mention yesterday, he only mentioned two days ago. So Turko asked the sixty-four-thousand-dollar question. "What happened yesterday?"

"Yesterday?" Neil asked blankly.

"Yes." I waved away some of the cigarette smoke at our booth. There was so much smoke hovering over the table it could have caused a smog alert.

"Well, that's when it got interesting." He smiled. "Yesterday the dean called me into his office and said:

" 'We have a problem.' "

"And I asked, 'Do we?' "

"Wait," said the Turk. "Were you wearing shoes now?"

"No, that's why I was there in his office. So the dean says to me:

" 'How many days have you been told to get shoes on your feet, Mr. Tilden?'

" 'At least three days.'

" 'And have you accomplished what I asked?'

" 'No, sir.'

" 'Why haven't you done that? It isn't a difficult task.'

" 'Not sure, Dean.'

" 'Why are you in school, Neil?'

" 'To get my law degree, sir.'

" 'Do you want to be a lawyer, Neil?'

" 'I've never thought about that.'

" 'Never thought about it?'

" 'No, sir.'

" 'Why are you in law school, Neil?'

" 'It just seemed like something I was supposed to do.'

" 'If you don't start wearing shoes, you're going to leave me no choice but to expel you from this school. You understand that?'

" 'Yes, I do.' "

Then Neil looked around at us and said, "Then he asked the big question." He took a puff on his cigarette. "He said: 'Neil, are you going to wear shoes?' "

We all stared at him. He had that poker-faced look which made it impossible to read what he was thinking ... and he milked it. We didn't ask the next question but Neil finally gave it to us.

"I said, 'No.' "

Turko said, "You said *no*? You got thrown out of law school your last year because you wouldn't wear shoes?"

Neil nodded. Stunned, we asked what he planned to do, and of course he had no idea. But the story got even stranger. After that, Neil said he went outside and decided to lie in the grass. The sky was filled with billowy clouds. As he stared up at them, he was lost in their beauty, remembering that as a kid he thought clouds were cotton candy and birds could fly up and nibble on them all day. As we listened, he began to ramble somewhat incoherently. We couldn't figure out what was wrong with him, but we said little. Part of the unspoken rule of Diner talk was that all conversation and behavior was accepted—up to a point. Neil was acting weird and we all knew it, but no boundaries had been crossed.

Annie filled in the rest of the details for me later that evening. Neil had been so still as he lay on the campus grounds, and he stared at the sky for so long, that some of the law students became concerned and thought that he might be in a coma or a drug-induced stupor. So the paramedics were called and Neil was taken to the hospital. Annie was summoned to the emergency room to see him. They hadn't run any tests yet. She watched him resting on the bed in the curtained-off cubicle, staring at the ceiling. He was still and quiet. Then, suddenly, he shocked her by speaking.

"Why did you come down here?"

Annie was relieved that he was coherent, but noticed that he seemed oblivious to his situation. He spoke as if nothing unusual was going on.

"So what are you up to, Annie?"

"Are you feeling better, Neil?"

"I'm fine. What do you mean?"

Annie was confused. She hadn't been a nurse for long, but this made little sense to her.

"Don't know why they took me away," Neil continued. "I was staring at the sky. That's all."

Then Annie said she began to get mad. She was relieved that

he wasn't ill, but his nonchalant attitude frustrated her. "They thought you were in a coma, for God's sake."

Neil gave his side of the story with his own logic. "They seemed to have a job to do, and I was busy staring. They had their thing and I had mine."

"God, you're impossible."

"I'm sorry."

"Are you taking LSD?"

"I was lying there and I could feel the blood flowing through my body. I could feel it, my blood, this working mechanism, you know, and when I shook hands with Dean Allen, I could feel all of his emotions in my hand, as if they were flowing into me."

Annie was almost afraid to ask.

"Why did you shake his hand?"

"Because he expelled me from school."

"Oh, Neil."

Annie tried to control herself, and although she was sitting by his side in a nurse's uniform, she began to cry. Neil continued, "You could feel it. He didn't want to. I didn't have to look at his eyes, I could tell he didn't want to."

Annie was confused. Was he taking LSD? Was he going mad? What was going on? She sat there trying to get her emotions under control. But she couldn't. This was her brother and she was losing him.

Then he said, in answer to her earlier question:

"Yes."

At last something made sense.

Eight

The next day, I started my work with Ranger Al and the gang—
Ozzie Rabbit and Doctor Fox, two hand puppets. They were
about two feet tall, filled with foam rubber, and to operate them
I stuffed my hand in the back of each puppet and grabbed at the
mouth, which allowed for a little facial movement.

The Ranger was an institution. A pleasant man, who dressed as a
forest ranger with a stiff brown hat, he had been doing the kiddie
show since the television station was founded. The Ranger did a
number of voices on the show, but because he was not a ventriloquist,
he had to pretape character voices. He gave Ozzie Rabbit a voice that
sounded a lot like Jerry Lewis when he was with Dean Martin, and
Doctor Fox resembled a white version of Louis Armstrong.

The voices were recorded on an audio cartridge. During the
show, all the audio man had to do was follow the script and, on
cue, hit the button so one of the puppet's voices would be heard.
Then the tape would self-cue itself to the next replay. This pretape system allowed the Ranger to be in the shot with the puppets, and it seemed very real. It was also cheaper than having
actors play the characters of Doctor Fox and Ozzie Rabbit.

The set was simple: a log cabin with a painted flat of the woods.
It was also flimsy—held up by a few sandbags to anchor the flaps.
The puppets would sit on the windowsill of the log cabin in front
of a black velvet curtain. Behind the curtain was the puppeteer—

that was now my job. I'd sit on a stool and watch on a small monitor so that I could see what shot the cameraman was on. That way,
I could, on occasion, have one of the puppets play to a camera.

"Hello, hello, hello," said Ozzie Rabbit. Ozzie was a fuzzy-
looking rabbit with a head about two-thirds the size of his body.
He didn't look as funny as Bugs Bunny but he was reasonably dis-
tinctive, dressed in just overalls and black and white shoes.

"Hello, hello, hello," chimed in Doctor Fox, who looked more
like a dog than a fox. He wore a goofy overcoat and a bow tie,
with one of those Scottish tam-o'-shanters on his head.

The Ranger walked to the side of the windowsill where the
two puppets were turned.

"And how is everyone today?" the Ranger asked.

Doctor Fox replied, "Lousy. Oops, sorry, sorry."

"You should say . . . ?" asked the Ranger.

"Less than perfect," replied Doctor Fox.

"Yes, that would be more polite," Ranger Al responded.

During the commercial break, Ranger Al nodded to me and
said I was doing a good job—my first compliment at the station,
and it meant a lot. Moving the lips on two hand puppets wasn't
exactly as triumphant a moment as that scene from *On the Waterfront*—Brando staggering along the docks coming back from a
bloody beating and showing the Mob that he couldn't be
beaten—but it *was* a compliment. At the time, I even thought it
might be a defining moment in my life.

Mickey, the other trainee, was kind enough to give me a tour of the
television station. Since the station also had a radio outlet, there
was a large record library, which stored stacks and stacks of LPs

and even the old 78s. It seemed as if almost anything that existed on record was in their archives. In the days, weeks, and then months that went by, I spent a great deal of time in that library listening to all of the different sounds—swing, big band, and bebop.

It was an education in itself. I discovered all kinds of trivia. For instance, the fact that Elvis Presley's "Are You Lonesome Tonight" was originally recorded by Al Jolson. When I told the guys at the Diner one night, they all laughed, Ben especially. "Elvis doing a Jolson song?"

He did a five-minute put-down and I was ridiculed unmercifully. In the Diner crowd, right was not necessarily might.

But the biggest and most impressive moment was when Mickey took me to the film library, with its massive collection of films, shorts, newsreels, stock footage, old cartoons, and novelty pieces. I walked down the halls and saw the titles of movies such as *Casablanca, High Sierra, Citizen Kane, The Best Years of Our Lives, It's a Wonderful Life, The African Queen, On the Waterfront, San Francisco* with Clark Gable and Jeanette MacDonald—all the movies they showed on *The Late Show, The Late, Late Show,* and *The Early Show*. There were a lot of titles of movies I'd never even heard of at that time, like *The Magnificent Ambersons* and *Sweet Smell of Success*.

Late in the evenings, I sat and watched a lot of these films. It was an experience that excited me in ways I wasn't really able to understand back then. I began to see movies not just as stories that could play into my fantasies but as something that needed craft and structure. I realized that choices had to be made and I was starting to see how fantasies were created. I began to understand how music held a scene together—it could move us emotionally or create energy. I saw how effective silence could actually be. Some of the old actors' styles seemed timeless, very contemporary, whereas others seemed hopelessly dated. I was beginning to realize that creative decisions were made from shot to shot.

I talked to Annie endlessly about the images I was watching and shared my revelations, my enthusiasm. But as far as she was concerned, a movie was a movie. You liked it or you didn't. It was nothing more than that for her, and in a way she was right. But to me, the fact that a given moment in a film could be either funny or dramatic, because of the way it was written, or that a camera angle could shape a mood, now consumed my thoughts. The end product was all that mattered to Annie, but the process of reaching that end product fascinated me like nothing else in my life ever had.

One night we sat in the film library together and watched *The Grapes of Wrath*, directed by John Ford. I'd never seen the movie when it came out, I'd never even heard about it, but I was amazed by the work and I ran it for her. I talked about the use of black and white and the starkness, the simplicity.

"It's so depressing . . . really sad. They're poor and have terrible lives. How can you pay attention to the images?" She was, as always, caught up in the characters and emotion, not the technique. "What an awful time that Depression must have been . . . the mother trying to keep the Joad family together . . . the appalling conditions . . ."

"I know, I know," I said. "I'm just talking about how good this John Ford is."

But Annie could only see and feel one thing: "It just breaks your heart, Bobby."

There were things I needed to learn and Annie understood that, but she just wanted to laugh or cry or be moved in some way by a movie. But I had the stirrings of ambition. For the first time it wasn't based on what my parents thought was best for me. I was motivated. *Obsessed*. These were new feelings, and ones I felt I had to keep to myself. I tried to tell Annie, but she didn't understand, so I kept quiet.

Since *The Ranger Al Show* was the only program at the station that was considered entertainment, as opposed to news-related, I began to think of ways I could use film and music to make the show more enjoyable. I wanted to be able to put together "a bit," as Ranger Al called it. There was no one to teach me, so I was left to my own devices. There were thousands and thousands of reels of film, and a music library that was massive. What could I do with all of this at my fingertips? I wasn't sure.

But I decided to figure it out. And I decided it had to be soon.

Nine

We all got postcards from Ben on his honeymoon in California—cards from Carmel, Big Sur, San Francisco, and Los Angeles. They looked like places seen only in dreams.

I remember watching the Rose Bowl games on television every New Year's Day. They were played in Pasadena, where everything was always light and sunny and warm. We watched those games on TV while outside our windows the world was cold and gray. We were in black and white, and out there everything was in Technicolor. When we were younger, we used to fantasize about what it would be like going out to Los Angeles. All the movie stars were there . . . Sandra Dee, Tuesday Weld. Somehow, in our minds, they would all be out on the beach.

Turko once said, "They might not be out there every day, but if you hang around long enough, no doubt you're going to run into them."

We were around eighteen when Turko blurted out those naïve words. All things were possible then. Life was a beach party, so why wouldn't Tuesday Weld be there?

I looked at the postcard Ben had sent from San Francisco—the Golden Gate Bridge. Neil pointed out that people loved to commit suicide there.

"A nice place to jump and die."

"Why?" I asked. "It looks so pretty."

He puffed on his cigarette and said: "It's the end of the line. The dream takes you west, and if the dream's not there, there's nowhere else to go. The end of land . . . the end of the line. No one dreams of going east, it's counterclockwise. Even the sun goes west, and if you don't like what you have there, what's left? Jump."

The idea of someone jumping off the Golden Gate Bridge fascinated Neil. He stared at the postcard, visualizing the suicide in his mind, and ran his fingers through his sandy blond hair, lost in his thoughts. "What do you think about when you jump?" he finally asked.

"You got me," I said.

"You have seven or eight seconds. You know you're going to die. The water is coming up to meet you. Within seconds you'll be hitting the cold water. What do you think?"

"I'd be thinking, I'm gonna fucking die," I said.

"No, you have to be thinking something else. You see, dying is a given. You have seven seconds for the last thought of your life." Neil was making a point now, trying to sort it out in his head. "What thought is worth that time, your last seconds on earth? Something frivolous? I don't think so. Something profound? I doubt it."

It was a riddle that intrigued Neil. He looked out the Diner window as if an answer might be outside, and then he quietly said, "Something ordinary, would be my guess. Something very ordinary. That would be poetic." And he laughed.

Neil was forever fascinated with death; it was an ongoing question for him. I didn't share his enthusiasm.

Years before this, we went over to Carlin's Park, a dilapidated old amusement center just off an area in Baltimore called Park Circle. The place was way past its glory days. It was shabby and a lot of the rides had been shut down, but they still had the Racer Dip, as we called it. It was a roller coaster that was built of wood, painted white and peeling. It seemed very rickety. You had the feeling it would collapse at any given moment. When it made the big turn near the Esso service station below, everyone would scream. Not Neil. Neil would sit there as if he was taking a pleasant drive on Auchentoroly Terrace—one of my favorite street names in life. He was not fazed by this terrifying ride, this death-defying roller coaster. We'd scream. Neil would sit and give an exaggerated yawn.

He once said, "How can you be scared of a ride?"

"It's scary," I answered, and all the other guys chimed in that they felt the same. Not Neil.

"It's a trick," he elaborated. "If the thing fell down every couple of weeks . . . if people were thrown out of the cars every other day, then it would be scary. But it's not real. It's only an illusion."

"We *think* we're going to die," Eggy said.

"Nonsense. Does the magician pull the rabbit out of the hat?"

"Yes," said Eggy.

"I mean, make it materialize."

Eggy had to say, "No."

"Of course not. It's a trick. Same with the ride. No matter how sharp the turn, no matter how fast, it is just a ride, and you're not gonna die. So it bores me."

We nearly shit our pants on that ride, and Neil was unfazed.

Then he mentioned little Freddie Krauss being blown up and sailing over the top of the Texaco sign. "Now that was a ride that could scare you."

Turko started the usual debate. "I don't believe he went as high as the Texaco sign."

"Higher," said Eggy. "Mulnick's brother was there, and he said higher."

That night the Diner talk was about life and death. None of us had ever had anyone close to us die, so we didn't understand the terrible pain of it. It was an abstraction. We were young guys fooling ourselves with the cockiness and naïveté that comes with youth. And we always came back to the Freddie Krauss story. Freddie would forever be floating over the Texaco sign.

And then there are gaps.

Ten

It was late in the evening, and I was on the stage figuring out an idea for *The Ranger Al Show*. Mickey was helping out. He was turning out to be a great guy, always in a good mood and a terrific laugher. He had moved from Ohio to get into this training program, and everyone said he had enormous potential—something I certainly never heard about myself.

We were playing with the hand puppets as I put together a routine using the Beach Boys' popular hit "Good Vibrations." Ozzie Rabbit and Doctor Fox sang along, and I had Mickey operating two worms I'd found in the prop box. I called them Flo and Wally.

As we developed the routine, I thought of giving Ozzie some type of hat, a bonnet, and letting him be a female rabbit—one who would give "good vibrations." I found a funny hat while rummaging through the costume closet. The idea was taking shape. We did a run-through to the music as a record player spun the song.

Afterward, Mickey and I assessed the situation.

"You think the Ranger will like it?" I asked.

"You kidding? He'll love it."

Then out of the shadows Annie appeared.

"*I* like it."

I was surprised to see her. "Hey."

"Hey, you," she said, and then looked to Mickey.

"This is Annie Tilden, my fiancée. Annie, Mickey Kolgin."

Mickey extended his arm to shake hands, but he had Flo Worm on his hand.

Annie looked around at the stage, the puppets, and the set. "So this is fun, huh?"

"Just trying to get a piece together for Ranger Al, you know . . . maybe come up with something."

"I see."

I wasn't sure what that meant. It didn't seem condescending, but it didn't seem enthusiastic either. I decided to let it pass and just asked, "What are you doing here?"

"Need to talk."

Mickey said he would put away all the puppets. I thanked him and led Annie over to a steel ladder that went up to the control booth. There was a longer way around, but I thought we could take the shortcut. The ladder seemed manageable for Annie. I told her to go first, that I would back her up. As she climbed the ladder she stopped and turned toward me.

"Don't look up my dress."

"I can't help myself."

I followed and suddenly she backed up and my head went under her skirt.

"Don't move," I mumbled, and she laughed, then quickly scrambled up the ladder.

The control booth area was dark, but the monitors offered some light. On one of them, *The Late Show* was playing a Bogart movie. However, there was no sound. It was late Bogart. He looked a little old, tired. He was some kind of a reporter or an editor at a paper. I couldn't figure it out, but I didn't pay a lot of attention either because Annie started talking.

She was having a problem with Neil, concerned about his recent behavior. Apparently her mother and father were apoplectic about him getting kicked out of law school. My parents were more subdued about *my* change. When I told my father that I'd quit law school, he just said, "Go get a job and make a living." When I got the job at WMAR-TV and I told him about working with puppets, he said little. This was not something he could brag about with his golf buddies. None of it made much sense to him, but he was never really negative about any of it. He couldn't give me encouragement because this was a line of work that was outside of anything he could relate to. But he never told me not to do it.

"Neil is impossible, Bobby. There's so much tension in the house."

It was hard for me to concentrate on her words because, standing there in the dark, Annie looked so beautiful. Sometimes her concern showed on her face as a strength, and there was a directness about her. Annie was never a girl. She was born a woman.

"I don't know what to do about him. He's like a car skidding out of control."

"Well, maybe he just didn't want to be in law school, you know. I didn't."

"First you give it up for *this*, and now Neil—"

"What do you mean, for *this*?" I asked. "You make what I do seem unimportant."

"You have a college degree and now you're working with puppets. It's cute, but—"

I cut her off. "Cute? I'm doing cute things? Thanks."

I could see Mickey down on the floor, through the glass partition. The studio was dark except for a work light casting a beam on the puppets as he put them away for the night. One by one they went into the box—Ozzie, Doctor Fox, Wally and Flo Worm.

Annie continued to explain that she wasn't being sarcastic and she didn't mean it as a personal attack. Then she added: "Can we deal with Neil right now?"

"Okay," I said.

"He trusts you."

I nodded. I didn't know what "deal with Neil" meant. I wasn't sure what I could say that would be meaningful to him. No matter how many times the guys had gotten on his ass for his unpredictable nature, Neil did what Neil wanted to do. But I said to Annie I would do what I could, as ill defined as that might be.

Eleven

The night had no moon and the air had the beginnings of a fall chill. Neil was sitting on his front lawn in a beach chair reading *The Great Gatsby* by flashlight.

I got out of my car and walked toward him. He continued to read, never looking up. Without so much as a glance, he said, "What's doing, Bobby?"

"Just thought I'd stop by. Check to see what page you're on."

Then he started to read:

" '*By the way, Mr. Gatsby, I understand you're an Oxford man.' 'Not exactly.' 'Oh, yes, I understand you went to Oxford.' 'Yes—I went there.' A pause.*"

"Neil, we should talk."

He looked up. "Sister sent you on a mission, old sport?"

He stood up and closed the book. He shone the flashlight on his bare feet, one at a time.

"Would it have anything to do with these?"

I smiled. "Naturally."

He moved around the front lawn sliding his feet across the grass, feeling the soft moist texture of the blades.

"Once upon a time, back in antiquity, a barefooted man was viewed as humble, maybe a prophet. Now just a jerk. A loony bird."

Then he started to recite the words from a Cole Porter song:

"In olden days a glimpse of stocking was looked on as something shocking, now heaven knows . . ."

He mocked a dance, à la Fred Astaire, and without me saying as much as one more word, he headed for the house.

"I'll get my shoes."

I was totally surprised. He had gotten himself kicked out of law school rather than put on a pair of shoes. Now, just like that, he'd decided to give up his barefoot ways. It was nearly impossible to understand what Neil's motivations were. Dealing with him was a little like roulette—sometimes the number came up, most of the time it didn't. On that night, my number came up.

When I pulled into the Diner parking lot with Neil in the passenger seat, I could see Turko and Eggy talking inside. Over the years, the two of them had some of the all-time classic Diner chats. They fed one another. They could come up with a topic and run with it for hours.

"I got this real problem with electricity," Eggy was saying as we joined them in the booth.

"Afraid of it?" Turko asked.

"How it works. Here's the thing, the electricity is in the wall socket, right?"

Turko nodded.

"Electricity is in there. You plug something in and it works. You don't plug anything in, the electricity just sits there behind the plug, waiting. It doesn't ever come out. It just sits behind the socket."

Turko mulled this over. "True."

"See what I mean?" said the Egg man.

"It's odd, huh?" Turko agreed.

Eggy had even more thoughts on the subject.

"You can't waste it. It doesn't trickle out on the floor. It's just there in the socket. You don't even need to put a cap on to keep it in. It knows to stay behind the socket."

Turko pondered this. "Right. How the fuck *does* it work?"

Neil took this moment to show off his shoes and the guys were duly impressed. Eggy said that this was a big step forward on a hygiene level, if nothing else.

"The ground has strange parasites," he went on. "In Africa they have something that slips between your toes, burrows through your body, and comes out your eyeballs. It leaves you paralyzed, or blind, or . . . I can't remember."

"No wonder all the colored people wanted to get out," Turko stated.

"What do you mean, they wanted to get out?" I said, incredulous. "They were brought over as slaves."

"Okay, okay . . ." Turko said, "but let me ask you this, when slavery was over, how many went back? How many, huh?"

"They weren't Africans anymore, they were Americans, so they would know as much about Africa as you would," Neil said.

We had very little understanding of the racial situation in Baltimore at that time, and depending on which part of the city you were raised in, you would see yourself as either a northerner or a southerner. Since we all grew up in the northwest section of Baltimore, we always thought of ourselves as northerners. We were supposedly the enlightened ones, and yet we never thought twice about the fact that blacks weren't allowed to enter white restaurants or country clubs or even attend city events. Integration of the school system took place in 1954, but until that point, as little kids, we never questioned the absence of black children in the classroom.

When civil rights demonstrations started up in the sixties, it took us a while to make sense of the situation—we were not aware that inequality even existed. We were middle-class white guys with college educations, and about as much knowledge of the history of inequality as provided in the movie *Gone with the Wind*.

Then suddenly we heard, "Thank you. Thank you." It was Shade, grinning from ear to ear. "I'm out. I'm out. Thank you. Thank you."

"The army?" Turko asked.

"Yep. Out." He explained how he finally went to see "Dan the Man" over at Knocko's Pool Hall. It seemed the timing for Danny was not the best, since he was involved, at that point in time, in a forty-six-hour marathon pool game. Fifty-two hours was the longest game he had ever played, against Mo Schultz, who came down from Pittsburgh to take him on.

Dan the Man always looked as fresh thirty-five hours into a game as he did when he first began. Periodically he would take a break. He would wash up and shave and put on a new set of clothes. He always had this thing about cleanliness and making sure he looked presentable.

Danny loved eight ball; he had a good touch and feel for it. Obviously he loved the film *The Hustler*, which he saw nineteen times, and marveled at how well Jackie Gleason played the game. He didn't really care for the story, it was just the pool segments that held his attention. "That Piper Laurie love story bullshit bored the hell out of me," he told me one day.

He enjoyed games of skill, and for a long time was addicted to pinball machines. Danny was about five or six years older than the rest of us, and the first time I ever met him was up at Cooper's, which was a little soda shop across from Elementary School 64. They had "coddies," which were a big favorite in Baltimore. They looked like small cakes, were spicy, and I assume were made from codfish, but I'm not really sure. They cost five cents and the best way to eat them was on a couple of crackers with mustard. The "coddies" would be laid out on the countertop, stacked high, and after school it was a good snack to go along with a Coke.

A lot of kids back then would pack the shop after school. Since the "coddies" were a self-serve item, it was a common practice to gobble down two or three but only pay for one.

It was over in the corner where I first saw Danny playing a pinball machine called "At the Races," his favorite game. It only had one ball, not five, and it had no flippers, which was extremely unusual. The object was to shoot the ball and try to land it in the slot corresponding to the one that was lit up on the panel. Each number was a racehorse. If a number 6 was lit up, you needed to get the ball to end up in the number 6 hole. Some numbers were easier to land on than others, and if you got a number that you thought was easy, you could put extra nickels in and build up the odds. Although it was against the law, Joe, who ran Cooper's, would pay out nickels for games, which made it as low-end a gambling operation as ever existed.

On the day I saw Danny for the first time, he had a 4—the easiest number to land on—so he built up the odds. Nickel after nickel after nickel he kept building until all of us young kids, twelve and under, started gathering around the machine. Suddenly, it was turning into the seventh game of the World Series. Danny had worked it so that it would pay out 120 nickels if he came up a winner.

There was tremendous tension in Cooper's, which was packed.

Danny was getting ready to shoot the ball. He was going for it. Then somehow, as if out of nowhere, fat Terry Tober moved through the crowded soda shop, desperately wanting to get a better look at the action. His ten-year-old fat little body bounced off one person after another as he moved toward his destination, squeezing, pushing, not wanting to miss the big moment. All of a sudden, he broke through the crowd and was there at the machine with the best view in the house. He was free and clear. But his momentum continued to carry him forward, and he couldn't stop his fat little legs. He tried to put on the brakes, but it was impossible. Almost in slow motion, his protruding belly hit the side of the pinball machine.

Cooper's went silent.

Danny's hands were on the glass of the machine and he felt the tremor. Being the expert player that he was, he knew that tragedy was about to strike. It was devastating. All those nickels that had gone into the machine were lost. All of Danny's hard work to build the odds in his favor was now meaningless. On the glass panel of the pinball machine, for everyone to see, the word TILT was lit up in bright red letters.

Danny turned to fat Terry Tober, and Terry could see the cold look in his eyes. But Danny said nothing. Total silence. Then, suddenly, there was the loudest wailing, the most mournful sound any of us had ever heard before, and Terry broke down crying uncontrollably. Tears squirted out of his eyes. His belly and his cheeks and his jowls were all shaking wildly. He dropped his head on the glass of the pinball machine and quietly murmured, "God, what have I done?"

It was a terrible moment. No one said a word. Joe's wife, Betty, who worked behind the counter, looked like she, too, was going to cry. Finally, Terry's head rose off the pinball machine glass, which was now covered with little droplets of tears. He looked at Danny but said nothing. Terry Tober then headed out of the soda shop and never stepped foot in that place again.

I ran into Terry about fifteen years later. I was walking into Read's drugstore on Liberty Heights and Garrison and Terry was coming out. We hadn't seen each other since that night at Cooper's. We exchanged pleasantries and then I mentioned the incident. He had to think about it for a moment. He had forgotten that Cooper's even existed.

"Oh yeah," said Terry. "Across from 64."

He was still heavy and now wore glasses that sat in a cockeyed manner on his nose—the frame higher on one side than on the other. I smiled and said, "Remember when you tilted Danny's pinball machine?"

He stared at me blankly. "Danny?"

"Dan the Man."

Terry just shook his head.

"Remember Danny? He was always over at the pinball machine in the corner?"

"Oh yeah, yeah . . . right. I remember knocking against a machine once. Was that him?"

"Yeah," I said, but I could see that the moment I remembered was not the same moment Terry had lived.

Sometimes I wonder if we ever remember the things in our lives as they really happened, or if they're always tweaked and rethought. Two people at the same event and yet two different stories. I once wrote a sentence that said: "Memories of times that never were are hard to forget." The older I get, the truer that sentence becomes.

What's real and what's imagined? What have we turned into myth? There was a line in *The Man Who Shot Liberty Valance:* "When legend becomes fact, print the legend."

And always there are gaps . . .

The night Shade came to see Danny during his marathon pool game, Danny was distracted, but he still eventually worked his magic. With five hundred dollars in his pocket, and after several hours of intermittent phone calls, he produced the crucial doctor's note.

"The whole thing worked. I'm out," Shade yelled to everyone in the Diner. "I am out! Not drafted!"

There was a smattering of applause, then, slipping into the booth with us, he said, in a very low conspiratorial tone, "The note worked like a charm."

"Told you," said Turko.

"You were right," Shade acknowledged.

"What's in it?" Eggy asked. "What'd the note say?"

"Don't know."

"Between us," said Turko as he slipped a ten-dollar bill to Shade. "After all, I'm the one who told you about the note."

"Never read it." Shade pushed the ten-dollar bill back across the table.

"Straight on this?" Turko asked.

"Yes. That was the deal. I pay the five hundred, he gives me the note, and I can't read it. Period."

"That's one hell of a note," I finally chimed in.

Neil didn't seem to care. He was staring at his shoes.

I saw headlights in the parking lot as I glanced out the window. A shiny brand-new '67 baby blue Cadillac was gliding in. It was so new that it caught every reflection. The car stopped, the lights went off, and then Ben stepped out proudly.

"Holy shit," I said, and we all raced out of the Diner.

We applauded as Ben stood by his treasure. He took a finger, pulled on his lower eyelid, and gave the familiar "You're me." He looked tanned and healthy.

"Beautiful car," said Eggy as he walked around it, running his fingers along the fender.

Ben opened the door. "Get in, start it. Listen to her. She hums."

Eggy turned the key and there was that beautiful low-end sound of the engine. The radio heated up. Music played. I hadn't heard the song before, but after that night I heard it a lot. It was Barry McGuire's "Eve of Destruction":

> *The eastern world, it is explodin'*
> *Violence flarin', bullets loadin'*
> *You're old enough to kill, but not for votin'*
> *You don't believe in war, but what's that gun you're totin'*
> *And even the Jordan River has bodies floatin'*
> *But you tell me over and over and over again, my friend*
> *Ah, you don't believe*
> *We're on the eve of destruction.*

We didn't really listen to the lyrics, and the escalating war in Vietnam was not much of a concern for us, except for avoiding the draft.

"You have a good time on your honeymoon?" Turko wanted to know.

Ben laughed and told a story about getting stoned before going to Disneyland.

"I got so messed up, I walked up to this couple and asked if they were a ride."

We all laughed appreciatively.

Then Ben turned his attention to Shade. "What are you doing here? I thought you got drafted."

"I'm out. I got the doctor's note," Shade said proudly.

Then Ben said a stunning non sequitur, "Janet's pregnant."

"So soon?" asked Eggy.

Ben gave him a look that said: Are you the dumbest person in the world? "Do you think maybe Janet and I had sex before the honeymoon?"

"Aaahhh," Eggy said as the realization dawned.

We all gave proper congrats to Ben, welcomed him back, and told him how glad we were to see him again. Then I said I needed to head home because I was assigned to write up the traffic report for the morning news. Neil didn't want to leave, so Ben offered to drop him off later on.

As I was leaving, Ben said to the guys, "Smoke a joint?"

On my way home I started to think about Annie. Although I had argued with her earlier about my work, it didn't lessen my feelings toward her in any way.

I drove down the quiet streets, not even listening to the radio. I was overcome by a strong urge to see her, to be with her. Heading toward my house, I stopped at a red traffic light and looked over at Read's drugstore. I remembered the Robert Mulnick scandal. Well, it was hardly a scandal, but parents talked about it for years. Mulnick was about nine at the time and he was looking at the Paper Mate pens in Read's. There was a new one on display— two-tone, pink and charcoal. It was as sharp-looking as anything he had seen in his life. He picked it up and held it in his small hand. He wanted it so badly. He didn't have the money for it, but he kept palming it and clicking it. The tip of the pen would come out and then vanish, come out and vanish. Mulnick *loved* that Paper Mate pen. He wanted it more than he'd wanted anything in his whole life. He couldn't help himself . . . he took it. As he opened the door to leave the drugstore, the pharmacist grabbed him by his coat and pulled him back inside. Mulnick was caught! He was a shoplifter. The unpaid-for Paper Mate pen was still clutched in his hand.

Word spread like wildfire through the community. Families would always tell the Robert Mulnick story as a lesson. "You don't take what doesn't belong to you."

Five or six years after the event, it would still come up in conversation at our dinner table, "Always make sure you have money enough to buy what you need. You don't want to end up like Mulnick one day," as if he had been sent away for thirty years. He was simply admonished by the pharmacist and told never to do that again, but in our community the idea of shame was a big thing. So the cautionary tale of Mulnick was one for the ages.

As these thoughts flashed in my head, thoughts of Annie intruded. I saw a phone booth and, in slow motion or so it seemed, I moved toward it. Then I was dialing. When I heard her voice I said, "I miss you."

"Well, that's very nice. I'm flattered, since I just saw you a few hours ago."

"I'm sorry, who is this again?" I teased.

"I really want you to come over."

"I'll be right there," I said excitedly.

"No . . . no . . . no . . . no . . . my parents just got back."

"Aren't we getting a little too old for this?"

"Yes, but come June, my dear boy, you just watch out."

"I'm coming," I said. "I'll sit in my car. If you want to come out and give me a good-night kiss, it's up to you."

"A kiss?"

"Yes. Just a kiss."

"Start your engines," she said. I hung up and was out of the telephone booth and in the car like a flash. I was in such a rush, I actually floored the car and burned rubber.

As I headed over to Annie's, one of the legendary Diner guys' adventures took place—a story that was told over and over again.

It started simply enough. They were all sitting in Ben's '67 Cadillac reveling in the beauty of its interior—how pretty the clock in the dash looked, the abundance of chrome, the placement of the radio, how smoothly the glove compartment panel opened and closed.

Eggy had a problem with the name "glove compartment." As best as he could remember, he had never once put gloves in that compartment or ever seen anyone else put gloves there.

"You keep maps in there . . . cigarettes, pencils. Never gloves!" he exclaimed. Then he went on with his ramble, "And why would you put gloves there? If it were cold, you would wear them. And there's a lock so you can lock your gloves inside? Now these gloves are so precious, not only do you have to break into the car, you have to break into the *glove* compartment? People desperately want gloves and nothing will stop them. Better keep 'em under lock and key. A *map* compartment, that would make a lot more sense."

It was then that Neil noticed that the car's odometer only had six miles on it. Ben reiterated that it was brand new and after that Neil asked the fateful question, "If you go backwards, does the mileage go backwards?"

"I'm not sure," Ben said.

"Let's back her up and find out."

A very stoned Ben said, "Good idea."

He backed up the shiny blue Caddie across the now empty parking lot. They stared at the odometer and there was the slightest movement backwards.

"It does," said Ben, amazed.

"Let's take her back to zero," Neil said. "Very cool idea."

Turko—the only sane one in the car—objected. "Not going backwards on a city street. Sorry."

"This could be exciting," Neil offered, but Turko got out of the car.

"I'm out of here. Egg?"

Eggy was unsure. Neil baited him.

"Come on. Driving backwards. Chance of a lifetime."

Eggy couldn't refuse.

Turko thought the guys were crazy. He slammed the car door and walked off as Ben backed the big Caddie into the street. And backwards they went.

Neil yelled out the window to Turko, "Back to zero. Yes!"

The Cadillac glided backwards down the quiet street. Eggy stared out the back window, almost frozen in fear. Neil sat calmly in the front seat smoking a cigarette, staring out the front window as the car moved away and the mileage gauge slowly went toward zero.

"Red light coming up," Eggy said nervously.

Neil smiled. "It can't be coming up, we must have passed it," and he laughed.

"Do we stop for red lights?" Ben casually asked, as if nothing out of the ordinary was going on.

"Your call," offered Neil.

"Nah . . . too late," said Ben, and he made no effort to slow down as they backed through the intersection.

They continued moving backwards through the empty Baltimore

streets as Ben fearlessly navigated the big car. They were on a mission, with Eggy as their terrified witness.

While taking a soft turn on Upper Park Heights, Ben lost control of the car and it swerved. He tried to compensate, and the next thing they knew, the car was on the sidewalk. Since it was trash collection day in the morning, the Cadillac mowed down garbage cans like dominoes. Then it was up on the lawns of the houses and through some hedges.

Eggy watched all of this through the back window, trying to help out. "Get back on the street. Left. Cut it hard. Left!"

After hitting a plastic birdbath, Ben maneuvered the car, and finally they were back in the street. As if nothing had happened, Neil said, "Two miles to go. Yes! Heading for zero."

They continued on, and not once during this strange rite did Neil ever look back to see where they were going. He was quite happy to see just where they had been.

"I ask you," said Ben, "is this the behavior of a married man with a child on the way?"

"Not a chance," Eggy offered up, still staring out the back window trying to anticipate the next potential obstacle.

"Thank God," Ben yelled, and the Caddie continued to quietly move backwards until Ben slammed on the brakes, jumped out of the car, stood in the middle of the dimly lit street, and yelled, "Zero! Back to zero!"

Neil calmly stepped out to stand next to Ben and pronounced, "This car, ladies and gentlemen, has never been driven."

"Brand new. Not a quarter of a mile, not an eighth of a mile. Zero. Never been driven," said Ben.

Eggy sat in the back as the guys enjoyed this marvelous accomplishment at three in the morning.

"How did it get here? A car in the middle of the street with no mileage?" Ben went on. "Magic." Then he said it again, but much louder. Not satisfied with that, he screamed it out: "MAGIC!!"

He yelled "magic" again and again and again, louder and louder each time.

"MAGIC!!!"

Eggy told me later he thought this was the "strangest" part of the whole escapade. Because rather than saying the word in triumph, Ben seemed to be yelling it in anger.

Twelve

I woke up in my car at 5:50, according to the clock on the dashboard, having fallen asleep with Annie in my arms. I had stopped over to see her after my phone call. She came out of the house in her frilly pink bathrobe and got into the front seat.

"When we get married, will you promise to wear that on our wedding night?" I asked her. "It doesn't get any sexier than that."

She snuggled up to me. "Promise you'll love me forever then."

"Forever . . . and a little beyond that," I said as I put my arm around her.

"I can't kiss you," she told me.

"Why?"

"I won't be able to stop there."

"Do we need to?"

"No, but we should," she said as she gave me a kiss.

"Want to debate the pros and cons?" I asked.

"For one, it's in a car . . ."

"It's uncomfortable," I added.

"Someone might see."

"So far, no pros. All cons," I said. Then I kissed her, and the debate ended as we made love right there in the car.

Now it was six-fifteen in the morning.

"Annie." I shook her, and her eyes opened.

"What?"

"I'm late. Damn! I've got to put together the traffic report for the morning news."

I hurried her out of the car, kissed her, and sped away. I couldn't screw up again. As I headed down to the television station, I created an imaginary traffic report.

> Traffic backed up on Jones Falls Expressway.
> Northbound traffic on Route 40 moving slowly.

I continued to write, scribbling quickly as I drove, making up every predictable traffic scenario I could think of. It was always pretty much the same every morning anyway. How far off could I be?

Then I pulled into the parking lot of WMAR, jumped out of the car, and raced for the front door of the building. As I entered the lobby, I heard the morning news theme playing on one of the television monitors, and I ran like hell down the hallway. I could hear the announcer's voice:

"This is WMAR with the morning news—first with the news in the morning . . ."

And I ran.

". . . We're going to give you all of the sports finals in just a minute . . ."

And I ran, holding on to my bogus traffic report.

I reached the studio, opened the door, and raced in. I could see Tom Estes, looking around waiting for the report. His introduction was beginning. I ran faster.

"First, let's get the traffic report, and for that information . . ."

With those words I slipped the report on Estes' desk.

". . . here's Tom Estes."

The red light was on Estes.

"Here's the way it is right now," he said. "Let's look at the traffic."

I was out of breath, holding my sides, as Mickey approached.

"That was close," he said.

"I had to make up the whole damn thing."

"What happens if they find out it's wrong?"

"If you're in your car stuck in traffic, you're not going to be watching the television," I explained. "To be honest with you, I never understood this whole goddamn traffic report. It's fine for radio, but for television it's nonsense."

Mickey smiled and walked away, and fortunately, no one caught on to my bogus report. I had dodged a bullet.

I went into the directors' lounge to catch my breath. There was a television set on, with the sound off, and as I poured myself a coffee, I started to pay attention to a news story about Vietnam. Although the images on the screen were shocking, the footage seemed very much the same as what had been on every other day—guys on stretchers, medics working on wounded soldiers, bags of blood and plasma, a lot of shots of helicopters.

But I didn't stay focused on the television set for long, my mind drifted to thoughts of Annie . . . of marriage and family. What would it be like? To have a child, to not just be some guy but be a dad to a little boy or a little girl? Try as I might, I couldn't visualize that dinner—me and Annie as mom and dad at the table, a young child in a high chair eating strained peas or applesauce or whatever it was they ate when they had no teeth. None of those images would come into focus. They were Polaroid snapshots of the mind that failed to develop. I stared at each photo, but no image would materialize.

I looked at the clock. It was twenty minutes after eight and I realized it was time to get ready for *The Ranger Al Show*.

I walked into the control room and saw Ranger Al in the audio booth laying down his audio tracks for Oswald Rabbit and Doctor Fox. The audio man was working the levels of the cartridge tape that was used to record the voices of the puppets.

"Well, I'm not sure of that, Ranger," said Doctor Fox—the Ranger using his Louis Armstrong voice.

Ranger Al nodded to the audio man that he was ready to do the next response. The cartridge tape was cued and then the Ranger did the voice of Oswald Rabbit: "He's never sure, Ranger Al. Never, never, never."

The Ranger continued to prerecord the voices of Ozzie Rabbit and Doctor Fox while I headed down to the studio floor to make sure everything was in order.

It was surprising how flimsy the sets really were and yet how substantial they looked on television. It was also impressive to think that a man with nothing more than a few scraggly puppets had been able to entertain boys and girls for over two decades.

It was easy to make fun of the Ranger, but he had a way of connecting with children. There was no denying the success of his show. It was on six days a week, fifty weeks a year, and was always the highest-rated program in its time slot. With all the changes that had taken place in that twenty-year period, Ranger Al was a constant. No matter what fads came and went—the hula hoop craze; the change in music styles from big band to rock and roll; the technical advances in movie making from Cinerama to CinemaScope to 3-D; the progression of television from black and white to color—and no matter the social changes occurring in an era that was beginning to define itself with sex, drugs, rock and roll, and a far-off war in Southeast Asia . . . Throughout it all, Ranger Al ruled the airwaves from nine to ten almost every morning.

I wandered around the stage trying on a few of the old hand puppets that were not in use. There was Martin Monkey, a little furry monkey with a sweatshirt and a big *M* sewn into it. He was popular once upon a time, but apparently his glory days were over. I was starting to realize that it happened to the best of us.

I walked into a little prop room backstage where there was twenty years of memorabilia—old photos of the Ranger on one of the earliest broadcasts, some miniature sets from old production numbers. I vaguely remembered seeing some of these props when I watched the show as a kid . . . half memories of sketches I couldn't really recall.

Then suddenly, Al was standing behind me.

"Bobby, I like your musical idea. Let's do it."

I turned, surprised and excited. "When?"

"This morning. The second segment," Al said methodically, then started to walk away across the dimly lit studio that in minutes would come to life.

I yelled after him, "Okay, I'll have it ready." I ran across the studio, up the ladder into the control room, and quickly got to a phone. I dialed Annie's number and heard her half-asleep voice.

"Annie . . . I know it's early, but the Ranger wants to do the Beach Boys piece. Watch."

Before she could even answer me, I hung up the phone. I had work to do. The Ranger was going to include an idea of mine in his show and I was euphoric.

Annie was having a cup of coffee in the kitchen as *The Ranger Al Show* played on the family's small black-and-white television set and things started to go terribly wrong.

I was sitting on a stool working the hand puppets inside the little Ranger Station. Ozzie Rabbit and Doctor Fox were sitting on the windowsill, and the Ranger was having his conversation with them.

"And how are you, Doctor Fox?"

Suddenly, we heard the voice of Ozzie Rabbit instead.

"He never said anything to me."

I whispered through my headset, "What the hell's going on up there?"

I could hear the audio man in the control room. "Shit, the tape isn't cuing correctly."

The Ranger realized that something was wrong. Using all of his great experience, he tried to compensate.

"He didn't say what, Oz?"

Now, instead of hearing Ozzie's voice, we heard Doctor Fox—a happy Doctor Fox.

"Hi, Ranger Al."

I was completely confused. Every time I started to move the mouth of the puppet that was supposed to be speaking, I would hear the audio of the other puppet.

I kept whispering into my headset to see if they could get this sorted out, but it was obvious that there were serious technical problems. Ranger Al desperately tried to make sense out of the dialogue but it was all one giant non sequitur.

"So how are you, Ozzie?" Ranger Al attempted a simple question and waited to hear the answer. But instead of an answer, Doctor Fox responded with, "He wasn't supposed to be there," and once again I worked the wrong hand puppet.

Apparently, Neil picked this moment to walk into his parents' kitchen, having just come home from the night before. After staring at the confusion taking place on the television, he smiled and said, "This is very nice."

Then Annie's mother walked into the kitchen and poured herself some coffee.

Up in the control room, they were desperately trying to correct the audio difficulties. The cueing device would not operate properly, so all the answers—the prerecorded voices Ranger Al had laid down—were coming up at random, and I kept working a puppet that didn't match the correct voice.

The Ranger, pro that he was, just kept smiling and said, "Well, you guys are really rascals today, aren't you?"

"Hi, boys and girls. It's Ranger Al time. Good morning! Hello, hello, hello," said Ozzie, as if the show had just begun.

In all of this confusion, my headset started to slip. I leaned over to pull more cord toward me and somehow, I still don't know how, my foot slipped and pushed away the sandbag which held the corner flat of the set in place. The set started to shake and then it toppled over. The entire front of Ranger Al's Ranger Station hit the floor and there I was sitting on a stool holding two hand puppets, staring right into the lens of the camera. I was on-air, for everyone at home to see.

I was on that black-and-white television in Annie's kitchen, holding two large furry puppets and trying to burrow behind them. Annie's mother stared at my feeble attempt to hide myself and said, "So this is my son-in-law-to-be. How happy I am." Then she walked out of the kitchen in disgust.

The Ranger got it together enough to say that a commercial was coming up, and asked the boys and girls to stick around because we were coming back in just a minute.

During the break, the Ranger was in a rage, asking, "What the hell is going on?" Over the intercom on the studio floor we heard the audio man's voice. "I'm not sure, Hal. I'm very, very sorry, there seems to be something wrong with the cueing device on the tape."

I started to put the set back up, and Mickey helped while I apologized to Ranger Al. "I don't know how I did it. I'm really sorry." Then the Ranger quietly said, "I think I'm going to have to replace you, Bobby."

I don't think any comment ever hit me so hard. This was the end for me. Between the news fuckup and this, I was out the door. The end of my brief television career. Mickey looked over at me, knowing how bad I felt, and quietly said, "It's not your fault."

We got the Ranger Al set back in place and I said nothing. What was there to say? All I could do was wonder what I was possibly going to do with the rest of my life.

Then I heard the director's voice blaring over the speakers onto the soundstage. "We have a three-minute wildlife short, then we're back, live. Set up for 'Good Vibrations.' " I had completely forgotten about the Beach Boys number I'd talked to Ranger Al about. I was in no mood to do it now, but I had to get ready.

Mickey yelled over to me encouragingly, "I'll get Wally and Flo Worm." I nodded, went back into the Ranger Station, put the bonnet on Ozzie, and slipped my hands into each puppet. Then I pushed them through the black velvet curtain and perched them on the windowsill. I was ready, although less than enthusiastic. The wildlife short seemed as if it was three hours long. Finally, it came to an end.

Ranger Al looked to the camera and, with great zest, as if nothing had gone wrong earlier, told the boys and girls that they were in for a special treat and that he was feeling so happy today—he was getting "good vibrations." Then the red light was on, and I worked Ozzie Rabbit and Doctor Fox while Mickey worked Flo and Wally Worm. We were cooking . . . the music was infectious. Ozzie looked genuinely funny in the falsetto parts; even I was amused. I worked those two furry little creatures for all they were worth, shaking them in an erratic dance, their pliable bodies moving around like big blobs of jelly.

The music drove our skit. I could see the camera guys caught up in the beat, obviously enjoying themselves. The little studio was rocking. The mix of the right music and appropriate visuals made for a fun "bit." My adrenaline was pumping and I loved every moment of it. Then, before I knew it, the sketch was over. Everything seemed a blur.

Suddenly, John Haynes, the general manager of WMAR, was in the studio. He was a tall man, dignified with gray hair, immaculately dressed. Within my cloud-covered mind, I heard the words, "You have gone from being the bum of the week to the man of the hour. I loved the vitality. I loved that music. It's new; it's fresh. It perks up the show, wouldn't you say, Hal?"

Al was just as buoyant. "My feelings exactly."

Haynes continued to throw around compliments. "We need more of that youthful vigor. The young ones love rock and roll." Then he walked closer to me, almost examining me. "What is your name again?"

"Bobby Shine, sir. Bobby Shine."

He stared at me for a moment, as if trying to memorize my name, then without saying goodbye or anything else, he abruptly left the studio.

The Ranger turned to me and quietly and supportively said, "You should really be pleased. John Haynes doesn't come around very often."

I was saved. I had been down for the nine count, but somehow I was back. Saved by the Beach Boys. One silly little sketch pulled me back up from the depths of despair. One silly little musical sketch.

Some things in life are a matter of timing. If the "Good Vibrations" piece hadn't been scheduled for that day at the exact time it happened, I might never have been there the next day. There might have been no more days after that. It could have been the end of my fledgling career. I always wondered what would have happened if I'd been fired. I was hanging by a thread but the thread didn't break, so I got a chance to see the next day . . . and each day that followed I got stronger. Each day I learned a little more. I couldn't wait for all those next days to come.

It was sometime that morning that Annie's father informed Neil that if he was not going to law school, "it's best that you find a job, and that means earning a living. I want you to find another place to live. It's time for you to be on your own."

All of Mr. Tilden's anger toward Neil bubbled up to the surface that morning—his disappointment in his son's choices and his frustration at his erratic behavior.

Neil listened, and then, when Mr. Tilden had finished, he looked at his father and, in the most understated way, simply said, "Ooooooh . . . family tensions," and walked away. Annie said nothing, neither did her mother. Mr. Tilden opened the kitchen cabinet, took out a few pills from a prescription bottle, and swallowed them with a glass of water. Then he walked out of the kitchen and left for work.

Annie was in her bedroom, putting on her nurse's uniform, when she heard the sound of her brother's voice. She approached Neil's room and could hear him more clearly now. He was reading aloud:

" *'I'm more beautiful than anyone else,' she said brokenly, 'why can't I be happy . . .'* "

Annie stood on the threshold of Neil's room. He glanced up at her for a moment, then went back to reading.

"Her moist eyes tore at her stability, her mouth turned slightly downward with an exquisite sadness. She says: 'I'd like to marry you, if you'll have me. I suppose you think I'm not worth having, but I'll be so beautiful for you.' A million phrases of anger, pride, passion, tenderness fought on his lips, a perfect wave of emotion washed over him, carrying off with it a sediment of wisdom, of convention, of doubt, of honor. This was his girl who was speaking . . . his own, his beautiful, his pride . . ."

Then Neil looked up at Annie. She had no idea why he was reading this out loud or why he said nothing to her. She said, "Are you going to move out?"

Neil closed the book and put it on his nightstand. "That's what they want. I'm a dutiful son." Then he pulled down the covers, climbed into bed fully dressed, and closed his eyes.

Annie watched him for the longest time, but Neil never acknowledged that she was still in the room. Finally she said, "Good night, Neil. I'm going to work."

She walked out of the room and closed his door quietly.

Thirteen

Some stories require guesswork. They're not all that clear to begin with. First-person accounts retold through cigarette smoke and coffee during late night Diner chats. Some stories show our character as unbecoming or unpredictable. Other incidents reveal the agonizing transition from youthful exuberance to the painful realities of adulthood. We can never be absolutely sure of the truth, however. We can only know what we are told.

What we know about Ben is that it started with a shiny 1967 Cadillac DeVille, slowly turning on a rotating platform in the Rawlings Cadillac dealership showroom. The room was a temple, a shrine to the gaudiness and glitz of the finest car America could make. It was everything that was good about the country. It was wealth and privilege and boyhood dreams.

Not ten feet away from the rotating pride of America was a sleeping Ben. He was dressed in a suit and tie with a glistening shine on his shoes. Ben had slipped into the costume of a salesman and had all the details down pat, but he lacked one thing: a passion for the job. He couldn't have cared less about it, and consequently, the reality of the job beat him up. Each day was drabber than the one before, and each day he was less and less interested, until he found it hard to stay awake. The honeymoon was over. The euphoria leading up to the wedding night was behind him now. He was supposed to be a man . . . supposed to be a grown-up. And all those "supposed to be's" were strangling him. In school when a class was boring you could cut it, but there was no such option now. You couldn't just cut your occupation. Or your life. If you skipped an hour, the rest of the day was still going to look exactly like it did before you left, and each day was exactly like the next one. And Ben couldn't stay awake.

A foot kicked Ben's metal desk, and the sound of it shocked him out of his slumber. Mr. Rawlings, his father-in-law, was standing over him.

"You may be my daughter's husband, but if you don't carry your load here, you're gone. This is no free ride, mister." That's all Mr. Rawlings said before walking back to his office.

Ben was embarrassed, because the other salesmen overheard what was said. And the embarrassment hurt more than the threat. Ben was the put-down artist; for him to have been put down in front of others was very difficult for him to deal with.

He got up from his metal desk, walked into the bathroom, and washed his face with cold water. As he did so, he saw a few hairs from his head fall into the sink. He looked into the mirror and examined the top of his head. He could see his scalp and how his hair was thinning, and then quietly Ben said, "Thanks, God."

For quite a few days after general manager John Haynes' encouraging comments, I was elated. Filled with excitement, enthusiasm, and new ideas—ideas that involved film, music, and puppets. I had been given a mandate and I felt challenged in the most positive way. For hours and hours I'd find myself in the music library listening to songs by the Beach Boys, the Mamas and the Papas, Dion, Dylan, the Lovin' Spoonful, Bing Crosby, Frankie Avalon. I'd sit at that turntable and sample one record after another, from *Slaughter on Tenth Avenue* by Richard Rodgers to novelty numbers by Spike Jones and the sultry ballads of Peggy Lee.

Hours and hours would pass. Mickey used to come by from time to time. He'd knock on the glass partition and shake his head, amused. Sometimes he would rap on the glass and mime eating, to see if I wanted to get some food with him, but I'd just shake my head no.

If I wasn't in the music library, I was in the film library, and I began to really study some of the great movies. That was the first time I'd ever seen a Busby Berkeley film. I loved the energy and the enthusiasm and particularly the kaleidoscope dance numbers.

It was also the first time I saw *Scarface*, *Public Enemy*, and *Little Caesar*, the tough-guy classics of the thirties. I was transported by some of the dialogue: "You're not gonna get me . . . see . . . I'm Little Caesar."

And James Cagney in *White Heat*, the weirdest, most psychotic gangster portrayal I'd ever seen. I remember, after seeing that film, I went to the Diner and said, "Top of the world, Ma! Top of the world." The guys thought I was crazy and didn't know what I was talking about. They'd never seen the movie, and I couldn't explain it well enough to hold their interest. Later on, at different times when we were sitting and talking in the Diner, I would suddenly blurt it out again and the guys would just shake their heads. Neil was the only one who took a liking to the phrase and he repeated it often: "Top of the world, Ma! Top of the world."

I came across a novelty series called *USA 1,000* in the film library. It was a compilation of silent footage of various types of goofy events: cowboys doing crazy tricks on horses and men trying to fly. There were reels and reels of silent film footage. On reel 28, one man was wearing feathers on his arms while jumping off the roof of a barn. Then a man wearing ice skates on a frozen pond had a rocket on his back. The rocket went off, the man immediately slipped on his ice skates and spun like a top across the frozen pond. There was one insane attempt after another to try and get into the air.

I kept notes on the different things I was seeing and the music I was listening to, and I began to formulate some ideas for Ranger Al. I was so in love with the possibilities. Television was no longer just holding my attention, it was consuming me. Although I didn't know where I was going with any of it, I was having the best time of my life. It did, however, begin to impact on how often I could see Annie, and even though she was more than accommodating, it did strain our relationship. But since we both knew it was an important period for me, she tried to support my newfound ambition.

Neil moved into a small, cheap hotel off St. Paul Street toward downtown. It had all the character of a Raymond Chandler novel, and I think when I mentioned that to Neil, he enjoyed the comparison. Neil was doing very little at this time except drinking alcohol, getting stoned, and taking various kinds of prescription pills for "the kick of it." He was always strapped for money, and Turko was quietly supporting him.

Turko was actually doing quite well in the bail bonds business. "The Turk," as he was known on the street, seemed to know about two-thirds of the criminals in downtown Baltimore. The city was becoming more dangerous in certain areas, but Turko *never* had a problem. He was too valuable to the criminal element. He was a human version of the Monopoly "Get out of Jail Free" card, except his card wasn't free.

The Turk now sported a pinkie ring that cost a lot more than the one he originally got at Ben Franklin's five-and-dime. It was a blue sapphire and dwarfed his pinkie finger. He only wore shirts that required cuff links, gold cuff links with engraved *T*'s. He was the first guy we knew who had a pair of shoes made. We'd never heard of such a thing. It took over two months for the shoes to be ready, and once they arrived the Turk would go on for hours about the comfort and necessity of a good handmade shoe. He thought these accessories would somehow bring him a touch of class, but it wasn't meant to be. Class was something Neil had without trying. Even without shoes. Even when he was down and out.

During this period, Neil seldom left his shabby room except to get lunch or dinner down at the Earl of Sandwich on the corner. It was surprising that he didn't venture out much further, because the area around him was beginning to change rapidly. In the parlance of that time, it was "a happening place."

More and more young people were beginning to inhabit Mount Vernon Place, taking over some of the old brownstones and moving into the buildings in groups of six, eight, or ten. They would throw mattresses down on the floor and use a few crates as tables or to store their records. Candles lit the rooms.

This was the beginning of the hippie period and it snuck up on us quickly and quietly. All kinds of different shops opened, selling tie-dyed clothes, sandals, handmade jewelry and candles. "Head shops" appeared, peddling drug paraphernalia, incense, and roach clips.

And there was a new vocabulary: *Man, I got wasted . . . Far-out . . . Can you dig it? . . . Groovy . . . Bitchin' . . .*

A small grocery store/restaurant opened up in the basement of a brownstone on Charles Street. It was called the Green Earth and that's where I first heard the term "health food."

Eggy was the first to discover the Green Earth and gave us this information at the Diner one night. "Health food isn't the only thing there," he said. "There's something else."

Having been there with Eggy earlier that day, Turko chimed in. He told us about the real value of this new find.

The second he descended the stairs and opened the front door, he whispered to Eggy, "Health food? What the hell kind of place is this?" Eggy, not wanting to reveal too much all at once, said, "It's not about the food."

"Then what's it about?"

Eggy nodded for Turko to look over at the library-type tables, and sitting there were a number of "hippie girls," dressed in tie-dyed tops, long skirts, beads, bandannas, leather vests with fringe.

Turko was overwhelmed. He was also suddenly uncomfortable in his suit and tie. His pinkie ring was definitely out of place.

In awe of it all, Eggy whispered, "Look at them. Look." And the two guys scanned the room, enthralled by the sight of girls with long flowing hair, no permanents, no hair spray, no beehive hairdos, no makeup. It may have been the sexiest moment of Eggy's and Turko's lives. They were Lewis and Clark discovering the Northwest Passage, stumbling upon a tribe never before seen.

"Chicks with no bras. No bras! You can see their nips," Eggy said excitedly.

Turko was duly impressed. "Nice find. This is a *very* nice find."

"It's all about free love," Eggy added. "These broads put out. They're living with guys. It's wild."

Turko was very curious. "You know the skinny on this? You have the whole lowdown?"

"I saw a sticker on one of these chicks' bags. It said, 'Make love, not war.' "

Turko smiled upon hearing this. "She'd have no argument from me."

Then Eggy suggested they get something to eat over at the counter, join the hippie chicks, and make their move.

They went to order from a long-haired guy wearing denims, a headband, and more beads than could possibly be imagined. "What are you guys into?" he asked.

Eggy responded sarcastically, "Other than food?"

The two guys looked at the menu board, which was filled with items they had never heard of. There were sandwiches made with goat cheese and bean sprouts, tofu and hummus, sun-dried tomatoes and sunflower seeds, and vegetable drinks with spirulina, bee pollen, and wheat germ.

A perplexed Turko asked, "You got any pastrami or corned beef?"

The counterman smiled. "That's not happening here."

The guys looked at the menu board again. "Shit, this is tough," said Turko.

The counterman, understanding their dilemma, said, "Close as I can get to what you want might be an organic turkey sandwich."

"Organic to what?" Eggy asked.

The counterman explained that organic meant the turkey was natural.

Turko thought about this for a moment—it was a concept he was not familiar with. "Aren't all turkeys natural?"

The counterman explained the philosophy of the Green Earth, which was that the turkeys were fed organic foods, free of pesticides and any preservatives whatsoever.

Turko grew impatient. "Personally, I don't give a fuck what the turkey eats. It's me that's hungry."

"You are what you eat, man," said the guy behind the counter.

Eggy nodded, then whispered to Turko, "Just get some soup and eye the broads. Then we'll go get a corned beef sandwich over at Atman's later." So they decided on garden vegetable, then went to make their move.

It was on one of their regular forays to the health food restaurant that Turko met Neddy. Neddy was a thinner, slightly more petite version of Mary Travers from Peter, Paul & Mary. She had a subtle smile, which for some reason was overwhelmingly seductive. Although she had that hippie look and seemed just one step above the poverty level, the reality was that she came from an extremely wealthy family in Hunt Valley, which was outside of Baltimore, and she was a student at the Maryland Institute of Art. She told this to Turko and he responded, "Art? Nice."

Turko was the type who thought Keane, known for painting women with waiflike eyes, was on a par with Picasso. "A fucking genius. How this guy can paint those eyes," Turko would say with such reverence.

Neddy also mentioned that she practiced yoga and macrobiotics. Turko said that he didn't really know much about any of that, and Neddy informed him, "It's all about mind and body." Turko gave her a little "come-on" attitude and said, "I like the sound of that."

Eggy supported Turko. "He likes anything with mind and body."

Then Neddy gave Turko that subtle smile and said, "*Do* you?"

"Without a doubt."

"Cool."

The two thought they had stumbled into the promised land. At one point Neddy asked if Turko felt comfortable all dressed up that way. He said he did and that he needed to be dressed in a suit for work.

"What kind of work?"

He lied that he was in the investment business. Eggy said they were partners.

"How old are you guys?"

They told her that they were both twenty-three, and Neddy was surprised. "Oh . . . oh . . . I thought you guys were much older."

The comment was like a jolt to their system. Neddy added, "Maybe it's because of your hair. It's so neatly combed and so in place." Since they were both Brylcreem guys, they didn't respond.

Turko tried to assess the situation. They didn't seem to be scoring overwhelming points with Neddy, but then again, she maintained some interest. However, it was clear that, at best, they were treading water.

Both guys had to get back to work. Eggy mentioned that he had a number of winter coats that needed to be priced. "Busy day at Sol Kirk's," he said with great importance.

Neddy looked at him. "I thought you were in the investment business."

Without wasting a split second, Eggy simply said, "I lied."

Neddy started to laugh so hard that Eggy was taken aback for a moment. Through her laughter she said, "That is *so* honest. So unabashedly honest."

Eggy looked at Turko. "Unabashed. I guess I am that."

"I just love that," Neddy added.

Turko asked how he could get ahold of her.

"You could probably find me here," she said. Then the two guys left.

At the Diner later that night, I'd noticed that Eggy's hair was freshly washed, minus hair lotion. Now I knew why. His hair was so white and fine, it was flying in all directions, a little like a circus performer who's been shot out of a cannon.

In the months that passed, there would be modifications in all of our hairstyles, as well as the way we dressed. Some of the changes were slight. Pants that were previously called dungarees became jeans, and the more worn and torn the better. Patches filled the holes, and the more holes, the cooler you were. Neil was as cool as it got. I was not a jeans guy yet. I was still wearing "slacks." And I still polished my shoes.

Girlfriends began to be referred to as "my old lady." All around us, guys and girls living together became a new lifestyle.

Music was changing too. Gone were pop idols Frankie Avalon, Bobby Rydell, Ricky Nelson, and the Everly Brothers. Even Elvis Presley had lost his crown as King of Rock and Roll. The English music invasion was in full force: the Beatles, the Rolling Stones, the Kinks, the Animals, Herman's Hermits, The Who, Gerry & the Pacemakers. The sixties now had a label—"the swinging sixties."

Black music exploded with the sound of Motown. Growing up in Baltimore, we had always listened to black music on what were referred to as the "colored stations." We listened to WEBB and WSID because both had a great roster of DJs, especially Fat Daddy, who could rhyme words in a fast barrage. "From the ghetto through the suburban areas comes your leader of rhythm and blues—the expected one, Fat Daddy. The soul boss with the hot sauce. Fat Poppa, showstoppa."

We tried to imitate him, but it was impossible. It couldn't be done, especially by a bunch of white guys. But now black music had crossed over and came to white radio stations in full force. Black entertainers of every kind were becoming popular, on television as well as radio.

And still, there are gaps . . .

While the world was changing, Neil mostly stayed in his hotel room ingesting every drug imaginable. We saw him less and less.

Things weren't getting any better for Ben, either. His boredom was overwhelming him and he was using amphetamines—"uppers"—more and more as the days went by. Then, one lunchtime, at his father-in-law's Cadillac dealership, everything came to a head.

It was the most ordinary moment imaginable that just went completely out of control. A delivery boy brought lunch to Ben, announcing, "Tuna sandwich, chips, and a Coke."

Ben pulled some bills out of his pocket. He always liked to have a wad of money if possible. It made him feel important. He handed the delivery boy a few bucks and said, "Keep the change." It was a good tip and the delivery boy acknowledged it with a "Thanks, sir." Then he turned to leave.

Ben called out to him, "Hey, what did you call me?"

"What?" asked the delivery boy.

Ben seemed agitated. "What did you call me? Did you call me 'sir'?"

The delivery boy was confused. "Yeah, why?"

"Do I look like your father or something?"

"No."

"Then what the fuck are you doing calling me 'sir'? I'm three years older than you are, tops."

Ben's anger seemed to be feeding on itself, but the delivery boy tried to remain friendly. "I was just thanking you."

Ben stepped closer to the delivery boy, moving past a shiny

yellow Cadillac which seemed to glow as it caught the midday sun. He yelled, "No. You weren't just thanking me. I am not some fucking sir!"

The other salesmen began to pay attention to Ben's yelling now. The delivery boy was starting to get pissed off. He tried to be pleasant and it didn't work, so he began to take a stand. "Don't make a big deal out of it," he said.

That only got Ben more and more agitated. He started to poke his finger at the delivery boy. "I'm not a sir. You get that? My father is a sir. I am *not* a sir!"

They were face to face. "I'm just delivering a sandwich. Period," the delivery boy yelled. The other salesmen realized that the situation was getting very tense. The "temple of Cadillac" echoed as Ben and the delivery boy screamed at one another.

"Period?!!" yelled Ben. "You have the balls to say 'period' to me? Period?!!!"

The screaming finally ended when the delivery boy said, "Go fuck yourself, *sir*!" then spun on his heels and headed for the door.

The final "sir" was like a dagger to Ben's heart, and he went at the delivery boy in a fury, a rage that was totally out of control. But the delivery boy was up to all that Ben could offer and he started slamming punches, hitting him in the face, the mouth, and the stomach with great speed. Ben lunged at him with a couple of hard punches, and then they fell onto the hood of the yellow Cadillac. Speckles of red marred the shiny surface of the Cadillac's hood as blood dripped from Ben's nose.

The salesmen tried to pull them apart, but Ben and the delivery boy kept going at it, the delivery boy getting the best of the battle. Even as Ben was taking hard punches, he was screaming, "I'm not a sir! I'm not a sir!"

It was at this moment that Janet's father walked into the showroom. He watched the fighting and the salesmen trying to pull the two men apart. One salesman saw Mr. Rawlings first, and within a few seconds, without Ben's father-in-law saying anything, everything grew still. The fighting stopped.

Mr. Rawlings looked at the yellow Cadillac DeVille and the blood dripping down the hood of his beloved merchandise. Then he asked, "What the hell is going on here?"

Ben pulled out a handkerchief to stop the flow of blood from his nose, but he didn't answer. Neither did any of the other salesmen. Even the delivery boy kept quiet.

"I deserve an explanation," Janet's father said, and then, because he had to, the delivery boy answered. "I called him 'sir,' " as if that would explain everything to anyone.

Later that afternoon, Mr. Rawlings fired his son-in-law. Ben said nothing. He left the dealership. But the ultimate humiliation followed moments later when Ben went to get into his loaner Cadillac. Janet's father raced out of the glass doors of the dealership and yelled, "You only get a Caddie when you work here. You don't work here anymore. Leave the keys."

Ben closed the door of the car and walked off.

Fourteen

Duke was directing the evening news. I sat at the back of the television studio observing, trying to get a better idea of how it was done. Even though he was only in his late twenties, Duke was the fair-haired boy of the station—talented, fast, always in control, confident, and very demanding. I worried, as I watched him, that I could never be as good. He handled the show effortlessly. Could I possibly do this? It seemed doubtful. But I was determined to try. I would stare at him, almost willing myself into his chair.

Morley Safer was on a monitor reporting from Vietnam. The news wasn't good. A U.S. cargo plane had crashed into a village, killing 125 civilians. As if that wasn't bad enough, another story stated that in Saigon government corruption was stealing up to 40 percent of U.S. aid. Then there was a Pentagon report admitting that the cost of the war was now two billion dollars a month.

Richard, Duke's assistant director, sat next to him, constantly feeding Duke information, giving him countdowns on various pieces of film, and alerting the Telecine area to stand by to roll the proper footage. It was a high-energy room, not unlike what you might expect from an air traffic control station—voices constantly intoning over headsets and intercoms.

"Three, two, one . . . roll one."

"Stand by on the floor."

"Stand by, camera two."

"Two—mike, cue him."

And then the commercial breaks. For one hour there wasn't a moment of downtime. Everybody had to be alert and aware of every second of time as the program moved toward seven o'clock. If a new story broke, they had to make room for it, adjust the other stories, drop some, abbreviate others. Duke was always in the center of the maelstrom.

I watched as he barked another order. "All right, have Tony wrap it up and have him introduce weather. Stand by on two."

Richard was right there, with more information. "Five seconds . . . slides on weather."

Duke raised his hand like a conductor and said, "One—mike . . . cue him," and then he snapped his fingers.

It was at that moment that I heard a tapping on the glass partition between the control room and the hallway. I turned to see Neil's face pressed against the glass, distorted-looking like some grotesque monster. When he knew he had my attention, he pulled away from the glass and indicated for me to come out.

"What's doing?" I said as I closed the control room door behind me.

"This how you spend your time? Watching television?" Neil had an alcohol smell on his breath. He hadn't just been drinking a glass of booze or even a bottle, more like a gallon of the stuff. Even so, he didn't seem drunk at all.

"I'm trying to learn," I explained. "Duke's the best director here. Trying to pick up what I can."

Neil looked through the glass into the control room as Duke snapped his fingers to indicate a camera change. "That's what you want to do?"

I tried to smile, almost apologetically, "Yeah," and it was then I could detect something was wrong. Neil seemed troubled and anxious, but he was not the type to ever reveal anything right away, so he peered back again into the control room. "It looks like the whole thing is all about the snap," and he mimicked Duke with the same finger snap. Then he grew quiet again.

"What's up?" I asked. "Why are you here?"

He pulled out a letter from his jacket and handed it to me. It didn't take long to figure out what it was all about. "Drafted?"

Neil nodded and lit a cigarette. "I have to report to Fort Holabird tomorrow morning, 6 a.m."

This didn't make sense. You didn't just get a letter from the draft board and report the following morning. I told him this and he offered up a very simple answer. "I've had it for two weeks."

"Shit! Why did you wait? What the fuck is wrong with you?"

He just shrugged.

Suddenly, there was a commotion coming from inside the control room. I looked through the glass and saw Douglas Shepherd, the weatherman, standing in front of a rear-screen projection that read "Weather," but the slide was upside down.

I could hear Duke screaming, so I walked back into the control room. Neil followed. We stood by the back door as Duke continued to yell into his headset.

"Goddamn it! Goddamn it! You think the next one is okay? You have that the right side up?!!"

They were getting ready to go to the national weather map. Shepherd was mentioning that a cooling trend was on the way, and as he said, "Let's go to the national weather map," Duke had no alternative but to say, "Change slide."

Now the national weather map came up on the rear screen, but it was also upside down. Duke went berserk. Veins were popping up in his forehead. "Goddamn it! Goddamn it!"

As angry as Duke was, Douglas Shepherd was as calm. Without the slightest hesitation, he took his pointer and indicated Florida, now at the top of the screen, and said, "Florida, eighty-two . . . and then down here in Maine, forty-one." Some of the crew in the booth were laughing as Shepherd continued to report the weather, completely unfazed, a seasoned pro.

Duke was yelling on the headset, "Mickey, if this is your doing, your ass is on the line, buddy."

Neil loved the drama of it all and quietly said, "The snapping finger guy seems a little frazzled," but I was thinking about Neil and his draft notice.

"Why didn't you call Danny and get the note?"

Neil looked at me for the longest beat, as if he had never heard about Danny's doctor's note and how it had worked for other guys . . . how it had just worked for Shade. He thought about it and then he did what Neil always did, and what he had done since we used to sword-fight with our bandaged fingers: he just shrugged.

We walked out of the television station, across the parking lot. The air was cold and damp, that Baltimore chill that cuts to the bone. Neil had come over by cab, so we got into my car and headed off in search of Danny. The most likely place to begin was over at Knocko's.

We rode in silence, my Chevy Malibu running smooth. The age of "muscle" cars was now coming into vogue, GTOs and the like. My Malibu might have been categorized as a "half-muscle" car.

Neil sat quietly smoking a cigarette, just staring at the passing lights. I didn't bother to ask, "Why did you wait so long?" again, since it was apparent the answer was never going to be forthcoming. Neil only revealed information when he wanted to, or when his mood allowed him to be straightforward.

I was looking out the window at the trees, stripped bare of their leaves—I always thought that trees in the winter months looked scared—and we drove in silence.

The radio was playing a song by Donovan:

"They call me mellow yellow . . ."

I was listening to the lyrics, but I couldn't stay focused long enough to make any sense out of them. Neil was blowing smoke rings that floated softly toward the windshield, and then I saw Knocko's Pool Hall up on the right, next to the Sinclair station.

We parked on the street, not half a block away, and quickly headed toward the pool room. The wind was kicking up, and I did a half walk/run to the stairwell leading down to the entrance. Neil seemed oblivious to the cold and walked casually, as if there was no urgency or even purpose to our visit. Before we went in I called him on this. "If you think I'm wasting your time, then fuck it. You're the one who's drafted, not me."

He shook his head and said, "No, no, no . . . get Danny." Then we went inside.

The joint was packed. Every one of the sixteen tables was in action. The place was a real shit hole, but the neon signs, the air filled with cigarette smoke, the crack of the pool balls, and the sound of the jukebox made for a seductive environment. It was a guys' place. The place reeked of "cool."

Knocko's was an institution. Not only were there rules of play, there were rules of protocol. No one was allowed in the establishment until they were at least sixteen years of age, and you had to be coming to Knocko's for over a year before you were allowed to say the supercool words: "Knocko, put it on my tab." Then you could get a five-cent Coke and a Milky Way, and Knocko would let you pay weekly.

Knocko wore flowered Hawaiian shirts all year long. He never recognized a season. Any season. And words were a premium with Knocko. If a four-word answer was considered concise, he made it three, and more often than not, two words were all he found necessary to utter. "Get out!" was his most frequently used sentence.

"Knocko, I got a problem with table seven."

"Get out!"

Perched on a stool, with a cheap El Producto cigar stuck in his mouth, he scanned the action in his pool hall. No one ever challenged or disagreed with him. This was his fiefdom and you played by his rules.

My eyes wandered the place until I spotted Danny, a cigarette hanging from his lips, wearing one of his fine suits, lining up a shot. I approached him and said that Neil had a real problem. I told him the whole story and how much Neil needed his help. Then he went back to playing pool, moving around the table with efficiency, examining his shots and manipulating the cue stick with grace and finesse.

I was bewildered, five minutes must have gone by and I was beginning to think I had never had the conversation with him. Neil seemed oblivious—didn't seem to care—and I didn't know what else to do. Danny made a difficult shot. He banked a ball off the cushion and sank a six ball. Then he scanned the table and spoke without looking up.

"You're one fucked-up soul, Neil. You come to me at the eleventh hour." He repeated the words, almost disbelieving. "The eleventh hour."

"It happened."

Without raising his eyes from the table, Danny spoke again, "You have five hundred?"

"Nada," said Neil, now sipping on a Coke, still seemingly without a care in the world.

"Oh, better yet." Danny looked up from the table for the very first time and rolled his eyes.

"I'll kick in a hundred. Some of the other guys will too," I offered.

Danny started rubbing chalk over the tip of his pool cue. "Why should I do this? This gesture . . . this service for you? Will you answer this for me, Neil?"

"Well," Neil said flatly, "I never fucked your sister."

Danny smiled. "You do get points for that."

I thought it best for me to get Danny back on the topic. Time was of the essence.

"Danny, can you get ahold of that doctor?"

"This late?" He put down the chalk and leaned across the table to line up a shot. "What do you think he's doing, this doctor? You think he's sitting in his office with a paper and pen waiting for my call?" He quickly made a shot and, without looking at Neil, said, "You're one big fuckup."

Then he walked over to a stool, sat down, and for some reason retied his right shoelace. After looking over his shoe and feeling satisfied that the bow was properly placed exactly in the center, that each half of the bow was symmetrical, he said, "I'll call." He nodded to the other player, said, "Give me five," and walked over to the phone booth.

Well, at least something was going to happen. Danny was going to go to bat for Neil, and I felt relieved.

Neil lit another cigarette and said, "You ever see Sinatra in that movie *Young at Heart*?"

"No, I don't think so. Why?"

He leaned against the pool table and, as if he'd seen the movie earlier that day, described it in great detail. Then he got to a part that absolutely fascinated him.

"There's this great scene. He's depressed and he's driving alone in his car, cigarette in his mouth. It's snowing outside and he's watching the windshield blades clean the window. Suddenly, he turns off the wipers and watches as the snow slowly piles up onto the windshield. He keeps driving, and the snow rises higher and higher until he can't see, until the entire windshield is covered in snow and it's all white. Then there's this crash. Great way to kill yourself, don't you think?"

"He died?"

"No. He ends up in a hospital. He's wearing one of those silly head bandages they always wear in those movies, and Doris Day showed up."

Suicide was an idea that was never far from Neil's mind. Too many conversations covered that subject. Too many times he had turned a discussion in that direction. Sometimes, when you look back on events, remember things that were said, you can find clues . . . signs that could explain behavior and what a person was about, what they were really heading toward. But nothing I remember about Neil ever offered any clarity. There was no way to predict what would ultimately happen to him.

Then Danny approached. "I called his home. Got no answer."

I asked him what the next step might be. He simply said, "We're gonna have to play this by ear."

Neil heard a song on the jukebox that he liked and began to dance to it. This pissed Danny off, so he went back to his game. "We'll keep in touch."

I said that we would head over to the Diner and be there most of the night. I reiterated that Neil only had until 6:30 a.m., when he had to report to Fort Holabird. Danny waved me off with a simple "I got it . . . I got it."

At the Diner, the night drifted on. At one-thirty in the morning there was still no call from Danny. Eggy and Shade were having a theological discussion that was quickly moving from the ridiculous to the sublime.

"Wait, wait, let me get this straight, Jesus had a brother named James?" asked Eggy, dipping his toast into a yellow egg yoke.

"Right," Shade said.

This revelation required a moment's thought on Eggy's part. He put down his toast and wiped a paper napkin across his mouth. "Jesus and James, the Christ brothers."

Shade corrected him, "Christ means Messiah."

"You know, it's bad enough when you have a brother who's all-American in lacrosse or the president of a fraternity or something like that—that's already hard enough to live up to—but can you imagine when your brother is the Messiah?" Eggy said this as if he had made one of the most profound statements anyone could ever utter. "Talk about an inferiority complex. Your brother is the Son of God, so what does that make you, chopped liver?" He dramatized that point by dipping his toast into the egg yoke again.

It was around that time that Ben walked in, his face puffy, a "mouse" under his left eye, his nose swollen. He looked like shit. He pulled up a chair. "No comments," he said. Then Eggy was back with his Jesus conversation again.

"Did you know that Jesus had a brother, his name was James?"

Without missing a beat, Ben said, "Yeah, James was the cool one."

"You knew he had a brother?" Shade asked.

"Jesus, really? I thought you were bullshitting me."

"Jesus and James, the Christ brothers," Eggy reiterated.

Shade was getting annoyed. "I told you that wasn't the last name."

Then Ben asked, "What *was* Jesus' last name?"

This question seemed to stump Shade. "I don't know. I don't think they had last names back then."

Eggy jumped in as if he was playing on a TV quiz show and snapped his fingers, "Judah Ben-Hur," and then Ben said, just as quickly, "Julius Caesar."

"Well, maybe some had last names," Shade backed down slightly, "but Jesus did not have a last name."

Again, Eggy, with a quiz show tone of voice, jumped in. "Jesus Steinberg."

Ben dismissed it. "Too Jewish."

Shade began to study Ben's beat-up face, the bruise under his eye, the red swollen nose. "So what happened?" he asked.

Ben responded with a condescending attitude. "Did I say don't mention my face, Shade? Was I very clear about that?"

The fight with the delivery boy was a story that hadn't been told yet. It was obvious something had happened, but nothing we said would make Ben reveal any more.

He ordered up some coffee while Eggy informed him of Neil's situation. After the surprise faded, Ben went into a tirade about how irresponsible Neil was. Then, noticing that Turko was not there, he asked Eggy, "Where's your better half?"

Eggy, proud that Turko was now involved with Neddy, said, "He's with that hippie chick again. She's death," which in Diner lingo meant an incredibly beautiful, voluptuous, outstanding girl.

Shade had to question that. "She's *that* good-looking?"

"Death. Trust me. A wet dream." And then, as if to get the guys hot and crazy, Eggy added, "No bra. Doesn't wear panties."

Ben liked the sound of that. "Very nice."

"The Turk is in heaven," Eggy said.

It was nearly two-thirty in the morning when Neil and I walked up the steps to Neddy's apartment. She lived off Charles Street, about a block north of Mount Vernon Square, which was where Baltimore's version of the Washington Monument stood. The streets around it were all cobblestoned. Every time I walked in that area, I imagined that I was in Paris—a student studying something esoteric like the writings of Rimbaud or the films of François Truffaut.

The smell of incense filled the hallway as we knocked on Neddy's door. The sudden noise did not make Turko happy. Neddy had been sitting astride him, blowing "pot" smoke into his mouth. But when she heard our continuous knocking, she left him and came to greet us, barefoot and wearing an outsized T-shirt.

"Is Turko here? It's important," I asked.

She turned in the direction of the Turk and said, "You have company," then motioned for us to come in.

I apologized for disturbing them and saw that Eggy was right—she was extremely attractive, and in the most natural way. Neil glanced at her and then began to look around the apartment. Turko came into the front room and asked, "What the hell's going on?"

"Neil's drafted. We need some money for Danny to get the note," I told him.

The Turk was irritated. "You guys can't wait? You're distracting me here."

"Drafted?" Neddy asked Neil.

"I leave in the morning," Neil said as he continued to study various sculptures and paintings which Neddy had apparently done in school. She seemed sympathetic to Neil's problem, but Turko was confused. "How's that possible? How could you leave in the morning?" Neil just shrugged so I explained the situation.

Turko grew angry. "You knew about Danny's note. What the fuck is wrong with you?"

I looked at my watch and asked Neddy if I could use her phone. She nodded. As I started dialing, I said, "We're hoping Danny gets ahold of the doctor tonight. Not much time left."

Neddy didn't know what the hell we were talking about and asked about the note.

Neil answered with another question, "You go to Maryland Institute?"

Neddy was surprised, "How did you know?"

"Looks a little like Giacometti. Not a bad influence."

Neddy was pleased and clearly flattered.

Turko immediately sized up the moment. "That's it, Neil, steal my girlfriend here."

"I'm nobody's girl, Turk," Neddy said sharply. "I told you that."

Then Neil flopped down on a mattress that was the living room couch and leaned against the wall. "I'm going, Turk . . . I'm going. No problem. I'm off to war. See me on the evening news." He began to imitate a TV newscaster, *"Thirty-six Americans die in Vietnam today . . ."* Then he smiled that weird Neil smile.

I had gotten through to the pool hall and was waiting for Danny to come to the phone, but could see Neddy's reaction to Neil's words. She was not exactly switching allegiance from Turko, but it was obvious she found Neil fascinating. I offered up some encouragement, "Danny'll get the note. He'll come up with it, you'll see."

Neddy had another suggestion. "You could go to Canada."

Neil lay on the mattress, smiled and put his hands to his lips, and said, "Shhhhhh."

Finally, Danny got on the phone. He still had no news to report. I told him that we would head up to the Diner and wait. He said he would let me know as soon as he had anything definite. Then he added, "Neil is one irresponsible fuck," and hung up.

I pulled into the Diner parking lot with Neil sitting shotgun. Turko was right behind me with Neddy. Light snow flurries were swirling around the night sky as the cool sounds of jazz from Berger's car filled the cold air. I was not a jazz fan, but it sounded like a Miles Davis piece, something from *Porgy and Bess.* I always had a rather basic understanding of jazz. I could stay with it as long as it remained melodic and mellow, but when a trumpet player like Miles Davis got into those shrieking sounds, it was goodbye for me.

I heard Turko say to Neddy, "You better stay here." When Neddy questioned why, Turko laid down our unspoken rule for the Diner: No girls allowed.

"What?"

"It just doesn't happen."

"Why?" Neddy asked, not understanding the senseless rule.

"It's just the rules of the game," Turko said, and walked off, leaving her standing in the parking lot.

Instead of getting into the car to wait, she just stood there. Snow continued to fall as she held her coat close to her. It was a long, brown, plain wool thing and looked like something worn during the Russian Revolution, but with her hair blowing lightly, she was still a prize.

When we got inside the Diner, Ben was on the phone at the cash register talking with Janet, explaining why he was out at three in the morning. "Janet, he's got a problem . . . Neil's supposed to report in the morning . . . Look, look, I want to be supportive . . ."

He was frustrated, hating the obligations that came with married life. He didn't want to explain why he was there, he just wanted to be there. When he saw Neil enter, Ben quickly handed him the phone. Neil immediately started talking in his most congenial manner, "Janet . . . hi, Neil. You feel that baby kicking?"

I headed over with Turko and sat at the booth next to Eggy and Shade. Eggy wanted to know what the story was.

"Nothing yet," I explained. "Just waiting for Danny's call." And Ben added the obvious, "Not much time."

Turko was still pissed off. "Fucking guy. It's one thing after another with him." The fact that Neddy had been paying special attention to Neil especially irritated him.

Ben glanced over at Neil, who was still on the phone. "Janet's giving me grief here."

Eggy said, "That's marriage," and once again launched into his theory that seeing prostitutes was a better way to go than dating or marriage. That night he presented it as an economic issue. "A hooker is cheaper in the long run." Love was never part of the equation with Eggy.

Meanwhile, Neil was deep in his conversation with Janet, discussing the anticipated birth of her baby. I heard him say, "For me, I want my first to be a girl, a little baby girl, but that's just me. You have a name picked out yet?"

Outside, Neddy wandered the parking lot listening to Berger's jazz selections. From time to time she would glance over at him in his car. He was lost in his music, sipping his usual thick cough syrup.

I was going to say something to Turko, that maybe under the circumstances Neddy should come in, but I thought I should leave that up to him. It was his girl, and guys didn't interfere, especially when sacred and inviolable Diner laws were involved.

Ben started a discussion about watching a Colts game with Janet. "I'm trying to watch the game one Sunday. Richardson drops the ball—I got the Colts and seven points, I'm betting a hundred on the game . . . ball goes right through Richardson's hand. I'm beside myself. Janet's reaction is, 'I bet he feels bad.' Feels bad! He could cost me some serious money and she's concerned about how he feels. She's watching the screen, 'Look, he looks really sad.' I tell you, I wanted to fucking kill her. You can't watch a game with a girl. Can't be done. She wants to know why they had to spit on the grass. 'It's unsanitary . . . you could fall on it,' she says."

Eggy was right there to back him up, "Broads don't know better. Prostitutes. You don't have to watch a game with a prostitute. Or you can watch it with her and pay her to keep quiet."

Ben continued. "There's a third down coming up, the Colts gotta make the first down. Janet's talking about something she saw on sale. I said, 'Janet, I can't talk now, the game is on the line here.' And she said, 'You could watch the game, and we could still talk about other things.' "

"She was killing the mood," Eggy offered.

Ben nodded and made a declaration: "Females are not equipped to see the subtleties of sports."

That was exactly the moment Neddy walked into the Diner. The whole place got silent. It was the equivalent of the feared gunslinger walking into a saloon in the old cowboy movies. Everyone was shocked.

Turko looked up from his coffee. "Oh my God."

"This takes the cake," Shade whispered. "I've never seen a girl in here. A waitress, but never a girl."

Neil sized up the situation and quickly hung up the phone on Janet. He walked over to Neddy. "Can I talk with you?"

"Sure, Neil."

And with that, he led Neddy back out the Diner door.

"I told her to stay put," Turko said disgustedly. "This broad is too much."

Shade shook his head. "Was that a bizarre moment, or what?"

I looked at my watch. Time was slipping away. Only a couple of hours left before Neil was going to be joining the army.

Ben watched Neil and Neddy through the Diner window and asked Turko, "You fucking her?"

"No, I'm just eating salads with her," Turko said sarcastically. Then he added, "Apparently, in a little wild run of hers a couple of years back, she fucked every guy north of Towson, but she has, as she puts it, 'just about sated that sex drive now.' She takes a more 'Zen' approach these days, whatever the fuck that means."

Ben stared back out the window of the Diner and mumbled, "Maybe I married too soon." He spoke quietly, but I could hear the anger. The frustration of married life was tormenting his brain again. Outside the window, I saw the opposite of anger as Neil began dancing with Neddy in the parking lot. They danced closely, sensually, to the sounds of Berger's jazz. Light snow fell on them as they held one another tight, lost in their private moment.

I saw them as I used to see those old *Look* magazine photos. I fantasized a scenario: He was trying to stop time as he held her. She had found her soul mate—a deeper love than she'd ever felt before. They danced—each breath filling the cold night air like an exhaust—and they danced. Two bodies running on steam, trying to turn life into a dream. But in reality, time was drawing to a close. Neil was only hours away from becoming a soldier in the

United States Army. Neddy's boyfriend was inside the Diner, tapping his foot impatiently. Still they danced . . . with the sun just below the horizon.

There was the sound of a phone ringing, and then I heard George, the owner of the Diner, calling my name. "Bobby, it's Danny."

As I walked to the phone, I realized I was holding my breath. Then came the words I was hoping for: "Come get it."

I yelled to the guys, "Danny's got the note!" and the small group cheered. "Dan the Man came through."

I opened the door and yelled out to Neil, "You've been saved, you fuck!" Neil looked toward me with only the smallest visible smile on his face, but Neddy screamed in joy as she hugged and kissed him. Berger lightly tapped his horn in celebration, and toasted Neil with his bottle of Robitussin.

We all quickly scrambled out of the Diner and piled into my car. It was like the old days. We'd go to the drive-in like that, four guys with four girls . . . each guy hoping and dreaming that he was going to get laid that night. We were ever the optimists, many times the fools.

It was 5:30 a.m. when we met up with Danny, who was having breakfast at the Toddle House. We exchanged money for the note, then immediately headed for Fort Holabird.

The snow was coming down harder now and we made the only tracks on the early morning roads. There was a partylike feeling in the car. It had all the celebration of a New Year's Eve night. It was the school year coming to a close . . . it was the Colts winning the championship against the Giants in sudden-death overtime . . . the Orioles winning the World Series over the Dodgers in four straight. Neil was not going to be in the United States Army. He had the treasured note from Danny's doctor. No Southeast Asia for our friend. He was home free.

We pulled into the army base with only a few minutes to spare. There was no need to say goodbye, Neil would be out within the hour. We decided we would go off for breakfast and return to pick him up.

Neil slid out of the car, slammed the door behind him, and headed for the front door of the army registration building, holding tightly to the note. Neddy watched after him, adoringly. As Neil reached the door of the building, he turned back to us. He waved the note and laughed and then he did the most surprising thing I had ever seen in my life. He tore the note up, threw the pieces into a wastebin, and without even looking back at us, he walked into the induction center.

We all sat stunned, unable to say anything for the longest time. Tears ran down Neddy's cheeks, and then quietly, almost reverentially, Ben said, "Son of a bitch, Neil."

Fifteen

Although Ben's father-in-law had fired him and their relationship was, to put it mildly, strained, at Janet's insistence he continued to go to the Bonnie View Country Club every Saturday night.

Janet always spent Saturday afternoons in the beauty shop with her mother, hair getting lacquered firm and high on her head, nails being done to perfection, preparing for "Saturday night at the club." She looked forward to the ritual all week. Afterward, she would slip into one of her dresses with the multipetticoats (which hid her pregnant stomach somewhat) and was ready to go.

At the club, the men were always appropriately dressed in suits and ties to complement the bright, frilly, layered dresses of the women. Alan Ackerman and his band would lumber through the classics of the forties, and make a feeble attempt at the rock and roll of the sixties. They used to plow through "Georgy Girl," giving it a cha-cha beat for some unknown reason. All the while, Ben would drink scotch and sodas and try to wish away the night. Periodically he would get up to dance, at the urging of Janet's mother.

"Go up there and do the twist. You young people love that dance, don't you?"

And so Ben and Janet would twist and sometimes they would do the Watutsi, but mostly Ben waited for the party to come to an end so that he could drop his wife off and quickly head up to the Diner to hold court.

It was on one of these Saturday nights that Annie and I joined Ben, Janet, and her parents at the club. Annie had still not gotten over Neil allowing himself to be drafted. She constantly questioned his motive for tearing up the note, and as we sat there at the table the topic came up once again.

"What was he thinking?"

I just shook my head.

"He didn't want to go in the army. There's no question about that. He makes so little sense, Bobby."

"You don't have to tell me. I keep seeing that moment over and over again . . . the pieces of paper falling into the trash can . . . Neil walking inside . . ."

"And now, not a word, not a note."

The Alan Ackerman Band broke into a version of the Monkees' "I'm a Believer." Janet's mother seemed to love it. "This is such a cute song—from that television group," she said. Then, to the two of us, "Go dance. You love this, don't you?"

I said, "We were talking, discussing—"

She cut me off, "Go . . . go . . . dance. Dance. Have fun."

Annie and I reluctantly got up and went onto the dance floor. As we moved across the room, Annie said, "I don't know how Janet puts up with her mother." Then she smiled. "Wouldn't you like to put a sock in her mouth?"

I laughed and looked over at Ben and Janet, dancing nearby. She looked so happy, but it was clear that Ben wished he were somewhere else. Anywhere else.

Alan Ackerman's band finished their decrepit version of the hit song and took a break. "The two young couples," as we were called, returned to the table. A few men were sitting with Ben's father-in-law discussing the "sit-in" at a local college. Mr. Rawlings was nearly apoplectic about the situation and said, "They're lazy bums. Foul-smelling, unwashed youth who have nothing better to do."

Joe Steinhorn joined in, "What do they know about foreign policy or what we're trying to accomplish?"

It was at that moment that Ben entered the conversation. "They're the ones who are fighting, aren't they? Those young people are the ones who are dying, aren't they?"

Mr. Rawlings offered up the analogy to World War II. "There was a war to be fought and everyone did his job."

Ben refused to back down. He said there was a big difference. "No one has declared war on the United States. I don't know much about the politics, but nothing seems very clear about this war, from what I understand."

Mr. Rawlings raised his voice at the comment. "The young people don't need to understand. There are times you have a duty to your country and you do it, for Christ's sake!"

Annie was concerned that the conversation was getting hotter by the minute, so she jabbed me in the side to make sure I didn't offer up my point of view. She knew that I agreed with Ben.

The consensus, according to the older men, was that this generation was too pampered and looking for the easy way out.

At some point, despite the look on Annie's face, I couldn't restrain myself any further. But I remained calm. "I think that's an overgeneralization."

As I started to put my two cents in, Ben cut me off. Out of frustration, he blurted out, "Then why don't you fat fucks all go grab a gun and settle the fucking war."

A pall quickly fell over the table just as Alan Ackerman's clunky music started up again.

Mr. Rawlings' face got beet red. "You disrespectful son of a bitch!" he yelled, and almost simultaneously picked up a glass of water and threw it in Ben's face.

Ben lunged for Janet's father. He grabbed him by the throat and laid him across the table.

The women started to scream, and before anyone could intervene, Ben and Mr. Rawlings tumbled to the floor, the tablecloth pulled along with them. Dishes and glasses shattered. And with that, Alan Ackerman's version of the Beatles' "I Want to Hold Your Hand" came to a halt.

Along with a few other men, I tried to pull Ben and his father-in-law apart, but Ben let loose with a solid right to his father-in-law's jaw. Mr. Rawlings' upper bridge plate flew out of his mouth and hit the floor a good ten feet away.

Finally, Ben was overpowered by the large gathering of country club men. Janet was crying and her mother shrieking. Everyone was shocked by the violent turn of events. It was an ugly scene. In the twenty-one years of the club's existence, a fight like this had never broken out, certainly not between son-in-law and father-in-law.

Annie immediately attended to Mr. Rawlings, who had a serious cut in his mouth and was suffering heart palpitations. She also could tell that his blood pressure was dangerously high. As crazy as the scene appeared, I couldn't help but be impressed by how Annie took control administering to him.

It wasn't long before the paramedics arrived. Janet and her mother followed the ambulance to the hospital in the family car, leaving Ben at the club. No one said a word to him. Including us. It seemed to take forever before we could get our coats, and as we waited at the counter of the cloakroom with Ben, he was forced to endure the scrutiny and disdain of all the remaining club members.

Finally our coats arrived and we made our way out of the

country club. As we crossed the parking lot toward my car, Ben said, "Drop me at the Diner, okay?"

"Don't you think you should stop over at the hospital?" Annie asked. "See how he's doing. Talk to Janet . . ."

Ben just shook his head. "There's a time and place, Annie. It's not the time . . . it's definitely not the place."

We headed down Slade Avenue, passing the new high-rise condominiums—something new to the northwest section of Baltimore. As more and more of their children moved out, people over fifty were moving from their family dwellings to the smaller confines of condominium living.

I turned left from Slade onto Park Heights Avenue and headed toward the Diner, several miles away. We passed Bancroft Avenue, and Ben remembered the terrible accident when Alan Simon lost control of his Pontiac Bonneville in a heavy snowstorm, crashing into a telephone pole and breaking his leg. "He's never been the same. Lost that basketball scholarship," Ben said.

I could see Ben through my rearview mirror as he continued to look out the back window. He seemed desolate. "Poor bastard," he went on about Alan Simon, and then, almost in the same sentence, "I was right . . . back there, wasn't I, Bobby?"

"You were right," I said. "You were right up until the punch."

"Did you see the way that bridge flew out of his mouth?" He began to laugh.

Annie was clearly irritated. "To be honest with you, Ben, it's not that humorous."

"Yeah? Well, it'll play at the Diner. It's gonna be one of the bigger topics to have come along in quite a while." Ben was excited at the prospect of sharing his story with the guys. I understood. When something happened—good or bad—it didn't become real to any of us until it was told and then rehashed over and over in the Diner. It's how our values were set. It's how we understood the meaning of our actions. It's the only way we knew if our actions *had* any meaning.

Annie looked at me as if I was supposed to say something, talk Ben out of going to the Diner. But all I could say was, "It will definitely be memorable."

A few minutes later, I pulled into the parking lot and Ben got out. As we watched him go inside, Annie shook her head. "The Diner. When do you think you guys are going to get past that? When are you going to move on?"

"Don't know if we ever will. It's the Diner. Cigarettes and coffee and talking . . ." I started.

"And no girls allowed," Annie finished.

"Well, that kind of came crashing down the night Neil went away," I said.

"How bold of you guys," Annie said sarcastically. "How did that happen?"

As I pulled out of the lot, Berger saw me and beeped his horn lightly, and then I told Annie about Neil and Neddy—the two of them dancing in the parking lot. I'd been reluctant to tell her since she was less than thrilled about the Diner to begin with. Annie felt that in some way the Diner came between the two of us. She hated the fact that some nights, after I said good night to her, I went on to other things, to a separate part of my life—to the Diner. I never told her what we talked about, never shared those conversations, knowing that she wouldn't find them as amusing or profound as I thought they were. This was a guys' place . . . a clubhouse for men only—and to be excluded was a very sore point with Annie.

In the last few years the Diner had no longer been front-page news between us, but dropping Ben off there rekindled the flames of anger within her. She was appalled that Ben would be recounting the tale of the Bonnie View fight, with laughs and coffee and encouragement.

We drove home in silence. When I dropped her off she gave me a cursory kiss, then slammed the car door as she left. And I went back to the Diner.

When I came in, the conversation was already zigzagging every which way. From justification to retribution, every nook and cranny of the country club incident was being explored.

As I sat down, Turko said, "Sometimes you have to punch out your father-in-law when all else fails." It went on for hours. And although the laughs were plenty and the sarcasm was laid on thick, in the end we knew it was a devastating night for Ben.

At around a quarter to six in the morning, we called it a Saturday night. Turko gave Ben a ride home, which was the last place he wanted to go. But he was a grown-up now. And even though his world was quickly crumbling, his obligations weren't over. He couldn't just flee, no matter how much he might want to. So Ben unlocked the door to his garden apartment and apprehensively entered. He didn't know what he would say to Janet, what he *could* say to her. But when he walked into the bedroom, the bed was empty. So he didn't have to say anything.

Sixteen

Time heals all wounds is one of the great clichés. But time didn't heal Mr. Rawlings' feelings about Ben. He openly despised him. He cursed the day Janet got married and he pleaded with her to walk out of the marriage.

Unfortunately, Janet's pregnancy was overshadowed by the animosity between her husband and her father. Ben's growing drug problem frightened her, but she kept quiet about it. She never confronted him, choosing instead to wish the problem away and hope for the best. What happened over the next few months—for Ben, for Janet, for the whole Diner crowd—could be described in many ways. But "the best" probably isn't one of them.

I was having one of my infrequent dinners with my parents. We met at the China Clipper, which wasn't too far from WMAR.

"You're like a ghost," my father said. "You come in when we're asleep, you go out before I get up. You're like a ghost. You come and go from the house and we never see you."

"What do you want me to say? The job takes up a lot of hours."

"That's a lot of work for fifty dollars a week," my mother remarked. "I think the box boy at the Food Fair gets more than fifty dollars a week."

I was having my favorite dish of shrimp and lobster sauce

mixed with pork-fried rice. The fifty dollars a week was a sore point with my parents since they didn't understand what I actually did. The only thing they *could* take pride in was how much money I made, and since, as my mother kindly informed me, I was making less than the box boy, they got very little satisfaction from my accomplishments.

I'd spoken with Annie earlier. She told me she was thinking of going back to school to get her master's degree, which would ultimately allow her to become a physician's assistant. This was an evolving category in the medical profession, and she was very excited at the prospect of moving beyond the position of nurse. I told my parents about it over the Chinese dinner.

"Why does she need a master's degree?" my father asked. "She's a nurse."

"She's doing so well," my mother added.

I tried to explain. "This'll give her, you know, more opportunity."

"Why does she need more opportunity? She's a nurse. Can't do better than a nurse," my father said.

I tried to explain about being a physician's assistant.

"But she's a nurse," my father repeated. "She's already assisting."

"Dad, I don't know all the details, but she thinks this is a better job. It's got more value to it. I don't know the whole thing, but she wants to do it."

"She looks adorable in that uniform. She going to have to give up that uniform?" my mother said as her body shook and her eyes started to water from overusing the hot Chinese mustard. She yelled, "Oh my God, is this hot! Whew!" and took a sip of my ginger ale.

"Why are you taking my drink?" I asked.

"I need ginger ale. I'm burning up here."

"Your Coke doesn't do the same thing?"

"No. You need ginger ale if you're burning up."

My father continued to ponder the subject of Annie. "A master's degree . . . a master's degree. She's too smart for her own good."

My mother added, "Smart as a tack."

"Too smart," my father said. And before I knew it, it was time to run back to the station and prepare for the late night news.

My mother had one parting comment. "Tell the weatherman—what's his name?—he's not accurate enough."

"I'll do that, Ma." And I left them at the China Clipper and headed back to work.

Not a fucking phone call," Eggy said one night at the Diner. "Almost two months, and not a fucking word . . . not a note."

Neil had ceased to exist. He'd become "Neil did." He was past tense and becoming almost mythical.

The "he did" stories would go on and on. The Atlantic City sunlamp story was repeated probably half a dozen times. "Remember when he tanned on the beach for ten hours, using baby oil mixed with iodine, then went back to the rooming house and used a sunlamp?" Eggy laughed.

"Yeah," Turko added, "he wasn't happy with his tan. He wanted to be darker still. We were only there three days maybe and he wants to be the most tanned guy on the beach."

Ben smiled. "He wakes me at 6 a.m., 'Ben, Ben, I can't see. I'm blind.' I look at him, I'm fucking exhausted, and I see his eyelids are swollen shut."

They all relished this story. None of the information was new, but the telling, the retelling of it all, was exciting. It was like taking one last cookie from the jar. You didn't need it, but you wanted it. And we wanted Neil, if not in person, at least alive in our imagination.

"We took him to the hospital," Ben went on. "So the doctor says, 'He's burned his eyelids. He needs to use this medication and wear bandages over his eyes and stay out of the sun.' "

Eggy laughed. "Out of the sun! We're in AC . . . nothing but sun, beach, and water."

Ben continued, "Neil doesn't buy one fucking word this doctor has to say. So he comes up with an ingenious idea. First thing he says is, 'Take me to the Rexall drugstore, get me some sunglasses. Fuck if I'm staying indoors for two weeks.' So we go there."

Then Turko jumped in, "But the schmuck I am, I put a pair of glasses on him and I say, 'How do these feel, Neil?' He says to me, 'They're fine.' He asks me how they look, I say, 'Good, they look good. Just great.' " Then Turko laughs and sips his coffee. "I didn't take off the tags that were on the lenses. There's stickers and all kinds of shit over the lenses, but I say nothing to Neil."

"And neither did I," Ben said. "So we head for the beach." He nudged Turko. "Remember this? Neil walks with us . . ."

"Yeah," Turko said. "He's looking okay, or so he thinks, and then he says, 'Let me walk between you and Ben so I can feel your shoulders. Then I'll look perfectly normal.' He's walking between us; but I see some broad I know, so I wander off. Next thing I know, you wander off, and all of a sudden we see Neil walking alone on the beach, blind as a bat." Turko laughs. "Then he steps on this guy—falls over onto the sand."

"Funny as shit," laughs Ben. Then he gave the kicker to the story. "All the broads take pity on Neil. 'He's blind, how sad.' So

Neil ends up popping any chick he wants. Week after his eyes are better, he's still wearing the gauze with the sunglasses on top." Ben shook his head, remembering that summer, reveling in the laughter.

Then Joe Tate, who was wearing a madras sports jacket in the dead of winter, approached us. Tate was one of the kitchen remodeling guys who worked over in D.C. They were a step above the tin men—the aluminum siding guys—but all were hustlers . . . wheeler-dealers.

"You heard about Freddie Krauss?"

"No, what?" I asked.

"You know he went to Vietnam."

We all looked at one another. We'd never heard that.

"So what's the story?" asked Eggy.

"This helicopter he was in crashed, but he survived uninjured."

"Lucky Freddie," Ben laughed.

"Yeah, but then there was a mortar attack that hit a convoy he was in. Blew his truck right off the road."

"Shit," the Egg man said. "What happened?"

"Nine guys died. But Freddie survived again. Not a scratch."

"Lucky goddamn Freddie." This time it was Turko laughing.

"But now they think he's dying. That's what I'm hearing," Tate said.

"What?" I said. I was surprised by my sense of shock. I hardly knew Freddie Krauss. We were never close. We were never even friends. Our bond was simply in the telling of the stories of his miraculous feats of survival. He was mythical. The image of Freddie, in his red windbreaker, sailing over the top of the Texaco station sign was one image that always replayed itself in my mind.

"Seems he was in a bar in Saigon. Some waitress didn't like his tip, or he said something that she didn't like. I don't know, it's kind of sketchy, but she stabbed him and he's dying in a hospital. Maybe he's dead by now."

He couldn't be dying. He couldn't be dead. Freddie Krauss was immortal. To die in a war zone at the hands of a waitress . . . it was beyond impossible.

"Could a God save you from so many disasters, to die in such a stupid way?" asked Turko. "Could there be such a God?"

I didn't have an answer. I still don't.

"Listen, I still don't understand World War II," Ben said.

"What do you mean, you don't understand it?" Eggy said, not quite believing what he was hearing.

Then Ben, as he casually dipped his roast beef sandwich into the broth, said, "We fought World War II for democracy, and then we let Hungary be taken over by Communists, as well as Poland and Czechoslovakia. So those countries just went from being under Nazi rule to being under Communist rule."

"Yeah, how come we didn't do anything about Hungary, Poland, and Czechoslovakia?" Turko demanded.

"That's the big question," Ben said. "But *now* we're concerned about Vietnam? Now we care? I never fucking heard of Vietnam before."

"There was a movie called *Saigon* with Alan Ladd," I said.

"What the hell's that about?" Ben asked.

"I don't remember."

Then Eggy stated, as if he was making some kind of proclamation, "It's this domino theory. That's what Vietnam's about. It's very complicated. Very complicated."

"So a major war was fought in Europe and we didn't even protect those countries from Communism?" Turko asked.

"What the hell do I know?" Ben chimed in. "I still don't know how the First World War got started."

I said, "It began when they killed the Archduke Ferdinand of Serbia."

"Where the hell is Serbia anyway?" Ben said.

I told him I didn't know, and we all laughed.

There was no real cynicism toward the government at that point in time. Its actions just made for more Diner discussion. Politics and policies were ideas that didn't make sense. I remember reading that sometime during World War II it became apparent that there were camps where Jews were being put to death. Military plans were made to bomb the rail lines so the Jewish people couldn't be transported to these death camps. Ultimately, it was decided that those missions would divert the focus from "more important targets." That's the phrase I remember. I also remember thinking: Six million people went to the gas chambers while the military faced "more important targets"? I didn't question the decision back then. I just wondered what targets could possibly be more important. The government had its reasons, I assumed. In those days the government was above suspicion. It was up to us to make sense of their decisions, and then to accept them.

And then there are gaps.

Seventeen

I was running a piece of film back and forth on the Moviola—a ballplayer being caught between first and second in a rundown. I made a grease pencil mark where I wanted to cut the film. I heard through the grapevine that the station, which aired the Baltimore Orioles games, was trying to work up some on-air promotions to advertise the various air dates.

I'd hit upon a piece of music up in the music library that had caught my ear. It was by Dave Brubeck, kind of a fanciful number which featured the alto sax of Paul Desmond. Brubeck called this cut "Unsquare Dance." I played it over and over again. Then it occurred to me that if I took a variety of baseball clips of guys being caught in rundowns between first and second, and also second and third, then cut it to the jazz version of a square dance, it might be a catchy spot.

I was working on it on my own time, and if it played out the way I thought it would, I would show it to the guys in the On-air Promotion Department. By this time I had done nearly a dozen Ranger Al sketches, so I was gaining a little confidence in myself.

Annie dropped by on her lunch hour, and still wearing her nurse's uniform, she watched me as I sat at the Moviola. She had a paper bag lunch that she spread out on a chair next to her. I knew the agenda and felt self-conscious, guilty. I hadn't been seeing her that much recently. I was being consumed by the work. It fascinated me in ways I was never able to explain to Annie, or my parents for that matter. I couldn't wait for the morning to come so that I could rush over to the station, and I never wanted the night to end because I didn't want to leave. Without an outlet, unable to find anyone who truly understood how excited I was by what I was doing, I had become much more defensive than revelatory.

"I think you're getting too involved in this, Bobby," she said, and I was surprised by the agitated tone of her voice. "You're always here." She took a small bite from a tuna sandwich and a sip of soda, then wiped her mouth with a paper napkin. "You missed the meeting with our parents last night. It was so embarrassing not to have you there."

"I'm sorry. I told you, they needed me to fill in for Mickey."

"It isn't just a onetime thing. We hardly ever have dinner together and we never go to the movies—"

She was right, but I cut her off. My reply was less than understanding. "You don't have difficult hours at the hospital?"

"Of course I do."

"It's no different. I'm trying to get a foot in the door. They almost fired me in the beginning. Duke still holds that against me, and it's keeping me off the news."

"I know, I know . . ." And then she started to mimic me—all the things I'd been telling her: *"Until I get through to Duke and get him to trust me, they're not gonna take me seriously."*

The mocking tone pissed me off. But I decided against accelerating the argument. Instead I switched on the Moviola and, for a few seconds, watched Mark Belanger running between second and third. Back and forth he went, caught in a rundown with nowhere to go. I froze the image as he was about to be tagged, marked it with the grease pencil, then turned off the machine.

Calmer now, I walked over and sat by Annie. "Nurse, this patient is going to be fine. Whatever wedding plans you make are going to be fine with me. We think alike. What you like, I like."

"Then don't complain later if I pick something you *don't* like."

My mind was suddenly filled with a picture of this scene—a nurse in a film editing room, some guy sitting next to her. If I took a photo of it and showed it to twenty different people, there would be twenty different stories. The incongruity of it all. But all I said was, "As long as I don't have to march down the aisle to that song from *Days of Wine and Roses*. What's that called?"

" 'Days of Wine and Roses,' " she told me.

"Oh." I laughed as she began to hum the song. I pleaded with her to stop, and finally she promised that when we marched down the aisle it would be to something more to my liking.

Annie offered me half of her sandwich. I made like a patient and she fed me a bite. Then the conversation moved on to Ben and Janet. Annie had spoken with her that morning. She said that their relationship had been very difficult since the fight with Janet's father.

I told Annie that Ben now had a job tending bar at Longfellow's, not far from the Green Earth, in the burgeoning hippie district. Annie was surprised; Janet hadn't mentioned the job. Then I offered up that she was probably too embarrassed.

Soon after that, I was walking Annie across a darkened studio, a shortcut to get to her car in the parking lot. Suddenly, I stopped her. "Wait a second," I whispered.

"Why?"

I nodded toward a very small lighted set at the far end of the studio. "I don't want Duke to see me." What I really didn't want him to see was me with a girl. I was afraid that he might think I was screwing around instead of doing my duties, reaffirming, in his mind, that I was a big fuckup.

"He looks so young. I thought he was sixty or something," Annie whispered.

"No. He came up quick."

"I always thought from our conversations that he was this doddering old guy. He looks like a hotshot."

We watched as Duke talked to a few members of the crew. It seemed as if he was discussing camera positions. I whispered to Annie, "I'm going to direct the news. I'm gonna AD it, and then get to direct. Duke doesn't know it yet, but I'm going for his chair."

"Well, I hope you get to do it . . . but let's not lose one another in the process. What do you say?"

I didn't know what to say. So I nodded, hoping that was enough.

"I understand ambition, Bobby, that's why I want to go for my master's. I want more. I want more gratification from my work too, but I wouldn't do it at the expense of losing you."

"This isn't about ambition. It isn't about just moving up . . ." I rambled on but I couldn't make her understand. I could never, with real satisfaction, explain my feelings, my fascination with the images and technology of film. It was too complicated to express. Or maybe I didn't truly understand it myself. So eventually I simply agreed with everything she said. I didn't want to lose her and I made feeble promises, all of which I believed. But I withheld a secret—I didn't know how to stop what I was doing. And I didn't know how I could hold on to the two things that I loved without losing one or the other.

We stood in the shadows of the darkened stage and looked at one another. We both understood that we were traveling through rough waters, but we didn't want to continue to burden ourselves with all the complications. We just wanted things to be simple, so we did the one thing that made us feel good—we hugged and kissed. There was a couch nearby, which was used on one of the public service chat programs, and I nodded to Annie, "That looks comfortable, don't you think?"

She smiled wickedly. "Are you crazy?" But without missing a beat, she led me toward the couch, on a lifeless set in the darkened corner of the studio.

We kissed and felt one another. Out of the corner of my eye I saw Duke and the other men leave, heard the large studio door slam shut. Completely alone, our passions built. Free and unrestricted, we made love on the public service couch. The absurdity of the scene was not lost on either of us—the young nurse, the young man in a suit, the frenzied passion. We looked like something out of a soap opera after it had gone off the air, and when our lovemaking was over, we laughed like we hadn't in a long, long time.

Eighteen

Turko continued to see Neddy, although things had not been the same since she'd met Neil. They were still sleeping together, but Turko felt her slipping away. At the same time, to the Turk's surprise, he was becoming more and more emotionally involved with her.

One early afternoon, Turko dropped by the Maryland Institute and took Eggy with him. Somehow, in a conversation, Turko had mentioned that the art school had live nude female models, and Eggy, with his constant hard-on, wanted to have a look-see.

They pulled up near the imposing large stone building not far from the B&O Railroad station. Eggy got out of the car wearing a beret and an ascot, along with his customary suit. His explanation was: "It's nice and artsy-fartsy."

They headed into the building. As they wandered down a corridor, Turko checked out various classrooms in search of a nude woman. He came to an art studio room and whispered, "Okay, this one. Just walk down the aisle, go find yourself an easel, and make like you're going to draw."

Eggy nodded, as if he was a spy on a secret mission, and went in. He passed other students who were drawing, then he saw a woman, totally naked, reclining on a couch. He was so excited, so immediately aroused, that he stopped dead in his tracks. He stared at the nude woman for the longest time, oblivious to anyone else around him, before finally moving on to find an easel with a fresh piece of paper attached to it. Eggy put up a thumb and extended it from his eye to the nude model, thinking this was a very artistic thing to do. But he never took his eyes off the reclining woman.

Meanwhile, Turko found Neddy in the student café. Her hippie attire was more elaborate than ever before—all types of beads, bracelets, and rings, with several feathers woven into strands of her blond hair. He was in a suit and tie, wearing his engraved cuff links and his blue sapphire pinkie ring, feeling more out of place than ever before.

Neddy pulled out a letter. "Listen to what Neil writes," she said, and began to read out loud:

"Monday came early this week . . . recollections of days gone by . . . mellow-hazed days of concrete grass and broken glass. This is a feeble attempt at a letter. It stinks! Neil."

Turko shrugged his shoulders, unsure what to say. He got a cup of coffee and moved the spoon around as if stirring sugar. He was absolutely crazy about Neddy and didn't know the best way to handle the situation.

He revealed these details at the Diner one night, in a manner that was not customary for Turko. He was straightforward, honest, and intimate about all the details. I'm not sure he would have said all these things if Ben had been present. There would have been too much temptation on Ben's part for the big put-down. But Turk was almost overcome by his feelings for Neddy. "I don't know why . . . I don't know what the hell it's about here."

Then he told us how difficult it was, knowing how she felt about Neil. "She was staring at Neil's goddamn letter as if trying to read words that weren't there."

Turko told us that he watched her as she held the paper softly in her hands. "If I thought Neil was really interested in you, I wouldn't have come a-knocking," he told her.

Neddy said nothing for the longest time. Then she raised her head, her eyes watery, and said, "I'm sorry, Turko."

Turko left the café and went looking for Eggy. He walked blindly down one corridor after another. He was not familiar with the deep ache he was feeling, and he took it as a sign of weakness. He was angry at his own emotional state of mind, his vulnerability, his lack of control. His own pain.

Finally, he gave up looking for Eggy and headed out of the Maryland Institute of Art. There, leaning against a car, was the Egg man, minus the beret and ascot.

"Where the hell have you been?" Turko asked.

"Some teacher threw me out of the classroom."

They made their way to the car, and Eggy told how the teacher had spotted him, approached him, saw his blank piece of art paper and his horny look, and said to him, "Let me guess, you are not a student in this class. Am I right?"

And Eggy responded, as fluently as he could manage, "Oui."

Nineteen

January 3, 1967, was the day the announcement came over the radio: *"He wandered from sad obscurity into epic tragedy. He fired the shot that frustrated the world. Jack Ruby, the man who killed Lee Harvey Oswald, died today."*

It was also the day Neil arrived back in Baltimore from basic training. He stepped off the bus at the terminal, looking impressive in his army uniform. He waited until his duffel bag was unloaded, threw it over his shoulder, and, in the late afternoon light, headed down the street.

Neil checked back into the same cheap hotel where he used to live, and carefully unloaded the few pieces of clothing he had into an old beat-up bureau. He had the radio on in his room and listened to more bad news from Vietnam. Thirteen U.S. helicopters had been downed in one day.

Neil took out a shoeshine kit and began to polish his boots, working the polish into the leather, buffing it until there was a fine reflection. Pleased with his work, which lasted some thirty minutes, he then lay down on the bed, lit a cigarette, and quietly smoked.

Later in the afternoon, he wandered around the corner to the Earl of Sandwich for a cold-cut sub sandwich. He sat there in his well-pressed uniform, reading from a book of Fitzgerald's short stories.

Neil was a curiosity in the sandwich shop, which had become something of a hippie haven. He was viewed as a member of the establishment. It was the ultimate irony. Here was the one guy they'd ever meet who truly marched in a parade of his own, and they thought he was an outsider.

A hippie named Gene Moss took it upon himself to sit down across from Neil. His friends were sitting over at the counter, and Gene told them that he was going to "goof" on the soldier.

Gene didn't know that Neil was just out of basic training and had never been to Vietnam, but he asked questions about how Neil liked the war over there and whether he understood "America's bullshit foreign policy."

Neil listened to him and said nothing. Gene Moss kept poking Neil with rhetorical questions—didn't he think that Americans were imperialists?—and spewed every antiwar doctrine that had ever been mentioned.

Neil was amused but didn't let on. At the appropriate moment, he said, "I'm with an advance unit in Vietnam. It's my directive to move through the back channels in the jungle, alone. Just me. One man with one mission. A sniper. To kill with impunity. I don't travel with a platoon—it's dangerous to have a Barnum and Bailey circus in the jungle. I move silently in deadly pursuit." He said it quietly, efficiently, like Clint Eastwood in those spaghetti westerns.

Then he said something that began to scare Gene Moss.

"Now, I'm back here to do my work."

"What's that?" Gene was almost afraid to ask.

Almost inaudibly, Neil said, "Covert operations. I take out anyone who interferes with the work that needs to be done. Some have very unfortunate accidents, others die from advanced forms of cancer. In some cases, they were driving on the wrong road at the wrong time." He stared at Gene for a long beat and said,

"Don't tell me your name. Don't let me see you too often." Then Neil stood up, paid his check, and left.

While none of us, his closest friends, had gotten even one letter from Neil while he was in basic training, he'd kept up a constant correspondence with Janet. She'd filled him in on the details of Ben losing his job at the dealership, the terrible fight at the Bonnie View Country Club, and how Ben seemed more and more despondent. She'd also told Neil that he was tending bar over at Longfellow's, which was within walking distance of Neil's hotel.

Neil strolled into Longfellow's sometime after eleven that night. The place was an old-fashioned bar that had been on its dying legs until the hippie migration. Now it was a happening place.

Neil sat at the bar, lit a cigarette, and when he saw the bartender kneeling down, stacking one of the shelves, he said, "Wild Turkey, please."

The bartender was Ben. Neil was surprised to see his longer sideburns and mustache and that Ben's hair had gotten even thinner on top.

Ben leaned across the bar, and as they hugged, he said sarcastically, "Thanks for all the letters. I was getting eye strain, you son of a bitch."

"I was practicing the art of war."

Ben sized him up. "You sure as hell look like a soldier."

Neil looked around the bar, checking out the crowd. "They want to have me qualify for the Green Berets."

"Are you?" Ben asked, as he poured the Wild Turkey into a glass.

"Any kind of beret is too much of an affectation for me." Then he held up his glass to Ben as if making a silent toast. Staring at Neil's uniform, Ben couldn't get comfortable. It was as if Neil wasn't really Neil.

Neil sipped his drink. "You go from working in your father-in-law's Caddie dealership to this? Trying to work your way down the ladder of success?"

Ben laughed. "Could be."

Neil, enjoying his buddy, happy to see him after all these months, said, "It's a long way down, Ben. A long way down."

Ben shrugged his shoulders and replied, "Maybe I'll get there before I lose all my hair."

Neil didn't smile. Instead, as Sonny & Cher's "The Beat Goes On" started to play on the jukebox, he said, "Janet's concerned."

Ben didn't answer. He just smiled as best he could, did the familiar pulling down on his lower eyelid, and said, "You're me."

Once again Neil lifted his glass to Ben, and this time he did make a toast: "To the King of the Teenagers."

"So when are you getting shipped out, or whatever they say?"

"Got me." Then Neil, as always, came up with a surprising statement. "All I know is, I'm not going back."

Ben was puzzled, and pressed, "What do you mean? You have to, don't you?"

Neil refused to elaborate. He just shook his head and said, "I don't think so."

Neil left the bar when Ben went over to serve drinks to a few patrons who had just sat down at a table. He never said anything. No "See you later." Nothing. He just quietly walked out.

At one point, Ben slipped an amphetamine into his mouth and washed it down quickly with a sip of water. It was only then that he realized that Neil was gone. Surprised, he asked a few people if they'd seen a guy in uniform. "Yeah, yeah . . . he just split," they told him.

It didn't take long for Neil to wander over to the quiet cobblestoned street that surrounds the Washington Monument in Baltimore's Mount Vernon area. He stared up at George Washington, carved in stone, then began to walk around the monument on the red-white-and-blue-colored stone walkway. He kept walking, moving around it and around it, his shiny black boots hitting the cement with purposeful stride.

A couple of hippie guys were sitting on a park bench, not forty yards away, and watched as Neil circled the monument, giving the impression that he was one lone guard protecting the first president of the United States. It seemed quite patriotic—a soldier, impeccably dressed in uniform, moving around the statue of the man who had led the nation to independence. It was such an unusual act of behavior that other hippies began to gather to watch this young soldier on his circular journey.

Neil never noticed the large gathering, and no one from the crowd said anything. He continued to go around the monument with a quiet determination. There was no end in sight. He was going in a circle, so how could it possibly end?

As time passed, the crowd grew. They didn't understand what they were witnessing, what it meant or why the man in uniform was doing it. Were they watching an act of defiance or an act of patriotism? It didn't matter. Everyone was pulled into the moment—a lone American soldier, a gathering of hippies, the Vietnam War lingering in the air.

If it had been a movie there would have been music playing and it would have been sad, but this was just life, so there was no music. Even in the quiet of the night, it still seemed sad.

Neil walked around the monument for another hour or so and then just walked away. He never told anyone why he'd begun or why he stopped. That was pure Neil.

Less than twenty minutes after Neil left, Neddy and Turko came into the small park area at Mount Vernon Square. The crowd was still abuzz about the soldier, but neither Neddy nor Turko made the connection to their pal. Since they didn't know he was in town and hadn't heard from him other than the bewildering "concrete grass and broken glass" note to Neddy, the hippie chatter was of no significance.

Turko hadn't been able to give up on Neddy, he'd kept trying to find a way to light her affections. She enjoyed Turko, found him comfortable to be with, but, as she put it, her one-night "flameout" with Neil kept her deeper emotions "close to her soul." There wasn't much that Turko could offer Neddy—her father's wealth precluded that—so it was only Turko's personality that could hold her attention. Unfortunately, he was well aware that when it came to charm, he played a distant second fiddle to one of his best friends.

They moved through the crowd, the sweet puffs of marijuana floating in the cold winter's night.

Neddy shivered, "I hate the winter."

Turko tried to perk her up with a story about how his grandmother, when he was a kid, would put his fur-lined leather gloves in the oven to heat them before he went off to school in the morning.

"One day, somehow she forgot that she put them in there. We smelled something like burning feathers and then we realized my gloves were cooking in the oven. Everyone I ran into at school that morning said, 'What's that smell?' And I had to tell them that my grandmother cooked my gloves." That story was usually good for a laugh, but Neddy was only mildly amused at best.

They walked quietly for a few more minutes, then unexpectedly she said, "It's just too cold. Let's go back to my place and get under the covers."

Turko wanted to howl, "Yes!" But he played it cool. He wasn't sure what had motivated this invitation, but he wasn't going to analyze it. He was off to get into bed with Neddy.

Twenty

I was in the control room with the audio man, Don Butler, and the video switcher, Cam Owens. I hadn't met either guy until that evening.

A Glenn Ford western, *The Man from the Alamo*, was playing on the station's *Late Show*. It was my job to roll the commercial breaks at various intervals. The movie hadn't been on very long and I was on the phone with Annie. She'd called, having learned that Neil was back in town but hadn't bothered to call her or their parents. She was absolutely furious, on a full-blown diatribe. "He is *so* irresponsible. Absolutely disrespectful! I mean, whatever his problems are, he has to have some obligations to the family. You realize how humiliating it is to find out that my own brother is back in town and I don't even know it!"

I asked, "Who told you?"

"Janet. He tells Janet, he doesn't tell his own sister, for God's sake. I swear, if I wanted to be spiteful I wouldn't even invite him to our wedding. To be honest with you, I don't even know if he would care."

"Let's not go to extremes here, Annie . . ."

"You're not offended? Your best friend doesn't even tell you he's back in town. You race all over the city at night trying to get him some note, trying to help him, and this is the way he repays you?"

It was at that moment that the film on the television monitor ran out, and all we could see was leader rolling on the monitor. "Shit! Go to slide," I yelled.

Quickly, Cam Owens punched up the "Late Show" slide on the screen. I spoke into the intercom, "Roll three," and as the movie came up on one of the film chains, I said, "Three and break." A commercial began to play.

I told Annie to hold on for a second, and then asked the guys, "Why did the film run out? Something doesn't seem right, does it?" Nobody seemed to have an explanation, so I looked down at the notes that were provided—giving information on the various commercial breaks. "According to what I see here, we should not have had a break for another ninety seconds."

Don Butler shrugged his shoulders and said, "Beats me."

I hit the intercom button to the Telecine area. Telecine was like the boiler room of the television station. It was where all of the film projectors, slide projectors, and videotape machines were housed. "Guys, something's wrong here. That break wasn't due for ninety seconds."

No one seemed to really give a shit. All I heard was, "Don't know."

The commercial continued to play: Mr. Clean moved around a kitchen creating miracles. All seemed okay for the time being, so I went back to the phone to talk to Annie. "So where's Neil now?"

"He might be with Ben. I'm not sure," she replied.

The commercial was about to run out. I told Annie to hold on again, then into the intercom I said, "Stand by for station ID and announce." And as the commercial ended I said, "Two . . . and announce."

The light in the audio booth came on, and the booth announcer, Roland White, said, "This is Channel Two in Baltimore. WMAR Television."

I snapped my fingers, said, "Change slide," and the "Late Show" slide came up.

The announcer continued, "You are watching *The Late Show*. Tonight's feature—*The Man from the Alamo* starring Glenn Ford." Then I called, "Roll four," and ordered, "Dissolve to four . . . and track," and once again the movie began to show on the television monitor.

I went back to my conversation with Annie. "What's Neil doing here?"

"I have no idea. That's the point I've been trying to make, Bobby. Are you even listening to me?"

I looked up at the clock. It was almost 11:40. "The movie should be over at one, and then I have sign-off. After that I'll go over to Longfellow's. Maybe he's there."

Then, very quietly, Annie said, "Bobby, you realize you're working a sixteen-hour day?"

I knew she was right. Some days were seventeen, even eighteen hours long. It was my own choice to stay that long, but I just said, "I'm filling in one night, that's all."

Then I heard a voice on the intercom from down in Telecine. "Bobby, it looks like this reel is gonna run out." I told Annie to hold on. I threw a switch connecting me to the Telecine area. "How's that possible?"

Before I could act, even think about what to do, the monitor that was showing the movie said "The End," and the credits started to play. "Oh shit," I muttered.

In rather a matter-of-fact voice, I heard the Telecine guy say on the intercom, "The reels must have been tagged wrong."

The closing music and credits continued to play on the monitor. To no one in particular, I said, "*The Late Show* ends twelve minutes after it starts?"

I threw the switch so I could talk to Roland White in the booth. "We have a fuckup here, Roland. I'm gonna go to *The Late*

Show slide. You announce the movie again." Then I faded the music out and went to the title slide one more time.

Roland announced, with great dignity and drama in his voice, "And now for the beginning of *The Man from the Alamo*, starring Glenn Ford."

I gave a few directions, then the movie came up on the screen and began to play, this time from the beginning. I picked up the phone. "I screwed up," I told Annie. "We ran the last reel first."

"Is that your fault?"

"No, I'm filling in for Kevin. It's his job to check the reels, but I'm gonna get the hit. I'm in the chair."

"But it isn't your fault."

"Believe me, I'm gonna catch the shit tomorrow morning. Goddamn it!"

We weren't connecting at all. She didn't understand the problem.

"If Kevin's responsible, he'll get the blame, not you."

She didn't understand the way things worked and I couldn't make her understand. Soon she started to talk about being accepted at Hopkins, where she was going to pursue her master's degree. I wanted to listen to her, I knew how important all this was to her, but I couldn't pay attention, couldn't focus. My mind was running a mile a minute.

The guys around me didn't seem to be the least bit bothered by the fuckup, but I was overcome by guilt. Annie sensed my distance, that our conversation was one-sided, so we hung up. I felt bad. I wanted to call her back but knew that would be pointless. I wouldn't have anything new to say and neither would she.

Now that the reels were in order, the rest of *The Late Show* ran without a hitch. But the damage was done. Once again I was "Mr. Fuckup."

When *The Man from the Alamo* finally ended, we did the sign-off, but I didn't go down to Longfellow's. I was still too angry, still beating myself up. I should have been more careful. I should have checked the reels.

As I drove home, I convinced myself that this screwup was just about going to do it. It would be the end of my career in television. Why didn't I notice that there were no opening credits? I shouldn't have let Annie distract me. I should have paid closer attention . . .

I quietly entered the house and went up to my bedroom. I lay there in the dark and reran the scenario in my head, over and over again. Then, at some point, I let the night go and I was asleep.

Turko and Neddy were under the covers, both stoned on marijuana. They'd had sex earlier and she was resting in his arms. Turko felt he had made a big breakthrough, although he had no idea why. Maybe it was the gloves-in-the-oven story, he thought. It was a very humanizing anecdote. He didn't ponder too deeply, however. He was with her. That was all that mattered.

Neddy got into a talkative mood. She started telling him about all the guys she had slept with. "So many guys . . . can't remember their names . . . not sure I remember all the faces."

She went on to talk about starting to have sex when she was about fourteen, how she really didn't care for it, but she did it just to do it. She told him all the things she had done, things he wasn't sure he wanted to know. Before she converted to her hippie look, she used to be called "Upstairs Nadine," and walked around town wearing only a raincoat—totally naked underneath.

At first the stories were laced with humor, then there were

tears in her eyes. She talked about a night she slept with six different guys. She didn't know any of their names—and she'd been the one to instigate the whole thing.

At some point she began crying, full out, and Turko didn't know what to do other than to hold her. Her tears eventually turned back to an uneasy laughter and she talked about how the things that had humiliated her had also made her stronger. Turko couldn't figure out what she was trying to say. He was stoned as well, his brain too dulled. Emotionally, he felt involved, but was unable to say or do anything that would help.

During one of Neddy's ramblings, she drifted off to sleep. Relieved, so did Turko.

Ben continued to hang around the bar after it closed at 2 a.m., bullshitting with a couple of girls who stayed late. They were employed by the Social Security office, and both were off work the following day. Ben teased them, "What's wrong? No one needs Social Security tomorrow?"

Rather than getting a laugh or even an amused smile, the girls just said, "Of course. Everyone always needs Social Security."

Ben decided they were too earnest, so he kept referring to them as "Tweedledum and Tweedledum." After an hour or so, he lost interest, sent them on their way, and locked up for the night.

At about 4:30 a.m., he let himself into his garden apartment and quietly moved to the bedroom, not wanting to wake Janet. Even though the room was dark, it didn't take him long to realize that she was not in bed.

He walked over to the night table and turned on the lamp. On

Janet's unmade side of the bed was a note: *"I waited for you until four o'clock. Where were you?"* That was all it said.

Ben went into the bathroom and noticed that a lot of Janet's toiletries were missing. He looked in the closet and saw that one of the small suitcases was also gone. He lay down on the unmade side of the bed and wondered what he was going to do.

The phone woke me from a deep and uneasy sleep. Ben was troubled and confused as he rambled on about Janet. He asked if I would meet him at the Diner. It was the last thing I wanted to do, but Ben seldom made a call for help.

"See you in a few minutes," I told him.

The Diner was quiet at five-thirty that morning. As Ben and I talked, Florence, the waitress, kept stopping by to top off our coffees. It seemed to me that Florence worked twenty-four hours a day, seven days a week. She was always there. In her late fifties, she had a feisty attitude and a smart remark for all of her customers.

"High school seems like a hundred years ago," Ben said, sipping his coffee. "A hundred fucking years ago."

"Five-plus years," I said.

"Don't be so fucking exact, Bobby." Then he looked at me for a beat and I saw fear on his face. "Do I look bland to you?"

"What?"

"Bland," he repeated.

"I know the word, Ben. What do you mean?"

"Boring. I'm getting boring. I bore myself. There's nothing amusing about me. Nothing."

I started to tell him that all he had to do was figure out what he wanted to do, what kind of plan he had for the future. I offered a few more pieces of advice before I suddenly stopped, realizing I sounded just like my father. It was a slightly nauseating feeling. I'd always thought how different I was from my dad, and that difference was important to me. It gave me hope that I might be better than he was and do something more interesting, have more of an impact on the world. Now I was saying the very things he had said to me over the years. And they made sense. They were *right*. It was the first time in my life that I realized I wasn't as different as I thought and that confused me. We were young guys breaking away from the past. We were on the eve of a cultural revolution that was defining and separating us from the older generation. But there I was with the same thoughts that were inside my father's head. The same reactions and responses. It was a revelation that would stay with me forever after that night, no matter how I fought it or resented it. I realized that no matter what I would do in the future or what I was about to become, I would forever be my father's son. It was surreal, like a nightmare moment in film—disconnected voices on top of one another, advice coming into my head, advice going out of my mouth . . . my father's face turning into my own face. A visual and spiritual collision of Mr. Shine and son.

As years went by, I saw more and more similarities to him—more than I ever thought possible. I fought against it constantly. For much of my adult life. Then one day, long after his death, I realized that I was proud of our similarities. But that was years away from that night with Ben. It was far into the future. And at the Diner the future was nonexistent.

"Oh shit, Bobby! That's fucking crap. My goal in life was basically to fuck around in school, have a good time, and graduate. That was my goal."

"Yeah, you did that part well. But that's kind of act one."

All of his frustrations began to pour out—how much he loved Janet, how much he hated her, how afraid he was to be a father. Ultimately he confessed, "I'm afraid of life."

Suddenly, Turko and Shade came in from the parking lot and up to the booth. Turko urged Shade, "Tell them." And before we knew it, Shade began to lay down the groundbreaking news.

"You're never gonna believe what George told me."

"How do you even know what the hell he's saying? I've never understood him all these years, with that crazy accent," Ben said, shifting back to his Diner persona now that other people were around.

Then Shade told us the unthinkable. "George said he was going to sell the Diner."

"Sell it?"

"Yeah."

Ben thought this over for a minute, shrugged, then said, "What the hell's the difference? So we won't have the crazy Greek. There'll be some other guy. The Diner's the Diner. Think the new guy's gonna sell French food?"

That's when Shade stuck the dagger in. "Supposedly, the guy that wants to buy this place wants to turn it into a packaged liquor store."

The end of the Diner, I thought to myself. In the wildest stretch of my imagination, that would never have occurred to me. Not once in our thousands of conversations had this possibility ever arisen. Some guys had stopped coming to the Diner, some had moved out of town, but now the Diner *itself* was leaving?

The Diner had informed us, shaped us. It was the magnet of the night. This little streamlined aluminum prefab building had pulled us in for years. A shiny neon-lit confessional booth that held some of the most memorable moments in all of our lives. I flashed on the nights when I drove by with a date—the cars I saw in the parking lot would determine how fast I wanted to drop her off, because hanging with the guys, the put-downs, the jabs, the sarcasm, was often so much more enjoyable.

Ben poured quite a bit of sugar into his coffee and stirred it. "I think you must have misunderstood his Greek accent," he said. Then he tried to make light of this deadly possibility. "He probably said he had a package he wanted to sell, something like that. Why don't you bring him your Nehru jacket and have him sell that, too."

"Don't fucking believe me," Shade said.

Turko chimed in. "You know, now that I think of it, how would you know, Shade? Since when did you become a close confidant of the Greek?"

Ben sipped his coffee and looked over at Shade with mock disdain. "Sell the Diner? What the hell's wrong with you?" He put his coffee down and pulled out a handkerchief to wipe his face. He was suddenly sweating profusely.

"You okay?" I asked.

"My heart's beating like crazy," Ben said.

"Maybe it's too much coffee," Turko theorized. "Or maybe it's the pills."

Ben tried to pick up a glass of water just to take a sip, but his hand was shaking too hard. "Is Berger still here?"

I nodded. Ben got up from the booth and walked out the front door. Concerned, I followed.

In his car, Berger was slipping a Charlie Parker album onto his portable turntable. He delicately placed the needle on the first track and settled back, relaxed. When he saw us, he asked, "What's up?"

Ben suddenly said to me, "Why don't you take off, all right?"

"What? You think it's a secret I don't know about, you asshole?"

Ben turned redder than he already was, then said to Berger, "What are the side effects of uppers?"

To my astonishment, Berger pulled out a medical book from under his car seat. "You shooting 'em or ingesting?"

"Swallowing," Ben said, annoyed. "Just taking them, for Christ's sake. Shooting 'em . . . fuck you!" Then, almost in the same sentence, he said to me, "Janet's not coming back. She's not coming back, Bobby. I know it. I fucking know it. I'm busting my balls working at that bar, fucking killing myself, and she takes off."

Berger, who was methodically looking through the medical manual, stopped on a page and read to himself for a long beat. Ben watched him. "What? What's it say?"

Berger began to read aloud, following the words on the page with his finger. *"Fever, sweating, dry mouth, headaches, blurred vision, tremors, loss of coordination"*—and then he turned the page—*"increased aggression, irregular heartbeat, visual hallucinations . . ."* The list seemed endless.

Ben finally cut him off, "I got it. I got it." Then he turned to me. "You're the lucky one, you know that, Bobby?"

I hadn't bothered to tell Ben about what had happened at the television station and how I'd screwed up. The lucky one, I thought to myself. I'll probably be fired first thing in the morning. And with the first light coming up, I realized I didn't have that much time. The guillotine was waiting.

"You mind if I rest in your backseat?" Ben asked Berger.

"Door's unlocked."

"Thanks."

"You gonna be all right?" I asked.

Ben pulled on his eyelid, said, "You're me," then got into

Berger's car and slammed the door shut. I stood watching him as he lay down on the backseat. Within seconds he was asleep.

The bebop of Charlie Parker and the loud snap of plastic as Berger opened yet another bottle of Robitussin were the last sounds I heard as I walked toward my car.

Twenty-One

I didn't have enough time to go home, take a shower, and change, so I headed straight from the Diner parking lot to the television station.

I went into the men's room and washed my face. My mouth felt dry and stale, but I had no toothbrush, so I just rinsed my mouth with water and ran my finger over my teeth. It didn't make me feel all that much better.

After a quick cup of coffee and a donut that I plucked off one of the snack trays left over from the morning news, I saw Kevin, the trainee I had filled in for the night before, setting up some chairs for a talk show. I immediately yelled at him, "Why the hell didn't you check the reels?"

"I heard what happened. It's my mistake," he said as he continued to dress the set. "I'm sorry."

"I got egg all over my face. I'm a big fuckup, thanks to you."

"I said I was sorry."

The response didn't sit well. I had my future on the line. "Sorry is not going to help me. I'm fucked, Kevin."

It was at that moment I heard Mickey's voice coming over the speaker system, and I looked up toward the control booth.

"Bobby," Mickey intoned, "John Haynes wants to see you."

"Now?" I asked. Mickey nodded through the glass window.

I felt so pissed off, so frustrated. "Thank you. Thank you very much, Kevin."

"You're not gonna tell him it was me, are you?"

"Why? You wanna tell him?"

Kevin looked terrified. "Fuck, no."

I turned and walked away, disappearing into the dark shadows of the unlit studio.

Kevin yelled after me, nervously, "What are you going to say?"

I kept walking.

"Bobby, what are you going to say?"

From the far corner of the studio, as I opened the steel doors to the hallway, I yelled back, "I'm not going to say anything . . . and fuck you, Kevin."

Haynes' office was on the fourth floor, but rather than take the elevator, I walked past it and headed up the staircase. I needed time to think. I knew I couldn't give Kevin up. Well, I could, but it didn't feel right. At that moment, nothing felt right. Especially standing at the door to John Haynes' outer office.

I had no game plan, not one idea what to say, no defense whatsoever, so I just walked in.

The secretary nodded to me, called her boss to announce that I had arrived, and within a few seconds the office door opened.

I stepped in tentatively. I wasn't able to read Haynes' face. And he didn't say anything. Not even hello. He just walked over to his telephone and dialed an intercom number. Finally, he spoke: "I want to play something for you." Then into the phone he said, "Okay, play it."

On the television monitor in his office, the "leader" popped onto the screen—10-9-8-7-6-5-4-3-2-1—and after that came baseball footage backed by Dave Brubeck's music. I had only finished the piece the day before, and had taken it over to the On-air Promotion guys to get their opinion. I hadn't heard anything back from them yet.

Haynes stared at the monitor. "You did this?"

"Yes, sir."

His question didn't seem like praise, but then it didn't seem like recrimination either. It was just a flat statement.

I began to mumble, "It still needs work . . . kind of a rough idea . . ." but Haynes waved for me to keep silent as he continued to watch. When the spot came to an end, he turned off the monitor and faced me. "I love this, absolutely love this," he said. "What a wonderful way to sell baseball on this station."

I waited for the other shoe to drop—the *Late Show* screwup—but it didn't happen. A huge sense of relief flooded through me.

As reserved as he was when I first entered the room, Haynes now couldn't stop raving about how much he loved the spot. "It's got humor and energy . . . Never seen anything like this . . . Love it!" I couldn't even get a word of thanks out of my startled mouth because he kept going. "Now, here's what I have in mind. I want you to continue to write those sketches for the Ranger—they're wonderful—but you don't have to work the puppets anymore . . . I'll put some of the new boys on that. I want to make better use of your time. I'm moving you up to assistant director. You're going to be working on the news with Duke."

"Great," I said, in a state of shock and disbelief.

"And if you want to keep playing with ideas for on-air spots, fantastic. Let's see what else you can do."

I was thrilled beyond belief. I showed it by nodding repeatedly, like an idiot.

"Now Duke is taking a week off," Haynes continued, "and Eddie Collier is going to fill in. Then you and Duke start together next week. Just check the schedule. And congratulations, Bobby."

"Thank you, sir. Thank you. I don't know what to say. Thank you."

John Haynes walked me to the door. "Oh . . . one more thing.

In the future, check the reels on *The Late Show*, or any of our movies, more carefully before we go on-air."

"Yes, sir. That was an oversight. I'm sorry."

"You're not the first trainee to mess up like that." Then he added, almost confidentially, "You know what troubles me the most?"

"No, sir."

He looked around as if he didn't want anyone to hear, "No one called in to complain. We show the last reel first and no one called to complain. I'm beginning to wonder if our viewers pay any attention to what they're watching."

"Well, thank you again, sir."

I thought it best to get out while the getting was good. But before I could do so, Haynes threw another compliment my way. "We have big plans for you, Robert," and then he closed the door behind him.

I couldn't believe my ears. It almost seemed inconceivable. My short television career had skirted one disaster after another. There had been highs and lows, depression and euphoria. But I was beginning to understand that this was life. The one truism seemed to be that nothing remained the same. Nothing—not family or friends, not even the city itself—was immune. Not even the Diner.

Something unusual was taking place over at Mount Vernon Square. Each evening a young soldier would walk around the Washington Monument for nearly two hours. He didn't say anything, he didn't do anything—except walk in circles.

No one knew his name, no one asked, but crowds had begun to gather to watch his peculiar act. Word of mouth had spread through the hippie community and the numbers grew. Neil never acknowledged their presence.

Stories began to circulate about the lone soldier. And when the "pot" was thick in the air, the stories became more fantastic. Neil's weird hike was being turned into a spiritual odyssey.

The Peabody Conservatory, a building full of budding musicians, was across the street from the monument. One evening a bass drum player, seeing what was happening, carted out his drum and began to accent Neil's circular journey. The crowd joined in, clapping methodically to the beat of the slow dirge. Neil continued, like the second hand of a ticking clock, sweeping around and around in his circle.

Neddy was coming back from the Green Earth when she heard the slow, rhythmic clap of the large crowd. She walked up the hill, away from Walters Art Gallery, until she could see the Washington Monument lit up, and the crowd. She had no idea what was happening, but she mingled with the hippies and other people, and eventually she saw the marching soldier. Neddy asked someone what was going on.

"It's kind of cool. This soldier . . . he does this every night," a stoned-out girl explained.

"Does what?"

"He just goes around it . . . walks around it for hours."

Neddy continued to move through the crowd, trying to get a better view so she could understand what had so mesmerized everyone. Then she saw who it was.

He looked different to her now; different from the way he looked the one night they had spent together. There was a determination in Neil's face, a ramrod posture. Neddy felt sad watching Neil's act of defiance, if that's what it was. And underneath the sadness there was a deeper hurt. She had thought about him constantly, had worried about him and cared about him. And yet here he was, back in Baltimore, and he had never even bothered to contact her. She told herself that she had only known him for one night . . . one brief night. Nevertheless, Neddy felt a sense of loss, just another member of the crowd watching a stranger.

After another half an hour or so, Neil stopped his march and walked away. Neddy did not follow him.

Twenty-Two

I sat with Mickey in the television station canteen area, a sterile room with half a dozen vending machines. I wanted to be the one to tell him that I'd been promoted to assistant director, rather than have him hear about it from someone else. Since I had leapfrogged over him in getting the position, I didn't want there to be any hard feelings. There weren't—the Mick was great about it.

He said, "There may not be anything flashy about me, but I'm steady, reliable, and I'll be just fine." He told me that he'd heard rumblings that Richard Towers was moving to the sister station in Durham, North Carolina, where he was to become a full-time director. "When I heard there was an opening, I was hoping it was gonna be me, but"—he shrugged his shoulders—"my time will come."

As I was heading down the hallway to go to the studio, I passed an editing room where Jerome Pilsner, one of the features reporters, was working on a video monitor. As I glanced through the glass door at the monitor, something took me totally by surprise. Neil was on the screen. I backed up and watched him walking around the Washington Monument in a soldier's uniform.

I slowly opened the door and entered the room. Pilsner was talking to the editor at his side. "I think right here, while he's doing the march, I can get some comments from the crowd, then we can intercut those pieces with the soldier." He sensed my presence and looked over his shoulder at me. "Who are you?"

"Bobby Shine. I'm gonna start AD'ing the news with Eddie until Duke's back from his vacation."

Pilsner nodded, not particularly interested.

"What's this about?" I tried to sound as nonchalant as possible.

Pilsner replied, looking at the screen, "Working on a feature about the hippies down in Mount Vernon and I stumbled on this soldier who keeps walking around the monument every night."

"Why is he doing it?"

"The *why* is what I'm trying to find out."

I stared at the screen, watching my friend perform one of the strangest acts of his strange life. "How long has it been going on?"

"I don't know. Maybe a week, maybe less. . . . maybe more. I've still got a lot of work to do." Then Pilsner turned to me. "Don't you have things to do?"

I said that I did and quickly went to call Annie at home. The cleaning lady told me she was out, working at the hospital. So I called there but she was in a staff meeting and couldn't be disturbed. I left a message, and when she called me back, I was working as a floor director on several different programs and couldn't talk. We played phone tag for the rest of the day.

That same evening I had dinner with Annie and her parents at the Chesapeake Restaurant, less than a mile from their son's circular march, about which they knew absolutely nothing. And since she arrived with her mother and father, I never had a moment alone to tell Annie privately what was going on. I didn't particularly want to be the one to break it to her parents. So throughout dinner I kept quiet, and was feeling rather anxious.

My anxiety wasn't helped by Annie's father's unrelenting diatribe against Neil.

"Here's a boy with talent, imagination. He would have been an outstanding lawyer. Absolutely outstanding. He had all of the connections set up for a very successful law practice. He's charming . . . very affable when he wants to be. But he hardly ever wants to be. It's frustrating beyond belief. You have no idea," he said, pointing a finger at me, "what it's like to have a son you don't understand and who can commit such moronic, frivolous, stupid acts of behavior . . ."

There was no stopping Mr. Tilden on the subject of his son. "Wait, see how you feel, Bobby. You and Annie have a boy, you raise him, you'll understand what I'm talking about. Only then. Doesn't have the courtesy to pick up a telephone and call. He's here in town, doesn't even call. Gets himself drafted for no apparent reason. He's a mess."

Mrs. Tilden, who had consumed at least three martinis, was drifting off all during dinner. Her eyes would flutter, and just when it looked as if she was about to fall asleep, she'd light a cigarette and, as was her habit, cough violently after the first puff.

A few times, Annie would reach out and take my hand for comfort. The dinner was initially set up to discuss our wedding plans, but there was no opportunity for that. Halfway through the meal—and Mr. Tilden's tirade—I couldn't hold things in any longer. I had to tell Annie the news.

"I've got to talk to you. Now," I whispered.

I cut Mr. Tilden off in the middle of his rant and said, "Excuse me. I have to go to the bathroom."

Annie said, "Maybe I'll go as well."

In a small, confined hallway outside the doors of the bathrooms and the kitchen, I told Annie about Neil's latest misadventure. It was not the ideal locale—waiters were flying in and out of the kitchen doors, carrying trays stacked high with food. Shouts of "Coming through!" peppered our entire conversation.

"When are they going to show the story?" Annie asked, stunned.

"Within the week."

"Oh my God," she sighed.

"Coming through!"

"What the hell is Neil doing?" she continued. "What could he possibly be thinking?"

"That's what Pilsner's trying to find out," I said.

"Don't be so flippant."

"I'm not being flippant. I'm just telling you that's what he's looking into. That's the story."

Someone was standing behind me as if I were in line for the bathroom.

"It's not a line," I explained. "Go on. There's no one in there. We're just talking."

"Thank God," he said. "I feel sick to my stomach."

He went inside and I heard the door lock.

"Why won't he call? I don't understand this," Annie said, nearly in tears.

"He's obviously pissed off with your parents for kicking him out of the house."

"I don't think he *cared* about being kicked out of the house."

Another waiter with a stack of plates squeezed by. "Coming through!"

"No matter what the situation," Annie continued, "Neil at least owes us a phone call."

Suddenly, from behind the men's bathroom door, I could hear the guttural sounds of a man throwing up.

"Oh Christ!" I said, and guided a shaky Annie back into the dining room. "We'll talk more after dinner, okay?"

She nodded and we sat back down at the table. We made it all the way through dessert, and at the end of the exhausting meal we were able to say our goodbyes. I was going to drive Annie home so we could spend a few minutes alone and talk privately, but her father said, "Don't be silly. We're going home, we'll take her. Why two cars?"

Annie objected, but her father couldn't understand the two-car logic. Then he threw a dig in my direction. "Bobby needs his rest. Doesn't he have hand puppets to work in the morning?"

With all the concern about Neil, I had forgotten to mention my promotion, so I told them all about it as we stood outside the restaurant. Annie was delighted, even after all the trauma of the dinner, but Mr. Tilden's reaction was less than enthusiastic. He showed as much emotion as if he were listening to the weather report and hearing that the next day's forecast was going to be partly cloudy. I politely said good night to Mr. and Mrs. Tilden, kissed Annie goodbye, and watched them drive away. In one car.

It was a little after ten when I walked into Longfellow's bar. The place was fairly crowded, the jukebox blasting away, and the dance floor area packed. There was a real mix, ranging from hippies to young business executives.

Turko was hanging out, nursing a beer, giving Ben the latest update on Neddy.

"Cut down on some of the romantic shit," Ben said. "More details on the sex."

"Did you ever fuck that Donna . . . what the hell was her name?" Turko asked Ben. "Lived out at Loch Raven?

Ben thought for a second. "Donna . . . what the hell *was* her name? Yeah, everyone fucked her. Why?"

"She was good. Right?"

"Very, very," Ben agreed.

"Well, Neddy is better."

"Nooo!"

"Plus, she completely knocks me out."

Ben poured me a beer and I told them what was going on with Neil.

"He's been walking around the Washington Monument?" Turko was incredulous.

"Doing what?" Ben wanted to know.

"I don't know what the hell he's doing," I answered. "He's just going around the monument."

"Fucking Neil's back, and he didn't let anyone know?" Turko now turned belligerent.

"He came in here once, then walked out. Not a word since," Ben told us.

"How come you guys didn't tell me he was back in town?" Turko demanded.

Ben cleaned out an ashtray. "I thought you knew."

"Knew? How am I gonna know?"

"From the broad," Ben said. "You told us that Neil writes to her."

"He wrote a *note*. One fucking *note*! Not *notes*! One fucking note!"

"How am I supposed to know?" Ben said. "You told me he wrote her a letter."

"It wasn't a letter. It was a *note*. Period. And it wasn't a *love* note." Turko continued his tirade. "It was nothing. Just a fucking note! She read it to me. I couldn't even read it. She had to read it to me."

Then I decided to jump in. "The point is, Neil's walking around the Washington Monument, and to make matters worse, they're going to do a news story on him sometime within the week."

Turko took some coins out of his pocket. "I'm gonna call Neddy and see what the fuck is going on here. How could she not tell me he was back in town?"

He practically ran over to the phone booth at the other end of the bar and closed the door. We saw the overhead light go on as Ben told me about the conversation he'd had with Neil. "He said he's not going back to the army. It sounded like he's going AWOL."

"Oh shit!" I said. "Like it's his choice. 'Sorry, army, I don't think I'll be coming back.' "

I looked over to the phone booth and could see Turko, agitated, as he hung up the phone.

"She knew," he told us when he got back to the bar.

"And didn't say anything to you?" Ben asked.

"She says she only saw him from afar. That's exactly what she said: " 'I saw him from afar.' "

"So why didn't she tell you she saw him from afar?" Ben pressed.

"I don't know. That's what I asked." Turko sighed. "Shit," he said. "I yelled at her. I shouldn't have yelled. All she did was see him from afar." He sighed again. "When's Neil supposed to go back? When's he gonna be a lot farther afar?"

Ben told him of Neil's AWOL plans.

"Oh, that's just fucking great!" Turko knocked back his beer and Ben immediately poured him another.

While Ben and I discussed the few alternatives Neil might have, Turko wandered off to the other end of the bar. He didn't want to hear another word about his friend, turned romantic rival.

"I'll tell you one thing, Ben, if he goes AWOL, there ain't no doctor's note in the world that's gonna clear up this situation for him. It's not like going to Atlantic City and suddenly getting a little bored halfway through the season," I said.

"He could run off to Canada or Mexico."

"Yeah," I said, "or go underground, something like that, maybe." But we were just throwing ideas around, since neither one of us knew what the hell Neil had in mind.

While we talked, Turko started dancing with a secretary who worked for the Baltimore Colts organization. She was in her late twenties, a few years older than any of us. A little later on he brought her over to the bar. He was in a better mood now and we told her stories of our many years following the team.

As a kid, his father never had enough money to buy him season tickets, so Turko was always looking for inventive ways to sneak into the games at Memorial Stadium.

"Sometimes I used to just rush the gate. Once I got past the guy collecting tickets I'd disappear into the crowd. But I always had to be moving around, otherwise one of the ushers would get ahold of me and throw me out."

"The best one," I said, "was when he got in under the guise of being handicapped."

Turko laughed. "That was an ingenious plan. Eggy, a friend of ours, had season tickets. He had them bring a wheelchair, you know, folded up, close to the gates, and then he waited for me over at section 39. I bolted through the gate with a big crowd surge, met him there, and then we opened up the wheelchair. I got in and he wheeled me down onto the field, right next to the Colts' bench. Best seat in the house. It was a brilliant scheme. They let Eggy stay with me because I needed assistance, you know, being handicapped and all. Then I really fucked up."

"How?" the secretary asked.

"Unitas throws this pass, sixty-four-yard touchdown, put the Colts in the lead. I jumped out of the wheelchair in celebration. I even hugged a couple of the players. One of the ushers sees me standing up, finds this suspicious, and comes over to me."

The secretary laughed.

"Tell her the punch line," I said.

"The usher's about to throw me out, thinks it's a hoax. I tell him I think it's a miracle. I make like I suddenly realize I'm walking. It's a miracle! Unitas has saved me! Eggy joins in with, 'Look, you can walk, Ronald.' To be honest, I thought we had the usher for a minute, but no such luck. Eggy was allowed to go back to his regular seat but I got thrown out."

The secretary seemed enamored with Turko, and although the Turk wasn't so taken with her, he was drunk and pissed off enough with Neddy not to pass up some action if it came his way. So he took off with the secretary for the night.

I hung around until closing time and walked out of Longfellow's with Ben after he'd locked up. It was only out in the parking lot, as I was about to get into my car, that he happened to mention that Janet still hadn't come home.

"What's the story?" I asked.

"I've got nothing else to add. Whenever I call, her father, or her mother for that matter, won't put her on, so I'm not sure what to do."

"Do you miss her?"

Rather than give a direct answer, Ben said, "I miss my life."

He pulled on his lower eyelid, but with no smile whatsoever, then got into his car and drove off.

Twenty-Three

It was early afternoon and the sky was steel gray when Neddy came down the steps of the art institute, bundled up in her brown army coat. She had a long red wool scarf tied around her neck. As she started up the street, a voice yelled to her, "Hey, young female artist," and Neddy turned.

There was Neil, casually sitting on a bus stop bench, still in uniform, boots perfectly shined.

She wanted to scream his name. She wanted to run to him, but she thought better of it. Instead, she just said, "Hi," turned her back on him, and kept walking up the street. She expected to hear him say something like, "Where are you going?" or "Let me talk to you," but she heard nothing. She didn't want to turn around and see what he was doing, so she kept walking . . . and waiting . . . and hoping that he would follow her. But such was not the case. Bracing herself against the cold air, she continued on her way, never looking back.

Crossing over to Charles Street and heading north, she reached her apartment building within a few minutes. Neddy started up the long stairway, and as she made the turn to head up the next flight, she was shocked to see Neil sitting on the steps, smoking a cigarette. "I'm sorry I didn't get ahold of you sooner."

"Why didn't you?" she asked.

"I don't know. Maybe I cared a little too much."

She was pleased and extraordinarily relieved to hear those words. Suddenly the hurt was gone, and as she leaned against the wall, the words quietly flowed. "I've never missed someone so much in my life, and I hardly know you."

"The more you know me, the less there'll be to like."

"I'll take my chances."

"At boot camp I kept looking in my wallet for a picture of you. But I didn't have one."

He leaned back on the step, resting his head against the wall. Then Neddy said, "Well, I'm right in front of you now, and I'm better than a picture."

Neil got up and moved toward her. "I don't always know what's real and what's not," he said.

Neddy lightly kissed him on the lips and said, "This is real."

Instead of going up to her apartment, they went for a walk. As they passed the Washington Monument, Neddy asked, "What's it about?"

"It's not about anything. It has no meaning. You can give it one, you can find some significance, but it has no meaning. I just started to walk around and kept going . . . and that's all."

"Then why are you doing it every night?" Neddy asked.

"For show. It's just a show. It created its own importance, which tells you what we're about. Something that is meaningless, insignificant, suddenly creates its own relevance . . . and that's the joke of life."

They headed north toward Druid Hill Park and the reservoir up near Eutaw Place, a section of grand old buildings now falling into disrepair. Neil pointed to a building as they approached it. "F. Scott Fitzgerald once stayed here when Zelda was having mental problems. She was institutionalized over at Sheppard Pratt. He would write here, then go and visit her at the hospital."

She surveyed the building, trying to imagine it in an age of elegance. "How do you know this was the place?"

"I'm full of useless information," Neil said. "Fitzgerald once wrote: '*All life is a process of breaking down, but the blows that do the dramatic side of the work—the big sudden blows that come, or seem to come from outside—the ones you remember and blame things on, and the moments of weakness you tell your friends about, don't show their effects all at once. There's another sort of blow that comes from within—that you don't feel until it's too late to do anything about, until you realize, with finality, that in some regard you'll never be as good a man again.*' "

"I'm not sure what to say," Neddy told him.

"You don't have to say anything. We should have fun, fun, fun till daddy takes the T-Bird away. The Beach Boys. Almost as wise as Fitzgerald." He held her and gave her a soft kiss. Locked in one another's arms, Neil whispered, "How foolish are we?"

"How foolish do you want to be?"

"Very."

They headed back down the street, away from the park, not saying anything else for a few minutes—just enjoying being close. Then Neddy broke the silence. "How much time do you have before you have to report back?"

Neil answered in the most casual way possible. "We have all the time in the world."

Ben woke up in the early afternoon. He was sleeping on a hardwood floor with a pillow under his head and an overcoat as a blanket. For the longest time, he couldn't remember where he was. Then he realized he was in his own living room.

When he arrived home the night before, the entire apartment had been stripped bare of almost everything in it—the bedding, the dishes, the silverware, the rugs, all the furniture. Nothing was left except Ben's toothbrush and toothpaste, his clothing, and a couple of things he'd brought with him when he got married—a torn ticket stub to the 1959 championship game between the Colts and the New York Giants; his high school ring from City; and a photo taken on the night he was crowned as "royalty," wearing a papier-mâché crown with stuck-on sparkles, a big smile on his face.

We found out later that Janet's father had some moving people come and take every possession that Janet had, or anything that had been provided by her father, out of the place. As Ben lay on the floor looking at his empty bookcase, only the autographed baseball from Orioles pitcher Bob Turley, remained. He lay there, too depressed to get up . . . too depressed to want to begin another day. So he didn't.

Twenty-Four

At 6 p.m. exactly, with its pulsating, overly dramatic theme music, the evening news began. I sat next to Eddie Collier—my first night as an assistant director. I nervously fiddled with the stopwatch, my most valuable tool. Everything about the news is timing.

The lead story was about the war in Vietnam. The casualty toll for the past week, as reported by the Pentagon, listed 144 men killed and 1,044 wounded. As the story continued to unfold, I gave Eddie information as to which film chain to roll and where certain slides were positioned.

"Ten seconds to out on film three," I said. "Stand by on camera one . . . five seconds on three."

"And one—mike, cue him," barked Eddie.

"Next piece of film is on four—footage on the casualties . . . twenty-five seconds of film," I instructed.

Acting on this, Eddie commanded, "Ready. Roll four and dissolve to four," and the image of wounded American soldiers came up on the monitor.

"The visual out cue is of the helicopter taking off," I told him. "You've got twenty seconds."

I watched the monitor. Guys younger than me wounded, bleeding—casualties of a war I hardly understood. I had no time to be emotionally involved in what I was seeing; I was too caught up in what I was doing. It was my first night as an assistant director, and I loved it. The jitters were gone and I felt as competent as a copilot of a jet plane.

But the images stayed in my head long after the news show was off the air. Stories of this horrendous war—of dying soldiers, bloodied civilians—played to audiences during the dinner hour. I could picture a kitchen somewhere in Baltimore, a small portable television set, a family eating their meal, the nightmare of Vietnam right there in the middle of that cheerful setting. Against images of napalm setting jungles on fire, there would be mundane chatter: "Why can't I have some dessert now, Ma? I ate enough." "You didn't eat enough. You didn't eat any of your vegetables." "But the pie looks so good." One of the most catastrophic events ever to take place in American history, played out against family scenes like that, night after night after night.

The show continued: the news, weather, sports, and special features. Throughout the hour broadcast, I supplied Eddie Collier with everything he needed to make it all run smoothly.

"Basketball scores on six . . . sports theme music cued . . . Dial soap commercial just been moved from film chain two to one. *It's been moved to one.* Chevrolet commercial on video two and a five-second lead-in . . . got a five-second roll."

It all went without a hitch, as did the next two nights.

Neil wandered into Longfellow's to hang with Ben, but Ben was nowhere to be found. The manager, Eric Moore, said he hadn't been in for the past few days. "He hasn't even called in. I don't know what the fuck his problem is."

Neil knew, having talked with Janet, that she had moved out. But he had been so caught up with Neddy, the days had slipped by and he hadn't had a conversation with Ben.

He dialed Ben's number at the apartment from the bar's phone booth. Ben's phone rang and rang as Neil waited for a response. He let it ring maybe twelve, thirteen times before he finally hung up. Neil sat there in the booth trying to figure out what was going on; where Ben might be. He decided he should find out.

In less than fifteen minutes, Neil pulled up, in a cab, into the Diner parking lot. He told the cabbie, "Go slow. I wanna see who's here."

He rolled down the back passenger window of the cab and leaned out, carefully peering in through the Diner windows. It was relatively early in the evening and not many guys were hanging, so it was easy to see that Ben wasn't there. Neil told the cabbie to take him over to the Greenspring Apartments.

Five minutes later they were at Ben's apartment building. Neil paid the cabbie, then walked around to number 9. He rang the doorbell but there was no answer. He knocked hard on the door, and still no reply. An older woman walked by. She took a good look at him in his uniform, smiled and nodded, and continued on her way.

Neil wandered around to the side of the garden apartment, trying to get a look through one of the windows, but the drapes were closed tightly. He stepped onto the side patio, where the sliding doors were, but vertical venetian blinds covered the view into the living room. Neil tried looking through the slats. He could make out that there didn't seem to be much furniture. Then he got down on his hands and knees to see if he could get a view of anything through the bottom of the blinds. The air currents from the improperly sealed door created just enough motion to allow a bit of flutter. It was then that Neil saw what looked like a foot lying on the hardwood floor. He crawled along the bottom of the door, trying to get a better look. That's when he saw Ben's hand.

Neil jumped up and tried to pry the doors open, but they wouldn't budge. He ran back to the window and tried to open it. Again it was shut tight. So he hit the windowpane with his elbow and broke the glass, stuck his hand inside, undid the latch, opened the window, and climbed into Ben's kitchen.

Once inside, he was stunned at how empty the place was. It felt desolate. He moved slowly through the darkness, feeling for a light switch. Near the counter, which separated the kitchen from the living room, he found one and flicked it on. He saw Ben lying on the hardwood floor of the empty living room.

His first impression was that Ben was dead. But as he moved toward the body, there was a slight movement in Ben's right arm. Neil crouched down and shook him, trying to wake Ben up. Then he noticed various bottles of pills, mostly empty and unlabeled.

As he continued to shake Ben, he could see that his friend hadn't shaved in days. Neil was also acutely aware of the odor of foul breath and the stench of urine.

Neil slapped Ben's face and kept shaking him, hoping to get some response. Ben opened his eyes slightly and mumbled, "Hey, soldier man."

Neil just stared at him. They'd known each other a long time, their whole lives, really. They'd been caught up in a lot of crazy scenes over the years—but this was the craziest. This was the one that made absolutely no sense. One of his best friends had just tried to commit suicide.

The King of the Teenagers was lying nearly unconscious in his own piss in a stripped-down bare apartment.

Neil ran back to the kitchen, looked in the refrigerator to see if there was any juice, but the shelves were empty. He found an old cup on the edge of the sink, filled it with water, went back to Ben, held up his head, and poured the water into his mouth. Most of it ran down Ben's face, but he did manage to take in a few drops.

The room remained dark except for the light coming from the kitchen. Neil sat down on the floor next to Ben, who kept floating in and out of consciousness, and pondered his next move. He gave Ben a little more water, got up, and went over to the phone. He dialed his home number. His mother answered.

"Is Annie there?" Neil asked.

"Who is this? Neil?" Mrs. Tilden said.

"Listen, I can't talk . . ."

"For God's sake, Neil, why can't you just come by and say hello or something?"

"Listen," he interrupted, "we can talk about that later on. Right now I need Annie. It's very important."

"Are you going to come by the house?" his mother asked angrily.

"I can't talk. This is important. Where is Annie?"

"She's at the hospital . . . but listen to me, mister, if you—"

Neil hung up the phone. Then he quickly dialed Mercy Hospital, and after being transferred from one department to another, at last he heard Annie's voice on the phone.

"Annie, it's Neil."

"Finally, you take the time to call."

"I can't talk about that right now. I've got Ben here on the floor. He's drifting in and out of consciousness."

"What's wrong? What happened?"

"I think he took an overdose of sleeping pills."

"Call emergency immediately."

Neil looked over at Ben, who made the slightest movement and then drifted off again.

"I don't want him to get mixed up with hospital reports, they'll call the police . . . attempted suicide. Do me a favor, will you? Get over here right away. I'm at his apartment."

"Neil, I think it would be best—"

Neil cut her off, "Annie, don't let's argue about this. I think we can get this under control here. I just need your help."

"Get him on his feet . . . move him around," Annie said. "Keep him as conscious as possible and I'll see you in a few minutes."

Neil went back over to Ben, lifted him off the floor, and leaned him against the wall. Then he started walking him around the living room. Ben was close to unconscious, so Neil ended up dragging him. It was as if he was dancing with a dead man.

Ben's eyes fluttered open and he mumbled something. Neil propped him up against the living room wall.

"What?" Neil said. "Talk to me."

"Let me sleep . . . let me sleep."

"I can't hear you. Say it louder."

"Put me down. I need to sleep. Put me down."

For the next ten minutes Neil tried to move Ben's limp body around the room. "Come on, you fuck! Stay awake!" He called him every name in the book, trying to get him angry. He tried to get him to talk about Janet. He did everything he could think of in an effort to keep him conscious. He gave Ben some more water, then sat down beside him. "This is lame, Ben . . . just lame. There's no poetry to this. The obituary says: *'Ben Kallin died from an overdose of sleeping pills in his garden apartment, in the suburbs of Baltimore.'* No poetry. Cold-water flat in Paris, maybe. But this?"

Much to Neil's relief, Annie finally showed up. She was efficient and unemotional as she assessed Ben's condition, checked his pulse rate, and listened to his heart. She looked at the prescription medication he had taken, all the time working on keeping him awake.

"Let's get him into the bathroom," she said.

Just like a fireman, Neil slung Ben over his shoulder and carried him. Annie felt he was conscious enough to give him syrup of ipecac. Neil asked what it was. "It's going to help him throw up. Hold his mouth open for me."

Neil did as instructed and Annie fed Ben a tablespoonful of the syrup. Then she said to her brother, "Unless you've got the stomach for it, I suggest you step out. It's not going to be a pretty sight."

Neil didn't move. And while they waited for the medicine to take effect, she asked him how he could have come back into town and not even bothered to contact her. "I don't think I'm exactly the demanding type, do you?"

Neil just smiled and shrugged his shoulders. Ben peered at the two of them through half-open eyes, then his body began to convulse. Annie quickly positioned Ben on his knees over the toilet bowl as he began to vomit.

Neil went to lean against the wall outside the bathroom and lit a cigarette as Ben's retching continued. Periodically Annie would flush the toilet; again and again Ben would vomit. To Neil it seemed as if everything Ben ever had in his system or had ever ingested in his whole life was coming up. The barfing sounds made Neil queasy.

He walked away from the bathroom and wandered into the empty living room—the tip of his cigarette providing almost the only light. The sounds quieted down in the bathroom now and he heard Ben arguing with Annie.

"Don't you dare look at my dick!" Ben screamed.

"I'm a nurse."

"You're Neil's sister, for Christ's sake."

Neil approached the bathroom and saw that Annie had taken Ben's clothes off. He was lying in the tub in his urine-soaked

Jockey briefs. She had the tap water running and was checking the temperature. When she felt it was right, she turned on the shower.

"It's too cold! It's too cold!!" Ben yelled.

She handed him a bar of soap and told him to clean himself up. "Take off your underwear." Then she told Neil to keep an eye on him. "Make sure he doesn't do anything dangerous. I'll be right back."

"Where are you going?" Neil asked.

"The deli, to get some coffee."

A short time later they all sat in the dark living room on the floor drinking coffee—Ben wrapped in a blanket, feeling weak.

As a diversion, not wanting to deal with what he'd just done, Ben began to reminisce. Janet's name came up—not the Janet of 1967, the fifteen-year-old Janet. The Janet who had once dated Neil. She'd been Neil's first girlfriend.

"Tell me about your first date with her again," Ben said. "Tell me that."

"Ben, I don't want to get into it."

"Just the part where you brought her home."

"You've heard it a hundred times."

"What happened?" Annie asked. "I never heard."

"The screen door . . ." said Ben weakly.

"What?" Annie was curious now.

Neil reluctantly told the story. "When we got up to her house—we were coming back from the Crest Theater . . . we saw something, I can't remember what. Anyway, we were standing at her door, between the screen door and the front door, and I went to kiss her. It was our first kiss. Suddenly, the screen door hit me from behind and we ended up banging our teeth together. It was this amazingly awkward moment."

Annie smiled. "That's so pathetic."

"I love that!" Ben exclaimed. "I love that moment."

"I never tried to kiss a girl good night at the door ever again."

"Never?" Annie was intrigued. "You never kissed a girl good night?"

"I kissed 'em, but it had to be before I got to the door. The door was too big a hang-up. I was afraid of screen doors."

"Did you ever kiss Janet again?" Annie asked.

Neil just shook his head and lit another cigarette.

"*I* did." said Ben. He closed his eyes, wanting to sleep.

"No, no, no, Ben." Annie nudged him awake and made him drink some more coffee.

"I'm tired," he mumbled.

"Just take a few more sips," Annie said, and Ben obeyed her.

"Who was the best kisser you ever had, Annie?" Ben managed to ask. "Your best kiss?"

"Bobby."

"No, besides Bobby."

"Best kisser?" She thought for a minute. "Eggy."

"Eggy?!" Neil said, surprised. "When in the hell did you date Eggy?"

"I didn't. It was on New Year's Eve down at the Alcazar. He just touched me on the shoulder, I turned around, and suddenly he kissed me. This big passionate kiss. He was a real good kisser."

Neil smiled. "I'm sick. Eggy is a good kisser? You kissed Eggy?" Then he turned to Ben. "How was Janet as a kisser?"

Ben just said, "Janet?"

"How would you rank her?"

"I would say she was fifth . . . no, fourth . . ." Ben thought for a moment. "Third . . . maybe second. A close first."

"Who else?" asked Annie.

"Marsha Cohn," said Ben. "That probably doesn't count because she only kissed me on the cheek, but she gave me such a hard-on I never forgot it."

Annie laughed. "You guys always had a thing about her, didn't you?"

"Are you kidding? She was death," said Ben. "Baltimore's finest."

They continued to reminisce in that empty dark apartment, talking about the past. The present was too painful for Ben. Only yesterday was soothing; only yesterday offered any comfort.

Ben said, "What about when you punched out that guy, Annie? What was his name?"

"Larry Mueller," Annie said.

"It was a punch heard around the school," Neil said proudly.

Ben started to doze off again.

"No, no, no, no, no, Ben." Annie and Neil pulled him up onto his feet and walked him around.

"Tell me the Larry Mueller story. I love it. I love it," Ben said, slurring his words as his feet did their best to move.

"I was sitting outside the cafeteria," Annie began. "Some of the girls were smoking cigarettes. Larry was up on the fire escape. It was one of those spring days and it was pretty out. I was wearing a very light sundress, which was cut out in the back—"

"Sexy," Ben muttered.

"Larry watched me," Annie continued, "and somehow, in his sophomoric demented mind, he decided to see if he could spit from the second floor of the fire escape onto my bare back."

"And he did," Neil added.

"I felt saliva sliding down my back, and there was Larry just so proud of himself. None of the girls around me knew what happened. I waved for Larry to come down as if I wanted to talk to him for a minute. When he came up to me I said, 'Come a little closer, I want to whisper something to you.' Then I just punched him in his face as hard as I could. He started bleeding . . ."

"I love a girl sucker-punching a guy," grinned Ben.

"The girls thought I'd just punched him for the hell of it,

because they didn't see what happened. I couldn't believe that I did it."

"You were 'One-Punch Annie,' " mumbled Neil.

Annie laughed. "After that he was always afraid of me. It was so peculiar to watch him in the hall. He would see me coming and duck away out of sight."

They all laughed, and more stories were told. Ben reveled in the glory of the past. Even two or three years ago seemed a long time in the past for Ben. When you're on top of the world, when you're the King of the Teenagers, you think all good things are forever, you think you are owed the continuity of good fortune and that the future will be consistent with the past. Reality may tell us it's a lie, but at that age, reality is denied access. Until, at some point, the present is not so perfect. The past is far more reassuring. But Ben's suicide attempt was not about the past or the present. Ben's pain came with the recognition that there was a future.

While this drama was playing out, I was in Studio A where *Ted Mack's Original Amateur Hour* was having local tryouts. Would-be talent lined the hallway and extended into the parking lot, hoping to move on to the nationally televised program.

Ted Mack's Original Amateur Hour presented a potpourri of acts—jugglers, dancers, singers, comedians, magicians—before a large studio audience each week. At the end of the program, the audience would vote for their favorite entertainer by applauding, and the act that got the loudest applause was chosen the winner. For those winners, it was the chance of a lifetime.

It's hard to imagine the level of talent that marched through Studio A during those auditions. Tap dancers tripped themselves, magic tricks didn't work, and comedians forgot punch lines.

"Man goes to see the doctor," one would-be comic began. "He says to the doctor . . . he says to the doctor . . ."

The comedian stared at the talent panel for about twelve seconds.

"No," he continued. "The doctor says to the patient . . ."

Then it was as if the man went into a trance. Nothing came out of his mouth. There was no body movement whatsoever.

One of the talent scouts finally said, "Thank you."

The comedian stood transfixed, almost in shock while the talent scout repeated, "Thank you *very* much."

Then, with the help of one of the assistants, he left the stage.

One of the oddest acts I'd ever seen was an elderly bald-headed man who played "Yankee Doodle Dandy" by hitting his bald head with a variety of different-sized spoons. He would shape his mouth to create the range of notes. The act took on a bizarre and unexpected twist when he hit himself too hard on his scalp and blood began to trickle down his forehead and nose. But he boldly played on, with a big cheerful look on his face. He finished his song by thumping his head with four spoons simultaneously, and took a quick bow. Then he pulled out a handkerchief and matter-of-factly wiped off the blood before leaving the stage.

The evening came to a premature end when a drum majorette set the studio on fire. The ends of her batons were soaked in gasoline and lit as she started auditioning. Used to performing outdoors, she misjudged the ceiling height and one of her fiery batons went up into the lighting grid and set fire to the curtains. Alarms went off throughout the building and I quickly ushered all of the talent outside. The firemen arrived and the blaze was soon under control.

It was during this time that Annie called to tell me about Ben's suicide attempt. I remember listening to the story on the phone in the control room, which overlooked the studio floor. I saw that the smoke was clearing and I thought of the absurdity of it all. The nature of life—drama and comedy playing out side by side.

And then there are gaps.

Twenty-Five

Neil moved Ben into Neddy's apartment, where she nursed him back to health with a diet of Green Earth health products. Ben was drinking carrot juice and miso soup and eating buckwheat noodles and broth with various vegetables and brown rice, which Neddy constantly reminded him needed to be chewed fifty times before swallowing. He took a liking to this macrobiotic diet, which was a long way from his usual selection of corned beef, burgers, and French fries with gravy.

Neil hung around most of the time, but ventured out nightly for his Washington Monument circular walk. Neddy convinced Ben to call Longfellow's and he spoke to Eric, the manager, who fortunately decided not to fire him.

In the time he stayed at Neddy's apartment, Ben never talked about Janet and never wanted to discuss what was depressing him. He just wanted to reminisce, and he and Neil did that for hours on end. They talked about the summers up in Atlantic City, and the South Philly crowd they always loved hanging with. Guys with names like Brother Feno, the Crow, DoDo, Shelley the Midget, and King.

Ben told a tale about the Crow. "You remember how tough he was. Not tall, maybe five seven, but tough as shit. We're leaning on a pole up at the boardwalk one night talking—I think it was the summer we graduated. So Crow lays this story on me about trying to rob this house. The police arrive, so he takes off. Suddenly, a police dog jumps right at him. The Crow punches the German shepherd right in the snout, knocks the fucking dog out. I'm amazed he tells me this, so I said to him, 'You punched out the police dog?' You know, I say that because it's an amazing thing to do. I never heard of something like that, somebody punching a police dog. The Crow comes at me defensively, you know . . . 'Hey, what was I gonna do?' " Ben laughed. "I love that. He's getting defensive—'Hey, what was I gonna do?' He was a piece of work."

Neddy laughed along with the stories that were told, but her fears, her anxieties, were just beneath the surface. Neither Ben nor Neil would openly talk about their troubles. Ben was on an emotional slippery slope and Neil seemed to be paying no attention to the fact that within days he was going to be considered AWOL. The image of Neil standing in front of the induction office on that cold, snowy morning, tearing the doctor's note into pieces of confetti, haunted her. On more than one occasion she had asked him to explain why he had done it, but Neil refused to discuss the subject.

He was just as evasive about his future plans. When Neddy asked him what he had in mind concerning his army report date, he would just say, "I've thought about Canada or Mexico, but I don't feel like traveling."

"We could drive to Mexico and live on the beach, or go further, maybe across the Yucatán peninsula," Neddy offered.

Neil thought about this for a minute. "Yucatán . . . Mayan culture . . . hmmm . . . I don't know. I mean, what the fuck happened to the Mayans? They're gone. This advanced civilization, gone just like that. I don't know if that's a place to go."

"Well, there are lots of other interesting places."

But Neil wasn't listening. "You know there's a story that when the Spanish first landed in the Yucatán, they came across the natives who lived there and one of the sailors walked up to one of these tribal people and asked who they were. Since these people didn't speak Spanish, they said, in their Yucatán language, '*Maya.*' The Spanish thought they were answering the question and that "*Maya*" meant who they were. But in the language of the natives, '*Maya*' meant 'What?' The Spanish are saying "Who are you?" and the natives are saying '*Maya,*' meaning 'What?' because they don't understand. So it ends up that the Spanish take *Maya* to be the name of the people and call them Mayans. The Yucatecs could have said 'Fuck off' and then today they'd be called the Fuckofferns instead."

Neil was full of useless information.

Sometime later, over brownies—which Neddy had baked with marijuana and the help of Duncan Hines—Ben asked, "Why don't you want to go back to the army?"

"Not a good enough reason yet."

"A reason for what?" Ben asked.

"To go back."

And nothing else was said on the subject that evening.

Annie and I decided to go and see Neil that particular night. We met Neddy and Ben at the Washington Monument. They arrived shortly after Neil began his walk, since he preferred to arrive and leave there alone.

A crowd quickly gathered as Neil walked his route. The musicians from the Peabody Conservatory were in place, the drums were being played, and the slow, rhythmic clapping started. The journey of the lone soldier was under way.

"If he doesn't want to go into the army, why doesn't he just take off that uniform and disappear?" Annie asked me.

"I don't know."

Conversations about Neil were always clouded with, "I don't know why he . . ."

Ben watched his friend, then turned to Annie. "Breaks into my apartment to save me. Your brother . . . he's so much crazier than me. So crazy."

As Annie watched her brother going around and around the monument, tears began to run down her cheeks. It all seemed so wrong, so pointless—a crusade without a purpose, a demonstration without a cause. She turned and walked away and I followed her. After half a block, she stopped and started to yell at Neil, not that anyone could hear, not that she really wanted to be heard. "Damn you, Neil! Damn you! Damn you!" Her voice was full of anger and frustration. His actions lacked reason, nothing was rational or logical. Nothing was understandable to her in any way.

I put my arm around her and we headed toward my car. Ten minutes later we stopped at Mandell's for a cup of coffee. Mandell's was a large delicatessen directly across the street from the Diner. It was the place to go when you had a date, when you wanted to eat with a girl. Over the years they had enlarged and fancied it up, but it was long past its fancy days. Its once modern fifties motif now was dated and worn. Only a few years earlier we used to stand in line, eager to get the next available table. There used to be a guy named Dave, a sort of maître d'/bouncer, and we would try to curry favor with him in hopes of getting a better table, acting like we were big shots. Dave also patrolled the place, so if we got a little too raucous, his big head would loom over our table like a giant moon. I can still hear his deep, resonant voice:

"If you can't keep it down in here, perhaps you would like to continue your loud conversation outside."

One of the most popular items on the menu was a hot dog wrapped in a piece of fried bologna. To our young palates there was no finer dish.

I recall some nights sitting in Mandell's and the date of my dreams was fading into the harsh reality of life—the realization coming that she wasn't what I had hoped her to be and that the prospect of having any sex seemed impossible—and I would stare out the window and see the neon sign of the Diner and wish I were there with the guys. Wanting to be where the conversation flowed freely and the laughs were always guaranteed.

At the Diner, "knocking," as we called it—sarcastic put-downs—was the language of the night. On the other side of the street at Mandell's, the conversation was polite, more respectful. Far less honest. During those years, girls were still aliens to us . . . another tribe. They were objects of our affection, but they were still objects. We spoke a "date language" to them, so nothing we said was instinctive or spontaneous. Which made it all slightly unreal.

It was a strange twist of fate that the Diner and Mandell's faced one another, separated only by Reisterstown Road. During our uncomfortable date nights, we could see the neon of the Diner calling to us, saying, You're on the wrong fucking side of the street!

Annie's anger toward Neil turned to introspection in our Mandell's booth. "He doesn't just get nutty one day, Bobby. He just doesn't *get* to be the way he is. It didn't happen suddenly."

She was looking for answers but I didn't have any to offer.

"There are people out there starting to protest. People who don't want to go to Vietnam," she continued. "Neil's never said anything like that. It's . . ." She was at a loss for words and so was I, so we sat in silence.

My mind drifted back to a time when Neil and I were about

seven years old, sitting at my kitchen table. We were both drawing spaceships—not just the exteriors, the fancy Flash Gordon or Buck Rogers drawings we had seen in comic books, but the interiors as well. We drew the areas where the space travelers would sleep and eat, the control room that would guide the spaceship, and the place where the rocket's engines would be housed. We discussed our competing designs and talked endlessly about our journeys to Mars and Venus and trips through the solar system. Neil was full of excitement, so eager to explore, and then it occurred to me that I hadn't seen that enthusiasm in his face in a long, long time. I mentioned this to Annie and we tried to remember the last time Neil really laughed—a laugh that is uncontrollable, where your sides hurt and you can hardly catch your breath. He was once that way. He wasn't that way now.

Mandell's was serving what they referred to as "the bottomless cup of coffee," and the waitress continuously topped off our cups. By the seventh or eighth topping, Annie and I had batted the questions about Neil around so many times that our so-called meaningful conversation began to seem frivolous. At one point she picked on my use of the word "enthusiasm," making fun of my choice of adjectives.

"When's the last time you had an *enthusiastic* week?" she said. "Have you been *enthusiastic* recently, Bobby?"

"I've been *very* enthusiastic lately, Annie," I played along. "Thanks for asking."

Then she slyly added, "I was very enthusiastic about the sex we had last week."

"Well, Annie, your enthusiasm is giving me an enthusiastic hard-on. Can one be enthused about that?"

I believe there is a doctrine that applies to things in life that are too complicated to deal with. One of the principles of that doctrine is, if a question can absolutely not be answered, the mind is allowed to turn it all into a game, to morph all conversations into pure nonsense. It's a defense mechanism, when the unanswerable becomes intolerable. Humor is a salve, frivolity a comfort. And I was all for this avoidance of painful reality. I was all in favor of meaningless conversation.

That's what I remember so vividly about my life at that time.

And then . . . more gaps.

Across the street, Turko nervously pulled up in front of the Diner. He looked around suspiciously, as if someone might be following him, then quickly went inside.

Eggy had suddenly become an ornithologist. He was expounding on the pigeon, and naturally had various theories about this particular species.

"I'm telling you, they prefer to perch on buildings rather than trees. No matter how nice the tree, how leafy, no matter how easily he can get his little claws around a branch, the pigeon prefers a building. And if a pigeon has a choice between a nut and a fresh berry, or whatever the fuck is natural, the pigeon would rather choose a hamburger bun, if it's readily available."

Shade was thinking this over. It did ring true.

The Egg had more pointed observations. "They eat French fries, sandwiches, potato chips. That's why they make that sound . . . that cawing . . ." Then he imitated a pigeon call. "You know what that is? Indigestion. They make that cawing sound"—he imitated it again—"because they're sick. You see a cardinal, it's perky, it's got color to it, it moves quickly . . . it sits on a tree. A pigeon is gray and it's slow . . . it's fat, it's tired . . ."

Turko slipped into the booth in the middle of the lecture. "I'm scared shitless. I'm a fucking dead man." He didn't give the details right away. Eggy and Shade had to wait for Turko to sort the story out. "I can't fucking believe it. Just my luck. That broad is nothing but trouble."

"Fucking give us a who, a what, a why . . . whatever those fucking rules of reporting are. What do you say?"

While Eggy was prompting Turko, Shade leaned over and took a couple of French fries and gravy off Eggy's plate. Then Turko gathered himself. "Remember I told you about that secretary, the one who works for the Colts' front office?"

"Who?" Shade said.

"That nymphomaniac you met at the bar?" Eggy asked eagerly.

"Yeah. It turns out her boyfriend is John Cromwell. He finds out I'm fucking his girlfriend, I'm like . . . a dead man. He's gotta be six five or six six."

"Cromwell?" asked Shade. "Is he a tight end?"

"No, second-string linebacker," said Eggy, "I think."

"He can't be," said Shade. "I'm pretty sure he's a tight end."

Turko broke in, "What the fuck is the difference?"

"I think he's a tight end," reiterated Shade.

Turko was getting frustrated. "You hear me? This guy, if he finds out about me, I'm dead. He's a huge colored guy."

Shade was blown away. "Wait a minute. This white girl is dating a colored guy?"

"A *huge* colored guy," Turko reiterated.

"I never heard of such a thing," Shade continued in disbelief. "I mean, is he just fucking her, or are they going out together?"

"They're really dating," Turko told him. "They're *involved* with one another."

"I've never heard of such a thing," Shade repeated in astonishment.

"Shade, I don't have time for your fucking prejudice or bigotry, or whatever, right now."

"I'm not a bigot."

Eggy jumped in, "What are you talking about? You went on and on about that fucking episode of *Bonanza*."

"That's not about being a bigot."

"*Bonanza?*" Turko asked, momentarily distracted from his dilemma.

"Shade was carrying on because this colored guy goes to the Ponderosa late one night and Ben Cartwright invites him in. Shade was pissed."

"I wasn't pissed. All I said was I didn't believe that reality—that a colored guy could show up on the Ponderosa at three o'clock in the morning and Ben Cartwright would say, 'Come on in. Have some coffee.' That's not true to life."

Turko shook his head in exasperation. "True to life? It's fucking *Bonanza* for Christ's sake."

"If I'm living on Park Heights Avenue," Shade continued, "and a colored guy knocks on my door at three o'clock in the morning and asks to come in, I'd say, 'Get the fuck outta here!' "

"That's because you're a bigot," Eggy stated.

"No. At three o'clock in the morning I'm not letting *anyone* in my house, whether he's colored, Chinese, or a Samoan."

"There's a lot of Samoans here," Turko said sarcastically.

"The point I was making is that no one lets someone in their house at three o'clock in the morning. That's all." Shade wouldn't let it go. "Fucking Ben Cartwright saying 'Sure, stranger, come on in.' I couldn't get over it. I could *not* get over it."

The *Bonanza* racial implications were played out for quite a while, until Eggy offered up that he had not one bigoted bone in his body. That he would "fuck any girl—white, colored, Chinese, midget—as long as she's a prostitute."

Then Turko asked the big question, "Would you date any one of them? That's the test whether you're prejudiced."

Without missing a beat, Eggy responded, "I don't date. Period."

"Hypothetically?" Turko asked.

"Yeah, hypothetically," Shade chimed in.

"There's no hypothetically. It's money from my hands to hers. End of story." Then Eggy shifted back to Turko's problem. "I don't get your problem, Turk. This football player, Cromwell . . . how's he gonna know? Who's gonna tell? It's only the secretary and you, and we can eliminate you, which leaves only her. Am I right?"

"Nice piece of reasoning, Egg. But flawed. *She's* gonna tell because she's mad at me."

"Why?" Shade asked, stealing a few more French fries and gravy.

"Because I told her I don't want to see her anymore. Then she breaks this news to me: 'You know who my boyfriend is? You know John Cromwell?' That's how I find out. I'm like beside myself, because I don't want to screw her anymore and she won't let go. It's like blackmail . . . sexual blackmail, that's what it is."

"Sexual blackmail? Hmmm . . ." Eggy pondered this. "So if you don't have sex with her, she's gonna send her boyfriend to kill you?"

"You got it."

"As long as you have sex with her, that's gonna keep the monster at bay?"

"That's right," Turko said.

"Well then," Eggy announced, "I suggest you keep screwing her. End of dilemma. *Fini*, as the French say. They do say that, don't they?"

"Do I give a shit?" said Turko.

Shade agreed with Eggy. "I mean, what the hell . . . so you screw her. What's the big deal?"

"I *mean*," said Turko emphatically, "I cannot perform on cue."

The guys laughed. "You're not turning into a homo, are you?" Eggy asked, and that comment totally put Shade away. He was out of control with laughter, which infuriated Turko.

"I checked this guy out. Cromwell. He's like half lunatic. The guy can bench-press an entire gym."

"Look, here's all you gotta do," Eggy suggested. "You fuck her, you let a week go by, you fuck her, you let two weeks go by. Next thing you know, it just falls apart and she gets on with her life. Just take the confrontation out of the whole damn thing."

Turko saw some sense in this, but had reservations. "Yes, but then I'm playing on her terms."

"So what?" Eggy said. "On her terms you're getting laid. On your terms you're getting the shit kicked out of you." He continued: "None of this would be happening if you saw prostitutes. You pay, you get laid, you go home, period. There's no other drama."

Turko wanted to talk to Eggy about Neddy and all that had happened since Neil was back in town. But he couldn't get to the subject as long as Shade was around. Shade was not part of the inner circle and this subject was way too personal. To relieve his frustration, Turko decided to give Neddy a call.

"I'll be back in a minute," he told the guys.

Over at the pay phone he dialed Neddy's number. Ben answered the phone and for a moment Turko was confused. "Who is this?" he asked.

"Turko, this is Ben, you stupid fuck."

Turko thought to himself, Why is Ben at Neddy's? It was all too confusing. "What the hell are you doing there?"

"I had the stomach flu," Ben lied, "and Neil set me up with Neddy . . . to, you know, get me back on my feet."

"Well, how kind of Neil," Turko said sarcastically.

"Turko, listen. We go way back, right?"

"Yeah."

"Since the days when you were called Alan."

"Yeah . . . so?" Turko said.

"I'm going to be straight with you. This thing you've got for Neddy . . . it ain't gonna happen. She's too crazy over Neil. I mean, I watch 'em. Believe me, she's crazy for him. As for what Neil thinks, who the hell knows, but her, she's a clear picture."

Turko knew that what Ben was saying was the truth. It hit him hard, but he didn't want to admit it. Not then, not to Ben, not for a long time after that. In fact, he was never fully honest about it, not until years later when the hurt had died down. The hurt never went away. It never does. But things do get easier to talk about.

So Turko hung up the phone and went back to bullshitting with Eggy and Shade, hiding his feelings, acting as if nothing had happened.

Turko never got a chance to implement the sexual withdrawal plan, as advised by Eggy. The secretary wasted no time in going to John Cromwell and giving Turko up. She painted a graphic picture of him as a sexual predator. The story was elaborate and full of fabricated details. The shorthand of it all was simply that she met Turko in a bar around Christmastime, he plied her with drinks and spiked the eggnog to make it a little more potent. Turko kept coming on to her, and in one of her weaker moments she gave in and had sex with him in the parking lot of the bar. Then he drove her over to his apartment for more sex. She was beginning to get sober, and told Turko that this was a terrible mistake, that she was dating John Cromwell of the Baltimore Colts. To add fuel to the fire, she told Cromwell that Turko said he didn't give a shit, he didn't like the Baltimore Colts and was a devoted Washington Redskins fan. Not being a Baltimore Colts fan and living in Baltimore was unheard of. It was sinful, absolutely outrageous, and the probability of such a thing happening was about as likely as a Nazi working in a deli. Cromwell was beside himself.

The secretary was reveling in her character assassination of Turko, making him appear to be a truly sinister person. She claimed that he was going to blackmail her and tell Cromwell what she had done unless she submitted to him once again. Since that fateful night she had become so remorseful, so overcome by guilt, and she had desperately wanted to tell Cromwell the wicked details but was simply too fearful.

As she hoped, Cromwell went into a rage over Turko. The secretary played out her scenario to perfection. She even acted out her reluctance to give Cromwell Turko's address.

At 2:40 in the morning, Turko's apartment door came off its hinges—the six-foot-five 250-pound Cromwell having put a shoulder to it.

Turko, as it turned out, was lucky—he had just gotten out of bed and gone into the bathroom to take a piss. The sound of the door flying off its hinges scared the shit out of him. He didn't have a clue what the hell was going on. Then he heard a voice from the other room. "Turko! Come and say hello to John Cromwell."

Turko almost went into shock. His heart was beating like crazy as he quietly set the lock on the bathroom door. He could hear the crashing of objects as Cromwell moved from room to room.

Cromwell yelled, "Where are you, you motherfucker? Fucking my girl?!! Fucking my girl!!!"

Turko heard glasses and plates shattering, and then he heard the lunatic lumbering toward the bathroom. The lock on the door would never keep Cromwell out, he realized. He needed to make the big oaf think he wasn't there. As the footsteps approached, Turko quietly undid the lock and stepped back. At that precise moment, the door was kicked open. Cromwell stuck his head in but mercifully never checked behind the door, where the trembling Turko stood.

Minutes later, Cromwell was gone, but it must have been half an hour before Turko came out of the bathroom—so fearful was he that Cromwell was setting a trap, baiting him out. When all was safe, Turko quickly ran to the phone and called Eggy. All he said was, "Cromwell is on the loose. I'm coming over."

He didn't even bother to dress. He just put on an overcoat over his underwear and T-shirt. Then he grabbed his wallet, money, and keys, went out into the freezing cold night, got into his car, and drove like a madman over to Eggy's.

For the first ten minutes after Turko arrived, he could hardly speak, he was hyperventilating so much. Eggy tried to ask him questions, but Turko kept waving him off. Eggy asked if he wanted him to call for an ambulance.

Turko tried to answer that one but Eggy couldn't understand. "Don't try to talk. Just shake your head yes or no."

Turko shook his head.

"No, you don't want to shake your head?" Eggy asked.

Turko shook his head again.

"Why don't you want to shake your head?"

Turko shook his head again and managed to mumble, "*Don't call, you fucking idiot!*"

After a few more minutes, Turko got himself under control and ran down the whole sequence of events. It was clear in his mind that he was not going back to the apartment anytime in the near future.

"What happens if he comes over to the bail bonds office?" Eggy asked.

"I told the secretary I was an investment banker, so I don't have to worry about him showing up at work. But we've got to find a way to get to him and straighten this thing out."

"Who do we know? This we've got to think about."

For the rest of the night, the question of how to deal with John Cromwell was played out in Eggy and Turko's classic Abbott and Costello manner, with the conversation moving from the ridiculous to the sublime. Finally, a greatly concerned Eggy told his friend, "Stay out of sight. Stay out of all places where he might be."

This advice suited Turko well.

Twenty-Six

At six-fifteen in the morning, I woke from a deep sleep with an idea for *The Ranger Al Show* pounding in my brain. I had this image of playing the Simon & Garfunkel song "Sound of Silence." Doctor Fox and Oswald Rabbit would sing it while a few of the other puppets built something—hammering and drilling and making as much noise as possible throughout the song. It was a simple, silly premise, but I thought it could work. I continued to kick the idea around in my head while I showered and shaved. I didn't know what the Ranger had planned for the day's show, but he had become sufficiently comfortable with me that if he thought I had an idea that was good he would slip it in.

I stopped into the film archival library. I remember looking at some very old films of a factory with all of its machinery working away. I also recalled a scene with a street under construction, guys working pneumatic drills. I headed down to the videotape area in Telecine to have these pieces of film transferred to tape.

I was informed that Gil, who was working the morning shift, had run up to grab some coffee. So I hung around, waiting for him to return. There were stacks of tapes with segments that had been completed for various shows. Some were for public service programs, one was for the station's editorial, which always ran at the conclusion of the noonday and evening newscasts.

The label of one tape caught my eye. It was Jerome Pilsner's story on Neil, entitled "The Guardian of Baltimore's Washington Monument." Apparently, Pilsner had finished the piece. Once it hit the air, Neil's one-man exhibition would be known throughout the city and the attention would bring nothing but trouble.

I tore the label off the tape. Within seconds Gil arrived. "What's up?"

"I got a couple of film pieces I'd like to transfer over to tape."

Gil looked at the videotape in my hand. "Is it clean?"

"No. It's got some old bits on it."

"You need to keep 'em?"

"No."

"Then let me degauss it." Gil took the tape from me and put it on a metal plate. The process was simple. Since all video is magnetic, somehow the plate wipes off all images and sound. The video is once again pristine. Within minutes, unbeknownst to Gil, Pilsner's story on Neil ceased to exist.

"Just take the film clips over to projection," Gil told me. "They've been using 2 and 2A for film transfer. Let me know if it's any different."

I'd pulled off a small victory for Neil. His problems were far from over, but at least he wasn't going to be on the news that day.

Or so I thought.

Neil stood on a street corner, alone, in a cold wind, not far from Penn Station. In the distance he could see a northbound train coming out of the tunnel, heading into the station. It was not the idea of traveling north that excited him, nor the idea of traveling, period. It was the design of the train that caught his eye. The glamour days of train travel had come to an end. The streamlined locomotives of the thirties were a thing of the past. Those glory days had disappeared before any of us really had an opportunity to travel by train. But Neil loved trains. He had an HO gauge set when he was a boy—the scale was more realistic than the Lionel trains. He hated that the Lionel tracks had a third rail to power the engines. "Too fake," he used to say. "Lionel is just too fake. No authenticity."

A dark blue Cadillac cruised down the street, and as it approached, Neil stepped toward the curb. When the car pulled up, Neil opened the door. A very pregnant Janet sat behind the wheel. "Sorry I'm late," she said.

"I got plenty of time," Neil replied. He got into the car and Janet pulled away.

"You look great in a uniform. Like a real soldier," she told him.

"No. Not a soldier. Just a guy in a uniform."

Before Janet could question what that meant, Neil diverted her attention, asking her how her pregnancy was going, how she was feeling. Then they got into names for the baby.

"If it's a girl, I like the name Phoebe," Neil said.

"Phoebe?"

"Yeah, from J. D. Salinger's *The Catcher in the Rye*. Holden Caulfield's sister was called Phoebe. I like that name."

"Phoebe Kallin? Doesn't sound good. Phoebe Tilden might be pretty interesting."

"I don't see myself having kids, so you can take the name if you want."

Janet laughed briefly, then put her hand on Neil's. "How is he doing?"

"Right now he's staying with this girl I know—"

Before he could finish the sentence, she said, "He's with *some* girl?"

"Not *some* girl. *My* girl."

Janet was surprised. "You're going with a girl?"

As Janet drove, Neil ran down the whole story of Neddy. She especially liked the part about them dancing in the Diner parking lot. "It's so much like you, Neil. Always unexpected and surprisingly romantic."

Neil smiled at her and tipped the brim of his military hat.

They stopped at the Lotus Inn for a Chinese lunch—Neil manipulated the chopsticks effortlessly, Janet used a fork. He filled her in on Ben, complete with details of his attempted suicide. He downplayed it somewhat, not wanting to overly upset her, but he wanted her to understand Ben's state of mind.

"I don't know what to do with him. It's so terrible . . . his drug problem . . . and my father despises him now. Despises him."

Her frustration started to overwhelm her and she fought back tears. Neil told her that this was not a situation that had to be resolved today or tomorrow, but he wanted her to know that Ben did care for her.

"It's not like he walked out the door and forgot about you. You're important to him." Then he smiled. "God Almighty, who would ever think that one day our lives would become like a soap opera? No matter how you try to run away from it, no matter how interesting you think you are or how clever you can be, we're all part of this grand soap opera."

"There's only one difference between us and soaps."

"What's that?" asked Neil.

"They speak more softly." Then Janet started to imitate actors in a television soap and whispered: " '*I have to see you, Ken. Will you be around tonight?' 'Try to call after ten. She should be sleeping by then.' "*

Neil was always entertained by Janet. There was a sense of whimsy about her, even now with a child on the way and separated from her husband.

"Mark Twain wrote," said Neil, " *'The only difference between truth and fiction is that fiction has to be logical.' "*

Following lunch, he went with her to the doctor's office, where she was informed that all was proceeding well in her third trimester.

Turko stopped by Knocko's to see Danny.

"Details," said Danny, so Turko explained the entire Cromwell situation, step-by-step, as Danny proceeded to tie and untie his shoelaces, over and over again. Just when it seemed he had the perfect bow, Danny would untie it and retie it again until he was completely satisfied. This took almost as long as Turko's story.

When Turko finished, Danny nodded, racked the balls on the pool table, and proceeded to move around the table, making one amazing shot after another. He was light on his feet, every movement was effortless. Within minutes the eight ball dropped into the pocket—he'd run the table. Then Danny looked at Turko and spoke for the first time: "Interesting jackpot you got yourself into, Turko. Very interesting."

He racked the balls one more time and again began to play. Turko was growing impatient, but he knew better than to challenge Danny. Halfway through his second run, Danny stopped.

"Write this down." Then he gave Turko the information he was waiting for. Relieved, Turko was about to say something to thank him, but Danny gestured with his hand, a gesture that said: Go away.

So Turko went.

Twenty-Seven

Sitting at my metal desk, I came across something very odd. The scheduling report, which assigned directors and assistant directors to the various shows at the station, showed that Duke was still on vacation and that Eddie Collier, the station's other director, had the day off. The sheet also showed that I was to AD the evening news. The shorthand of all of this, as I interpreted it, was that no director had been assigned to the news that night.

It was possible that someone else was going to pick up on this mistake, but possibly not. If "not" was the reality, I came up with a plan.

I headed up into the newsroom at four-fifteen. Teletype machines were churning out the latest newsworthy events, and the reporters were busy at their typewriters. I walked back to a room where rear-screen projector slides were being made for the show. Mickey was working a large Polaroid camera as he lined up a photo of President Johnson speaking to troops in Vietnam, which had come across one of the wire services.

"I need your help," I said to him.

He stepped away from the camera's viewfinder. "What?"

I told him about the scheduling screwup. Confused, Mickey said, "So we need to let Haynes know?"

"No," I said as confidently as I could manage.

"No?"

"Let it just fall through the cracks."

Mickey didn't get what I was up to. "Then what?"

"Then I'll direct the evening news."

"You're crazy."

"Why not? I'll take my shot tonight. And you, my friend . . . you AD for me."

Mickey shook his head. "You're out of your mind. This is the biggest news show in town."

"I need you, Mick. Get somebody else to do the rear-screen slides, and don't let anyone know what I'm up to."

Mickey fumbled with one of his unfiltered cigarettes; I could see there was a slight shake in his hand as he lit it. Somehow his fear calmed me down.

Where I was getting this newfound confidence I wasn't sure, but I was now committed to my plan. "If they ask where Duke is, just say you don't know . . . maybe he's in the video room . . . or ran to get some coffee . . . you know, stuff like that."

"And if you blow the show?"

"Then I'm truly fucked. But hey, I'll tell Haynes I didn't notice the schedule screwup until it was too late . . . too late to notify anyone."

I walked out of the small darkened room, back into the large newsroom. Mickey followed. "You *sure* you don't want to locate Eddie? Because if this goes bad, it's gonna be like a multiwreck on the 695."

"Thanks, Mick. I appreciate the support. Get somebody to take over the slides."

As I moved through the busy hub of the newsroom, one of the news reporters called out to me, "Have you seen Duke?"

"No, he probably isn't in yet," I lied. "You need something?"

"I want to pull the civil rights demonstration piece off the CBS feed."

"I'll go over it with you until he gets here." I felt an adrenaline rush. It was a "go for it" moment and there was no more time to rethink my decision. In less than two hours, the evening news was about to hit the air and I was going to be sitting in the director's chair.

At 4:50, Jerome Pilsner approached me. "I've got a hell of a problem."

"What's that?" I asked.

"My story on the young soldier walking around the Washington Monument is lost or misplaced. I don't know what the hell happened."

"That's a shame," I said, hoping I didn't look too guilty. "So you'll have to start over?"

"Hargrove wants it on tonight. He loves the story. When's Duke coming in?"

"Should be any minute. Why?"

"Hargrove wants us to do the story live. It's gonna require a lot of pieces that we'll have to roll in—film of the soldier and film of various people making comments about him—and we're gonna need some voice-over segments to be done live. It's complicated."

"Live?" I was taken aback.

"Yeah," Pilsner said. "As soon as Duke gets in, give me a buzz. We'll have to go through this piece carefully." He walked away and I could see he was nervous, but he wasn't anywhere near as nervous as I was. My sleight of hand had backfired. Not only that, now I had to direct a complicated segment that would require film, video, and a live news reporter. I also had to face a new moral dilemma: What was going to happen to Neil if I let this story air?

I immediately called Annie at the hospital. She was in the midst of a crisis of her own. A patient had gone into cardiac arrest and they were short one nurse on the floor. She was frazzled when she finally came to the phone, and hearing about Neil put her on momentary overload.

"Damn him!" she said angrily, and I expected a tirade. Instead, she paused, then, in a much calmer voice, said, "What can you do about it, Bobby?"

I could hear confusion in the background—all the sounds that seemed so familiar from shows like *Ben Casey* and *Dr. Kildare*, as well as my many childhood trips to the hospital. It's amazing how many images flashed through my mind in just a few seconds: Dr. Gillespie patiently teaching Dr. Kildare a surgical lesson; Ben Casey enraged by the behavior of another doctor; me being wheeled down a corridor to the operating room. The rush of sodium pentotal being injected into my veins, and that sudden cold feeling before I lapsed into unconsciousness.

"I don't know," I said to Annie, snapping back into the present. I didn't want to confuse the issue by telling her that I was going to actually direct the evening news, or even that earlier in the day I'd destroyed the original story.

"If that gets on tonight," she said, "they'll have him arrested. He's already AWOL."

A few of the on-air reporters approached my desk. Things were starting to heat up with Duke not around.

"Listen," I whispered into the phone, "I'll see what I can do. I have some people standing at my desk right now . . ."

"Can't you find a way to kill the story?" she pleaded.

One of the reporters tapped his watch as if to say, Let's go. It's late.

"Look, I'll do the best I can," I told Annie. "I've got to go."

"I know you'll do your best."

We hung up and I was left with an uneasy feeling. I didn't think my best was going to be nearly good enough.

For the next half hour I hid the fact that Duke was not coming in from an increasingly nervous crew, all the while trying to figure out how to deal with the Neil situation. I called Neddy but there was no answer. I tried Longfellow's and Ben wasn't there. I even called Eggy, who didn't know where anyone was. Turko was nowhere to be found either. There was no way to warn Neil. I was frustrated and angry—angriest with Neil for refusing to deal with the consequences of his actions. Fuck him! I thought to myself. He created the situation; let him deal with the reality of it all. But the reality was that Neil didn't *care* about the consequences. That was Neil. That was always Neil.

I settled in and began marking up the news pages as they were being assembled. I made pencil marks in the margins, timed the introductions to film stories and video segments, checked everything with my stopwatch, making appropriate notes.

Mickey approached me and quietly said, "So far, so good, and Hargrove's got no idea."

Suddenly I was overwhelmed by insecurities. "Five-second roll for tape, three-second roll for film?"

"Yes." Mickey smiled. "You starting to panic?"

"Double and triple checking, that's all."

The most critical aspect of directing a news program is timing. Video and film clips need to flow directly into one another without dead air. The screen must never go black. A newscaster can't stare at the camera waiting for something to happen. As I looked at the placement of the stories I could see that "The Soldier at Mount Vernon" was going to run in the last quarter hour of the show, a six-minute segment. Suddenly, I had the flash of an idea how I could help Neil.

As Mickey started to walk away, I whispered, "Mick, don't ask any questions, but start spreading some of these segments . . . ten seconds here, fifteen seconds there. I want the show to run long so we'll have to make some changes."

"Why?"

"Just stay with me on this, all right? Nobody's going to know."

"You're full of surprises today, Bobby."

I was suddenly overcome by fear. So many things could go wrong. So many stories had to be handled correctly. And so many people were already looking to me to orchestrate the one-hour program. I scanned the room. The energy and excitement were building as we headed toward our deadline. The sound of the news service teletype machines pounding away was almost deafening to me—it meant that more stories were coming in, new elements were being added, news events were being updated. It was overwhelming.

I watched the faces of the crew. Everyone seemed to be talking but I couldn't hear what was being said. My face felt hot. It was almost as if I could hear the sound of blood pulsating through my head. What in the hell had I gotten myself into?

It reminded me of a time when I was seven years old. Neil and I were at a swim club and we decided to jump off the high diving board. We scrambled up the ladder, Neil ran across the board and leapt effortlessly into the water. I followed behind but the diving board suddenly seemed as if it was only one inch wide and I was walking on a tightrope hundreds of feet up in the air. I was overcome by fear and just stood there, not knowing what to do. Neil was in the water below yelling, "Jump! Jump, Bobby!" But I couldn't.

I tried to back up, to turn around, but I couldn't. I was frozen. Then suddenly everyone was watching me. All the kids below were yelling, "Jump! Jump!" I couldn't even look down. I just stared at the blue sky and listened to the voices in the distance. It seemed as if I was up there for hours.

Finally, I began to kneel down so that I could lie on the diving board and then crawl back to the platform. But I lost my balance and toppled into the water. As I was sinking deeper and deeper, heading toward the bottom of the pool, I felt humiliated. I remembered sinking as if the pool had an endless bottom . . .

Suddenly, it was 5:45 p.m.—fifteen minutes until airtime. The activity in the newsroom was as frenetic as it could get. I took a deep breath, walked into Sid Hargrove's office, and quietly said, "Sid, we have a problem."

"What?" he said, looking up from the news pages in front of him.

"I just checked . . . there's been a scheduling error. Duke's still on vacation, Eddie's supposed to fill in, but he's also off."

"Holy hell! You can't find Eddie? Did you call?"

"Sid," I said in my most deceitful manner, "I've been trying for the last twenty minutes. I can't find him. So I got Mickey up here to help AD and . . . I'm gonna have to direct."

"Oh my God!"

On that note, I spun around and walked out of his office. The clock read 5:59:30 and the newsroom was emptying out. I turned to Mickey, closed my eyes for one second, then said, "Let's do it."

We picked up our scripts and headed out of the newsroom and down a flight of stairs. Mickey looked at his stopwatch. "Twenty seconds." Then we turned a corner and exited the stairwell to the hallway. "Ten seconds," he said. We made a quick right turn down another hallway, "Five seconds," and then we were in the control room.

I yelled to the crew, all of whom were waiting for the director. "Stand by on music and effects." They looked at me, surprised, as I snapped my fingers and said, "Music and effects." But they responded to the cue and the high-energy up-tempo music blared—signaling the start of the six o'clock news.

"There's been a scheduling fuckup," I told everyone. "I can't find Duke, can't find Eddie . . . so stay with me, guys. I need your help."

"Five seconds to end of opening," Mickey said. I looked through the glass booth down onto the studio floor. Tony, the anchorman, was behind his lectern. Then I snapped my fingers again. "Stand by on Tony. Take one. Mike, cue him."

Up on monitor one was a medium shot of Tony. "Good evening, this is *News Beat*, Baltimore," he said, and so the show began.

I looked down at my script. "We've got a feed coming up," I told Mickey.

"It's on tape three."

"Got it," I replied.

The lead story of the evening was about twenty-five hundred women who had arrived at the Pentagon to protest the war. They were demanding to see "the generals who sent our sons to die." Defense Secretary Robert McNamara refused to deal directly with them but sent an aide. We had a film clip of all these dissident women carrying signs reading DROP RUSK AND MCNAMARA, NOT THE BOMB.

Other stories included President Johnson intervening in a controversy over Central Intelligence Agency secret subsidies to the National Student Association; he was demanding an end to all such programs. Former Vice President Nixon, talking with a reporter, indicated that he might, in fact, run for president of the United States in next year's election. And there was a strange report from Africa on the discovery of the world's first white gorilla.

The news program proceeded precisely, without incident. Neil's story was still to come, but as I'd planned, we were gradually falling behind. At six forty-five, I spoke with Sid Hargrove on the headset and informed him that we were running long. He looked at the remaining segments to see what could be cut, and I said, "If you don't mind me throwing in my two cents' worth, why don't you save the story on the soldier over at Mount Vernon. That's not going to lose its freshness."

"Not a bad idea," he said, and I informed Pilsner that we were dropping the story for the night, due to time constraints.

I played the scam perfectly and smiled with satisfaction. Mickey whispered to me, "I don't know what the hell you just accomplished, but whatever it was, you did it."

The next thing I knew, Tony was signing off with his customary closing line, "That's going to do it for us. So from this time until next time, good night."

I snapped my fingers. "And . . . go to network." Then I saw Walter Cronkite's face. The *CBS Evening News* had begun, and we were out.

I got a nice round of applause from the crew in the booth. I looked over at Mickey and thanked him. Then I heard that voice: "Bobby."

As I turned around, there was John Haynes standing at the door.

Twenty-Eight

I picked up Annie over at the hospital and we headed downtown to Longfellow's. She wanted to go home to change first but I was in such a euphoric mood I didn't want to waste any time. I wanted to have something to drink. I wanted to let off steam.

Annie had managed to catch the program and realized that the story on Neil had been killed. What she didn't realize was that I had directed the show, and she was genuinely happy for me when I told her what had happened. For the first time, the commitment I had made to my work was beginning to show results. My obsessiveness was paying off. My work was becoming more defined for her, and she seemed to be comforted by that clarity.

I told her about my conversation with John Haynes at the end of the show. "He said, 'You did one hell of a job, Bobby. Very commendable. Excellent work. Excellent.' And then he joked that I was a bargain at fifty dollars a week."

"How much money do you make if you become a director?" she asked.

"Fifteen thousand dollars a year. And that's just to start."

"Very nice," Annie said with a little sexy attitude.

"I might need a little private nursing care later," I told her.

I almost revealed Eggy's fantasy about me having sex with a

nurse in uniform, but decided against it. That was a story that needed to remain in the Diner.

When we pulled into the parking lot at Longfellow's, we heard music coming from a VW van in which half a dozen hippies were partying. The Beatles' "Strawberry Fields Forever" was playing on their van radio. I couldn't see them clearly since they had thin East Indian throws draped on the inside of the van windows, but I noticed the front logo of the VW had been reinvented as a peace sign.

Neddy was the first hippie I'd seen in Baltimore, but I was seeing more and more all the time. A guy with long hair dressed in a denim shirt, leather vest, beads, and moccasins, crossed the parking lot and knocked on the van door. It opened and he stepped inside. We were probably almost the same age, but the fact that I was wearing a suit—the uniform of an assistant director—made me feel older and out of step with the times. It was not a comfortable feeling.

In his song "Ballad of a Thin Man," Bob Dylan wrote: *"You know something is happening here, but you don't know what it is. Do you, Mr. Jones?"* At that time, I still didn't know what it was. A cultural change was under way that would rock the country politically and socially, but all I saw was a costume party. In some ways it was an omen, a signal, a flashing yellow light that meant CAUTION. Good and bad would come of it all and everyone would be caught in the wave of change. I didn't understand it, so for the most part I ignored it. But I have never forgotten the image of that hippie opening the door of the VW van and stepping inside. He didn't look at me as he crossed Longfellow's parking lot. I don't remember if Annie even noticed him. It was not a dramatic moment in any way; it was quite ordinary. And yet it stuck in my memory bank. The image doesn't have a caption but it will forever linger in my mind.

When we got into Longfellow's, the place was half crowded with an equal balance of hippies and preppies—a mix of Bass Weejun loafers and sandals, button-down shirts and sports jackets, tie-dyed T-shirts and calfskin vests. The jukebox was playing the Beatles' "Norwegian Wood," and as we crossed over to the bar I was glad to see that almost the whole gang was there—Neil with Neddy, Eggy, and of course Ben working behind the bar. Turko was staying away, afraid that he might run into the secretary or, even worse, John Cromwell. Eggy mentioned that Danny had set up some kind of meeting for Turko which was going to happen later that evening.

Since I was feeling so ecstatic I bought drinks for them all.

"What's with you?" Ben asked me. "Never seen you so free with the nickel."

I told everyone that I'd just directed the evening news. "And, Neil, I also buried the story about your antics over at the Washington Monument. You fuck!"

Neil somehow seemed surprised. "Me?"

"Yeah, but believe me, it's gonna run tomorrow. So you'd better decide what to do."

Neil just gave me a blank look. Exasperated, Annie jumped in, "Don't you get it? Once that story airs, everybody's going to know about you. And since you're AWOL, it's gonna make it easy for the military police to come and find you."

Neil shook his head. I couldn't tell if he was thinking of an answer to the dilemma or simply listening to the Beatles tune. But there was no question he was going to have to face his predicament now. Everyone had a different solution. Neddy still wanted him to go to Canada or Mexico. Annie wanted him to report back to the military immediately. "Father's lawyer friends might be able to find some kind of medical deferment for you," she told him.

Neil shrugged that off, not wanting anything to do with his

father. "Fuck him! I'm an orphan with a sister," he told her. Then he did something I'd never seen him do. He put his arms around Annie and hugged her. She was equally surprised and it affected her very deeply. As strong as she was, I saw the tears that welled up in her eyes.

Turko walked along Baltimore Street—"the Block," as it was called—filled with strip joints. The area had always looked run-down, but now it seemed as if it was actually decaying.

He entered the Two O'Clock Club and scanned the room. A stripper was lackadaisically moving about on the stage, dropping her clothes. As a few customers watched with halfhearted interest, Turko just waited until he saw a man at the far end of the bar give him a hand gesture and wave him over.

Without bothering to go through the usual introductions, they only established that they were there because of Danny. The man was immaculately dressed and Turko noticed that his fingernails were manicured and buffed.

"I don't want to mention his name right at this minute, but I'm having a real problem with this guy," Turko said.

"This is a big problem?" the guy asked as he sipped his drink.

"Let's just say it's a very serious problem, and I'd like to find a way of resolving it," Turko quietly replied.

The man stared at him for a good five seconds before he nodded. "This can be done."

A new stripper came on the stage but seemed to be just as bored as the one who had just walked off. A three-piece band started to play "Goldfinger."

"I know just the person for this," the man said with very little emotion.

Turko was relieved and elated. "You do? Fantastic! Great!"

"It's gonna cost you two thousand."

Turko was beside himself. "Two thousand fucking dollars?! Are you crazy?" He actually yelled it out, but the place was noisy enough that no one paid any attention.

"You want him dead or what?" the man asked.

"Dead?"

"You want him killed?"

Turko was in a state of shock. "Killed?! Holy shit! I just want to resolve this problem I have."

"I only know how to resolve matters through death. Then everything is clearly defined," the man said.

"Oh, for Christ's sake! I thought we were going to resolve something. But kill him! God!" Turko thought to himself, Shit, this guy could have killed JFK.

The man threw some bills on the counter and stood up, buttoning his jacket. "Well, should it ever come to that, you know where to find me."

Neil had been in a phone booth for about five minutes having a conversation. None of us knew who he was talking to or what it was about. Then he hung up the phone, slid the phone booth door back, and the light went out. He walked over to us with a stoic look on his face. "I just spoke to Lieutenant Dill."

"Who's that?" I asked.

"He's the guy I'm supposed to report to."

"What does that mean?" Annie wanted to know. "What did you say?"

"I told him I'll be reporting back tomorrow morning, 6 a.m."

We couldn't believe the words coming out of his mouth. Always the unexpected from Neil.

"I told him I had some family problems, so I don't think the AWOL's going to be a big deal."

It was a moment of very definite mixed emotions. On the one hand, the crisis was over. But on the other hand, Neil was going back to the army and ultimately to Vietnam.

"All right. So no more talk about this. It's over. It's done. Too much talk about this shit already," he said. Then he turned to Neddy and asked, "Can I have this dance?"

There was a lot more that could have been said, with many questions to be answered, but of course it wasn't to be. Neil was an unsolvable riddle, but now, as he danced with Neddy, he seemed satisfied with his decision. It was obvious that she didn't want him to report back to the army, but for the time being she said nothing.

I told Ben, who had been busy working the bar, about the new turn of events, and he seemed pleased. He was perspiring heavily and his hand was jittery as he poured me a drink.

"You know, maybe you should lighten up with the 'bennies,' " I told him. "Is that what you're taking tonight?"

"Uppers, downers . . . whatever it takes."

"You can't keep doing this, Ben. Christ, it's only a few days since Neil came over and found you."

"Fuck you!" he said angrily. "Just take care of your own shit, Bobby. I don't need any fucking advice."

"Ben, I'm just—"

"Fuck you! Stay out of it. Just fucking stay out of my life!"

"What the fuck are you getting so pissed off about?" I yelled back at him.

Ben was enraged, way beyond a normal response. "I don't need another nursemaid!" he screamed.

I got angry at Ben's response. After all that had happened that day, I wasn't in the mood to take any shit. So I screamed back, "That's exactly what you need—a nursemaid." Disgusted, I said, "The fucking King of the Teenagers. Fuck you!"

With those words, Ben flew across the countertop at me. As he did, I grabbed him and a few beer bottles crashed to the ground.

Annie ran over and tried to separate us. "Cut it out!" she yelled. "Just cut it out!"

Ben couldn't control himself. I had him in a headlock, otherwise I think he might have tried to kill me. The whole place turned quiet. Everyone was staring at us. And then Ben's rage ended as quickly as it began. I could feel all energy just leave him. I let go and he slumped to the floor.

"Let's go," I said to Annie.

"Good idea," Ben spit back. He managed to stand and walk back down the bar.

We went over to Neil, who was still dancing close with Neddy, and we said our goodbyes. He was so involved with her, so lost in their dance, that he was the only person in the bar and completely unaware of the flare-up between Ben and myself.

When Annie went to kiss him goodbye, Neil took her into his arms and began to dance with her. No words were spoken. Then she slid out of his grip and we left Neil behind.

We drove in silence, passing the Druid Hill reservoir and the large mansions that overlooked the water. This was once Baltimore's most elite address. Now the estates were falling into disrepair, boarded up, on their way to becoming run-down apartment houses.

It was not lost on me how our lives suddenly seemed so complicated. The simplicity, the innocence of the past—of our youth— was quickly fading. When you are young there are those euphoric moments that stand alone—a first kiss, a first love, the pride that comes with early success—and nothing can interfere with them. Nothing can temper that joy. It is a narrow view of reality, maybe pencil thin, but the highs are so high and so clear. The new reality of adulthood—the reality I was so aware of that night—carves a wider path where laughs and tears exist simultaneously. Those mansions along the lake were just another reminder . . . nothing stays the same.

We kissed, parked in front of Annie's house, and talked about sneaking up into her bedroom. I walked her to the front door, and as soon as she opened it, I quickly dashed across the foyer and up the stairs toward her bedroom. Maybe I was just trying to recapture those youthful moments, not wanting to be the young man in the suit and tie. But it scared the hell out of her. For some reason, her caution made me start to laugh, and emboldened me. I could hear the television on in her parents' bedroom, but I continued to inch up one step at a time.

My playfulness took over and I kicked off my loafers and dropped my pants. Annie was shocked, "Oh my God, Bobby . . . please." I went up one more step of the darkened staircase and said, "Come to bed with me, Annie. Come on . . . throw caution to the wind."

I was closing in on the top of the stairs. I could see down the hallway—the light under her parents' door, the sound of Johnny Carson on the *Tonight* show, and the laughter from the audience.

Annie remained at the bottom, looking up at me as I stood there in shirt and tie, jockey shorts and black socks. I undid my tie and tossed it down toward her. Then I took another step, and quickly and quietly, she ran after me. She grabbed at my shirt and literally tackled me. I fell backwards with a thump, my head near the top of the stairs now. The thump scared her, thinking I might be hurt, but once she realized I was okay, she just kissed me. The kiss turned passionate as my hand slipped under her skirt . . . and then the door to her parents' room opened.

Annie's father, in his robe and slippers, started toward the stairs. His walking slowed as he tried to make out the darkened forms ahead of him. He stopped, stared at my pants, spread out in the middle of the staircase. Then he said: "Annie, when you find the time, please bring me a glass of milk . . . and . . . good night, Bobby. Drive safely." He went back to his bedroom.

Our passion quickly faded, replaced with an awareness of the absurdity of the moment and our deep and heartfelt youthful laughter.

That moment, lying on the stairs with Annie, was an exciting and immensely romantic fragment of time. It seemed as if I wasn't really there. I was separate, just watching her laugh—watching this girl who was going to be my wife. And I tried to picture myself laughing along with her, as her husband. All of a sudden, I worried that, as the moment faded, there might never be another one like it again. I don't know why I thought that. I only know that I didn't want to let it go. But just like holding water in the palm of your hand, moments only last for so long.

The crowd thinned out at Longfellow's. Neil talked to a much calmer Ben at the bar; Neddy was at the jukebox examining the play selections. A hippie-looking guy named Doug Stanley approached her. "You Nadine?"

"Yes," said Neddy.

"You used to go with a friend of mine, Jerry Berk?"

"Sure . . . yeah. Nice guy." She dropped a quarter into the jukebox and started to press keys to select songs.

Doug played with the bottle of National beer in his hands and looked over at Neil chatting with Ben. "I'm surprised you're with that guy."

"Well, don't be." She walked over to stand beside Neil. "I wish you would have decided on Mexico instead," she told him.

"You have to understand, I'm not the renegade type."

Ben laughed. "Oh yeah . . . sure."

Doug strolled over, put his beer on the counter, asked Ben for another. He tapped the counter with his hand, and with the half a dozen rings he was wearing, he made a lot of clicking sounds. Then he looked at Neil purposefully. "Does that uniform make you feel proud?"

"Should it?" Neil stroked Neddy's hair as she leaned against him.

"You tell me," Doug said, continuing to tap his rings on the bar.

"I don't tell much."

"You're not that soldier who goes around the monument, are you?"

"As I said, I'm very thin with the information."

This seemed to piss Doug off. "You ashamed or something?"

It was at this point that Neddy jumped in, "Okay, why don't you just cool it. Give my best to Jerry."

Ben, almost itching for a fight, glared at Doug, who seemed to calm down. So Ben put a fresh beer on the counter. Doug took a sip and stood there quietly. Ben moved off to clean the other end of the bar. Neddy once again relaxed into Neil's arms as she listened to one of the songs she had selected—Buffalo Springfield's "For What It's Worth":

> *There's something happening here*
> *What it is ain't exactly clear . . .*

As the antiwar song filled the bar, Doug said to Neil, spitting out the words, "You like the idea of killing all those Asian babies and families, all in the name of democracy?"

Neil looked down at the floor. "Let's not have a conversation about this country's Southeast Asia policy. What do you say?"

"Fuck you!"

"Let's go, Neil." Neddy started to move him away, pulling on his army uniform.

"Fuck you, Private!" Doug yelled, and that was all it took. Ben quickly jumped over the top of the bar. Doug pushed him off, but Ben went at him again with a quiet fury. Doug could do no more than try to defend himself, blocking the punches.

Pinned against the jukebox, Doug went slack and Ben let up. "I want you out of here, you understand?"

Doug nodded and Ben released him, but the truce was a momentary one because Doug immediately threw a wild roundhouse punch, clipping Ben over his right ear. Ben staggered backward but managed to stay on his feet.

Just as Doug was about to hit a defenseless Ben, Neil moved in. He blocked Doug's punch and tried to tie him up in a clinch, but Doug had too much fight in him and pulled free of Neil's grasp.

Ben seemed to have regained his senses and moved toward Doug again. His movement distracted Neil, who turned in Ben's direction. Doug delivered a hard right hand straight into Neil's face. Neil went down instantly, like a tree, slamming his head against the tiled floor.

Eggy, who had just returned from a "quickie" with one of his prostitutes, walked in amidst this turmoil. Although he was never one to fight, he went after Doug, who now had Ben in a headlock and was dragging him around the bar. Neddy raced over to Neil, who lay unconscious on the floor.

Eggy pulled Doug off Ben and Ben went completely out of control. He ferociously slammed Doug up against the wall and punched him continuously in the face. Blood began to pour from Doug's mouth and nose, but Ben wouldn't stop. Eggy had to jump in again and pull Ben away. "It's over, it's over," he kept saying.

Doug slid to the floor in a pool of blood as Ben stood over him. Neddy, who was tending to Neil, screamed out, "Call an ambulance."

Eggy ran to the phone booth. Just as he was about to dial, Neddy saw Neil's eyes open. He was dazed but managed to smile.

It seemed as if time had stopped. The tableau was becoming familiar—a soldier wounded in battle. In this instance, the battleground was Longfellow's bar.

"Let's take him over to Mercy Hospital," Neddy said. Neil muttered that he didn't understand why. He felt completely at peace, he said, and added: "Probably for the first time in my life."

From the phone booth Eggy called out, "Do we want an ambulance or not?"

Neil mumbled "No," and Neddy yelled back, "We'll drive him over there."

Neil sat in the back of the car, resting on Neddy's lap. Eggy drove, Ben sat shotgun. When they arrived at Mercy Hospital's emergency room, Neil said he felt much better. His head had cleared and he decided he didn't need to get checked out. "Since this is my last night before reporting, there are better things to do with my time."

He held Neddy close to him and danced slowly, wobbily, under the canopy of the emergency room entrance, but Neddy was determined that he be examined, so to please her, he stopped their dance and dipped her down to the floor with a great flourish.

Ben gave polite applause and said, "Very nice, Fred Astaire. It's time to get your head examined."

Eggy added, "Which should have been done a long time ago."

The emergency room was packed. The crowd of patients was so dense that there was nowhere to sit, so after Neil signed in, they crouched in the hallway, leaning against a wall.

Several times Neil made pleas to take off, arguing that he didn't want to waste his last night waiting on line. To reassure them that he was not losing any motor skills, he touched his nose with his finger and recited, *"Peter Piper picked a peck of pickled peppers."*

Finally, his name was called and he went off with a young doctor for an examination.

About twenty minutes later, Neil came back out. They had done a battery of tests and he had to wait for the results. He seemed in an especially good mood and became very talkative. He started on about the early settlers in America and how they viewed the Indians as savages. "These nomadic tribes lived in tents, hunted and fished. They danced at campfires. That's why the white man called them savages. We destroyed almost the whole race of Indians and put the remaining ones in reservations."

It was an odd topic for him to fixate on at this moment, but that was Neil and he wouldn't let it drop. "We thought these were uncivilized people. Nowadays, civilized man can go hunt and fish and sleep in tents, and we call it a vacation. If you do it all year long, you're a savage, but to be able to do it for two weeks out of the year, that's a vacation. It's all in how you perceive it." He seemed to delight in the absurdity of it all.

Eggy said, "You're not gonna find me camping out. Fuck that. I remember being sent to camp once. We were in this pool that was fed by a stream, and I'm swimming. All of a sudden, there's this snake swimming next to me . . . uh-uh . . . no sir. I like how the camp counselor said, 'It's only a snake.' Only a snake! 'Only' and 'snake' are two words that should not go together. Just give me a chlorine pool with chaise lounges."

Neil was feeling antsy, so he walked up to the patient registration desk and asked how long before he got the results. The nurse replied that it might take up to another hour.

Neil returned to the group and said, "Let's get out of here. I don't have that much time left."

Neddy tried to argue, but Neil added, "Look, I have to report to Fort Holabird first thing in the morning. You can get the results and if there's anything there, pass it on to the army." Then he said, "Why don't we all go up to the Diner?"

Eggy pointed to Neddy. "Hey . . ."

"Oh shit, Eggy," complained Neddy, "are you going to start with those Diner rules, too?"

"Rules is rules," Eggy insisted emphatically.

"Let's pass over the golden rule," Neil said as he looked to the guys for approval. "What say?"

"Aw, what the hell," Ben chimed in. "The place is supposed to be closing anyway, if anyone can understand the Greek correctly. Come on. This'll be a smile."

And so they walked out of the emergency room, not waiting for the results of Neil's tests.

Almost thirty minutes later, Dr. Atherton was looking at an

X-ray of Neil's skull. The X-ray wasn't conclusive, but it was his impression that Neil was suffering from a subdural hematoma, which translated into a small blood clot at the lower part of the brain. If the clot moved, this condition was potentially fatal.

"I think we should run a few more X rays . . . do some more tests. Why don't you bring Mr. Tilden back in here?" Dr. Atherton instructed a young intern.

The intern went into the emergency room waiting area and called Neil's name several times but got no response. He walked back to the registration desk and checked Neil's file. Neil had filled in a telephone number, and the intern called it. A man answered the phone in a groggy voice. The intern said, "I hate to disturb you, sir . . . I'm looking for a Neil Tilden." The man was angry at having been awakened, but the intern explained he was calling from Mercy Hospital and had a medical emergency.

The man was now more awake and asked to hear the name again, and the intern repeated, "Neil Tilden." The man then said, "We bought the house from the Tildens, but that was sixteen years ago."

The intern considered that for a moment. It seemed a curious thing for Neil to do. He thanked the man and apologized for the inconvenience.

The intern thought about the Tilden name. It sounded familiar to him. Then he remembered there was an Annie Tilden with whom he had worked on a number of shifts. He thought they might be related in some way, so he looked up her number and called. He awakened Annie from a deep sleep and quickly explained the situation. She agreed that Neil's giving out a number from that long ago was more than slightly suspicious, and was concerned that the head injury could be more serious than Neil realized.

Turko, who was already at the Diner, saw the guys and Neddy enter. He yelled out, "Forgive them, Father, for they know not what they do," and the group laughed as they headed down the aisle and squeezed into his booth.

Neddy sat next to Neil, leaning affectionately against him as he smoked. Turko said nothing, but it was obvious that he was being eaten up by jealousy.

At a quarter to four in the morning, I got a frantic call from Annie. She told me the whole story. She had called Longfellow's and Neddy's but had not gotten any answer. She'd also been calling the Diner but the line had been constantly busy.

"Let's go there, Bobby. It worries me that he gave out that telephone number. It really worries me."

I told her I'd pick her up right away.

Back at the Diner, Neddy asked with great curiosity, "So what do you guys talk about until the wee hours of the morning? Getting laid?"

"It does come up," Ben said, signaling the waitress for coffees all the way around.

Eggy offered, "And other things too. Like why in the Flash Gordon serials do all the people in the future seem to wear band uniforms?"

"Band uniforms and tights," Turko corrected. "They wear a lot of tights in the future."

"And then we talk about sex again," Ben said, smiling.

Neddy wanted to know more. "What about it?"

"Well," said Ben, "there hasn't been enough sex in my life."

Neil seemed tired, but since Neddy was resting against him, she didn't notice that he was not very attentive.

"You guys count how many girls you've slept with? I mean, you keep a record of that?"

"One night I counted how many girls I'd slept with," Ben told her, "but the big revelation was, I forgot to include my wife."

Eggy and Turko broke up in laughter. Neddy also found it funny. Neil just stared out the window.

The guys started telling stories about first dates, awkward moments with girls, the first time they got laid. They told the story of Marvin Simon, a middle-aged man who died of a heart attack, having sex in Harry's Barber Shop.

Neddy laughed. "How's that possible? I don't understand."

"There was a small back room in Harry's Barber Shop," Turko said, "which he used to rent out. Marvin was in there being sexually pleased when he suddenly died."

Eggy colored it. "Darlene Somerville was her name. She comes out half dressed and whispered to Harry that Marvin had *expired*, that was her wording. She takes Harry back to the room, and there's Marvin . . . dead on this bed, but with a full hard-on."

Neddy completely broke up.

Ben chimed in, "It's true . . . true. Absolutely true."

Neil remained quiet, still just looking out of the Diner window.

"How can you die with a hard-on?" Neddy asked.

Nobody seemed to know, but as Eggy said, "It's true. Documented. The best part is, after the paramedics came and declared him dead, they put a sheet over him. The sheet goes up like it's on a tent pole. Honest to God. Harry asked the paramedics if there was something that could be done about this erection, since if Marvin's wife came down to see him, she might think he was getting something other than a haircut."

Ben finished it off by describing how they had to get Marvin dressed. "It was no easy chore with his life-after-death hard-on."

"A rigor mortis hard-on?" Neddy was curious to know. "How is that possible?"

None of the guys had the slightest idea; they just knew that the story was one hundred percent gospel.

Neil's hand started to touch the window. He ran his fingers along the glass. "Ben, you better put on the windshield wipers," he said quietly. "There's too much snow. It's all going white."

"What?" Ben asked, bewildered.

Neddy still had a smile on her face, but the smile faded when she turned and saw Neil.

We pulled into the Diner parking lot and quickly got out of the car. I could see Neil's fingers on the Diner window. There was something about it that didn't seem right.

Inside, Neil whispered, "The snow's building up. It's all going white . . ." Then he slumped in his seat, unconscious. We saw him fall.

"Oh God!" Annie said, and ran toward her brother. I could see Neddy grab Neil.

As Annie entered the Diner, she heard Neddy scream. It wasn't a scream of terror. Or even fear. It was a sound filled with a sense of loss and mourning.

For some reason I didn't run after Annie. I watched the images unfold through the Diner window. Somehow I understood that there was nothing I could do. Or perhaps the sense of loss was so overwhelming that I couldn't move.

Within minutes, the paramedic truck was in the parking lot, its red lights blinking against the chrome and glass of the Diner.

I stared up at the window as the paramedics worked on Neil, who was out of sight below the window frame. I could see the concern, the fear on the faces of Ben, Turko, Eggy, Neddy, and Annie as the minutes passed.

It was like a scene out of an Edward Hopper painting, slightly surreal, just an image without sound. But in real life, a moment is not frozen in time, the next moment follows, and then the next, and the moment that came that night was tragic. I could see tears streaming down Annie's face. She had a valid reason for crying—her brother was dying right in front of her.

I continued to stare at all of my friends framed in that window. I thought of all the movie images that had run through my head in the past year. Funny images, slapstick, dramatic, murderous, and beautiful. I wished desperately that what I was seeing now was just a movie, but I knew that it was all too real; no movie could ever be this sad.

Then I went inside.

Twenty-Nine

In the limousine on the way to the funeral, I held Annie's hand and looked across at the devastated faces of her mother and father. All three of them had been so frustrated with Neil and his antics. Now that frustration was replaced with an overwhelming sense of loss.

I always wanted to make sense out of life and death and give things some purpose, but in the end it's impossible. Neil could be many things—irresponsible, infuriating, and a million other adjectives his friends and family might want to throw in—but never had I imagined him existing in the past tense forever. But from that day on, that's all there would be.

I started to backtrack in my mind, trying to link all the events that had led to this meaningless death, as if somehow I could change what had happened. If he hadn't been wearing the uniform in Longfellow's an argument never would have started. If he hadn't ripped up the damn note, he wouldn't have even *been* in uniform. Then I realized that if the evening news segment on him had aired, if I hadn't stopped it, he might not have gone to Longfellow's that night. He might have understood the need to remain secluded until he came up with some kind of plan. If he'd only had a plan for his future, I thought, maybe he would have *had* a future.

During the service, an image began to play out in my mind—a smiling Freddie Krauss floating over the top of the Texaco station sign wearing his red windbreaker.

We all mourned. Ben stood with a very pregnant Janet, and Turko and Eggy and Neddy and Shade and Berger and Danny. The crowd was still. There were many tears. The image of Freddie Krauss floating over the top of the Texaco station sign never left my mind. It wasn't a haunting image; it didn't frighten me. It was simply an image that I couldn't define.

Looking back, perhaps that explains it all. Maybe you can never understand the significance of a moment. And that which you cannot define or explain will continue to play itself over and over again in your mind. The brain is like a computer, forever seeking an answer, and it's possible that until the question is solved, the question remains on that screen in the back of your head forever.

It was late in the afternoon when we gathered in the Diner parking lot for our private memorial service. None of us had been to the Diner in the three days since Neil's death, so we were not prepared for what we saw. A CLOSED FOR BUSINESS sign hung on the front door. The Greek's comments to Shade had been true. The Diner was sold. The sign announced that a packaged liquor store would soon be opening on the site.

It seemed to all of us that things had happened so quickly, and without warning. But, of course, there had been a warning; we'd simply chosen to ignore it. And now the Diner, too, was gone. Closed, darkened. No more neon.

We leaned against our cars and softly, reverently, told some classic Diner stories. No one was in the mood for laughter, but eventually the laughs came. It was unavoidable. Like tears, laughter often comes when you least expect it.

Then our attention turned back to Neil.

"It's going to happen, so we might as well face it," said Turko. "It's definitely going to happen to every one of us, one way or another. One day it'll happen. It'll happen."

"No!" That was Eggy, mocking Turko's statement.

Ben chimed in, "Last month, so help me, this happened. It was when I was still with Janet. We were driving—you know my life's not exactly going great—and I realized . . . I know this is going to sound ridiculous, and you can laugh . . . I'm listening to the radio, and for the first time, I realize Puff is dead."

"What?" I asked.

"Puff is dead," Ben reiterated.

"Puff the Magic Dragon? The song?" I asked.

"Yes," said Ben. "I guess I never listened to it before, I mean, really listened to it. It was so sad. It's the passing of youth. Anyway, I'm listening to the radio, and honest to God . . . honest to God, I'm crying."

"Stop it," said Turko, "this is too tragic," and we all broke up laughing.

But Ben kept going, "I'm telling you, Puff died. I mean, I really got emotional about it."

Turko thought this over, then said, "Why did it suddenly occur to you that Puff is dead?"

"Because," Ben said emphatically, "Puff died and Little Jackie Paper went on to play with things kids don't play with anymore. And I always wanted to have that joy. I never wanted to lose that, you know . . . that thing."

I had a pretty good knowledge of the song, since I had used it on one of the sketches on *The Ranger Al Show*. "Not beating 'Puff the Magic Dragon' to death," I said, "but can't you return to Honah Lee anytime you want?"

Ben thought about that for a long moment, then shrugged and said, "Sure," which completely broke us up again.

Shade's car pulled into the lot and he stepped out carrying a cardboard box filled with coffee cups.

"That was deep, Ben. Well . . . semideep," Turko said, still laughing.

Then I brought up the subject I knew we'd all been thinking about. "He didn't want to go in the army, he had Danny's note, but he went anyway."

"I think he was proud of the uniform," said Ben.

"But he was opposed to Vietnam."

"Maybe," said Turko, "but Neil never said that."

"True." And I thought about it. "You never knew with Neil. Maybe you're right. He died in uniform, and in some ways he was like a casualty of war . . . but a war much bigger than Vietnam."

We lifted our paper cups of coffee up into the air. "To Neil," everyone said.

Silently, I turned to the building behind me, lifted my cup in the direction of the darkened door, and I said goodbye to the Diner as well.

Thirty

I sat in the film library late at night. I had been there for over seven hours, alone, smoking cigarettes, drinking coffee, and watching films on the small projector. I wanted to be alone. I wanted to think, but I really couldn't, so I just stared at films.

I had seen *Public Enemy*, John Ford's *Stagecoach*, and Howard Hawks' *His Girl Friday*, and now I was watching Fred Astaire and Ginger Rogers as they danced on a shiny black floor, looking dignified and regal. I didn't turn the sound on, which made the dance more impressive. I remembered the comment someone once made about Ginger Rogers: "She did everything that Astaire did, except backwards and in heels." I don't know why that came to mind.

I'd never before experienced the death of someone so close to me. There were a couple of aunts that had died, but I hadn't known them well. And they were old, at least they seemed so at the time. Neil was from my own generation. The prospect of death had never frightened me, probably because I had been so close to it during my years in and out of the hospital, but now I was frightened, not for myself, but that others I was close to might die. As I looked at the screen, Fred and Ginger continued to dance. But I also saw myself wheeled into one operating room after another. They kept dancing as I was lying in a hospital bed, bottles hanging from stands and tubes running out from under the sheets. There was the distant sound of a nurse. "His blood pressure is dropping. It's dropping!"

They continued to dance as a flurry of nurses and doctors rushed to my bedside, raised my legs, and packed me in ice. Then Fred and Ginger were dancing at Fort Holabird on that snowy morning as Neil tore up Danny's note.

The images on the screen went in and out of focus . . . and then I fell asleep.

One of the virtues of living in the East is that there are seasons—four distinct periods of change. Neil died in March, when it was brown and bare and cold, the end of winter. Within weeks, everything was sunny, trees were green and flowers were in bloom. It made it seem as if Neil had died long ago in another place.

One afternoon Eggy, Ben, Turko, and I went to be fitted for tuxedos for my upcoming wedding to Annie. When Eggy showed up we had a good laugh at his expense. He was dressed as an up-scale hippie.

"Laugh, guys. Laugh," he said. "We're selling this stuff like hotcakes over at Sol's. Hotcakes."

His wardrobe consisted of a red-white-and-blue-striped shirt that was open to the chest, and dark blue velvet pants, not quite bell-bottoms but slightly flared. He also wore a neckerchief that had white stars on a blue background.

"I'm a vision, don't deny it," Eggy said, so proud of his look.

Ben was measured and got pissed at the tailor for adding two inches onto his waist size. But after double and triple checking the tape measure for accuracy, he had to face the fact that he'd put on yet more weight.

Janet had given birth to a seven-and-a-half-pound baby girl, but Ben had never seen his young daughter. Janet's father had forbidden him access. Since they weren't legally separated, there wasn't much he could do about it.

One evening, in Mandell's, we sat for hours as Ben went into a drug-induced tirade against his father-in-law and laid out a plan to get to see his daughter.

"I'm going to kidnap the family dog," he told us.

"Dog?" I asked.

"Yeah. The old fart loves that dog."

"What good is it kidnapping the dog?" asked Turko.

"Then," Ben said, "I can make a trade. I get to see her, he gets his dog back. He loves that fucking stupid wire-haired something or other . . . corgi or Jack Russell . . . who the fuck knows what that piece of shit is, that goddamn dog that he loves. He'll be whimpering like a baby when I tell him I've got his dog. It'll drive him crazy. He won't be able to see the goddamn thing; he won't be able to walk it with that stupid little blanket that he puts on, that bullshit blanket he puts on that weaselly four-legged creature. I'll tell him, You're not getting it back. You're not getting it back until I see my baby girl, you understand me? You're not getting the dog back. I don't give a fuck. If you want to call the police on me, call them, because you're never going to see that dog. So let me see my baby or I'll kill the dog if I have to. I'll kill the dog!"

This preposterously moronic monologue went on for a good fifteen minutes, in great detail. Then it turned into the planning stage, with all the strategy of a war movie, and we were minutes away from saying, "Let's synchronize our watches."

I started to hum the theme from *The Guns of Navarone*. That caused a quick confrontation between Ben and me. "Your fucking pissy attitude is getting on my nerves, Bobby."

"I just thought you needed a little music to accompany the dog caper."

"You think this is funny? You think this plan is funny?" he asked angrily.

"Yes, I do," I told him.

With that, Turko and Eggy broke into laughter. Ben turned his attention to the other guys. He looked at them for a long beat as they laughed and somehow his anger died. Then he said, "You're right, Bobby. Stupid idea," and pulled on his lower eyelid and gave us his familiar "You're me."

It's hard to watch a friend fuck up his own life, but there was little I could do to change the course Ben was on. Eggy and Turko were also concerned, but we all felt helpless. There was no such thing as drug rehab or counseling back then. The attitude was, You fuck up, you pay the price.

As we talked the night away, I couldn't help but look through the big glass window of Mandell's and over at the closed Diner across the street. A sign had been installed but not yet lit, which said HILLTOP LIQUORS. The shiny aluminum exterior was in the process of being covered by a fake brick façade.

The liquor store opened a few weeks after that, but over the years, to the best of my knowledge, not one of my friends ever set foot in that place to buy a six-pack of beer, or anything else for that matter. Not one.

Certainly Berger never did. His cool sounds of jazz had filled the night air, providing the sound track for the Diner years. Now there was no need for the music, and so Berger was gone. When the Diner closed, he just disappeared.

As Turko was being fitted for his tux, he admitted, slightly embarrassed, that he was seeing Neddy again. "Just seeing her . . . talking, you know."

"How is she doing?" I asked.

"Like we're all doing," he said.

He mentioned that, in addition to going to the Maryland Institute, she was getting more involved with the antiwar movement and had participated in several demonstrations in Baltimore and Washington. The war was now becoming a part of our daily lives, and more and more a part of our conversations.

"Does anybody understand this fucking 'domino theory' yet?" Eggy asked.

And that set us off on that topic. There were the pros and cons. Eggy's approach was, "Why do we need to fucking get involved? Let the north kill the south, the south kill the north. Who gives a fuck?"

Turko's opinion was that if one Southeast Asian country fell, they would all turn Communist. Ben would go back to one of his old arguments. "We didn't care that Poland or Czechoslovakia got to be Communist. Why are we concerned with what's going on in Southeast Asia?"

Later, as we were changing back into our street clothes, I asked Turko, "What's been going on with the Cromwell story? Has that faded from sight?"

"No," he said.

In fact, he had heard indirectly, through somebody who knew somebody, that Cromwell was still pissed and still looking to get him.

"But there's a glimmer of hope," Turko said. "The Colts dropped him from their roster. Maybe he'll get picked up by another team and get the fuck out of town. I should be so lucky."

But he wasn't so lucky. No one picked up Cromwell after he got cut, so he stayed in Baltimore, and there would be that inevitable meeting.

As the weeks passed, I continued to AD the evening news, now with Duke. He had heard about my one-night directing stint and had given me more responsibility. On several occasions I got to direct the weekend news. I was now officially a young hotshot kid being groomed for a full-time directorship. There were rumors that Duke was moving on to the network.

I was in the directors' lounge early in the afternoon, bullshitting with Mickey and a couple of the new directors, when I got a call to go and see John Haynes.

"Oooh, this could be trouble," Mickey said.

"Trouble?"

"Yeah. I hear they're looking to make cutbacks."

"Really?"

"I'm fucking with you. Go on, go see him."

That evening Annie and I had made plans to have a parents' dinner. It wasn't as if they needed to get acquainted since they had known one another almost since I was born. But we thought it would be a nice thing to do. As it turned out, it was perfect timing for me to share my news.

We were at Hausner's Restaurant, one of Baltimore's more unusual restaurants. Every inch of wall space in the various dining rooms was covered in artwork. Some of it was good, but most of it was dreadful. I knew something about ugly artwork since I had attempted to paint several times in my early life.

Everyone was in a jovial mood as I began to tell them about my meeting with John Haynes. I played it out for all it was worth, milked the story. Finally, Annie interrupted and made me get to the punch line.

"Then Haynes said, 'I pride myself on having a top staff and I know a news director when I see one.' " I looked at everyone listening to me attentively. "He said this as he stood behind his desk. His desk was very clean, very few things on it."

Annie shook her head, smiling, but I still took my time because the best part of the story was about to be revealed and I wanted every bit of drama possible.

"So Haynes looks me in the eye and says: 'I'm going to offer you a director's position at fifteen thousand dollars a year to start.' "

Both sets of parents applauded and Annie hugged me. They were all thrilled.

"You're a director!" my father yelled proudly.

"Not yet," I said.

"What do you mean, not yet?" Annie asked.

"This is a big step."

"Especially when they're only paying you fifty dollars a week now," my mother said, a huge smile on her face and a little piece of lettuce stuck between her teeth.

"Fifteen thousand!" said Annie's father. "That's gonna be a big help for you two."

"Haynes told me to think it over this evening and give him an answer tomorrow."

"What's to think about for God's sake?" my father asked.

"I don't know. He said think about it."

My father laughed. "You should have said, 'I already thought about it. It's a done deal.' "

I could see how pleased my father was. Suddenly I had legitimacy. Annie was ecstatic, the first time she seemed happy since Neil's death.

"You did it, Bobby," Annie said excitedly, "on your own terms."

It was an extremely pleasant dinner. My news seemed to let

them all move on from Neil's death. It was as if it made them aware that life was going on—and would continue to go on—all around them. At the end of the meal, we all toasted. Annie's father said, "To health and happiness . . . and I couldn't be happier, Bobby, that you are marrying my daughter."

As we clicked our glasses, it was impossible to imagine that our worlds would be turned upside down within twenty-four hours.

Thirty-One

At nine-thirty in the morning, I found myself walking down the hallway to Mr. Haynes' office. I was clean-shaven and had put on my good suit. A couple of guys passed me on my way and congratulated me, saying they'd heard the news. I felt pumped up. A director at twenty-four years of age, I marched into Haynes' office triumphantly.

As I sat in the chair in front of his desk, he talked about my future at the station, how much progress I had made, how I'd learned from my mistakes, and how I should feel proud of my accomplishments. He mentioned the money a number of times, fifteen thousand dollars a year, and how much that represented to someone my age. It was so overwhelmingly positive, and yet the more I thought about the fifteen thousand dollars, the more it scared me.

I had images of carrying a bag of cash into a bank and a wide-eyed bank teller saying, "That's fifteen thousand dollars." I thought of myself up in the directors' lounge, the fifteen thousand dollars spread out on my desk. I opened the trunk of my car and before my eyes were stacks of money, piled high.

I heard myself saying to John Haynes, "If I take the fifteen thousand dollars, it's going to be very hard to ever quit. That's a lot of money."

Haynes smiled. "Yes, it is."

Not believing what was coming out of my mouth, I added, "When you make fifty dollars a week, it's very easy to quit. So with all due respect, sir, I quit."

I couldn't believe it. It was as if some part of my brain had thought about it and made the decision but hadn't bothered to inform me. In effect, Mr. Haynes and I both were hearing this for the first time.

He stared at me for what seemed like forever. "*What?*"

"I just can't accept it, sir. I'm going to get up and walk away from that fifty-dollar-a-week job because I won't be able to walk away from fifteen thousand dollars. I'll never be able to give it up."

"Why would you *want* to give it up?"

"I don't know, sir. Believe me, I'm as surprised as you are."

And before John Haynes could say anything else, I stood up, shook his hand, said goodbye, and walked out of his office.

I headed down the hallway, stunned by my own actions. A chill spread through my whole body. As I crossed the reception area, the television was on—the Ranger Al theme was playing and the show was about to end. Then I pushed the front door and left the building.

I sat in my car, not moving, in a state of shock. I had just done the single craziest thing I'd ever done in my life. I stared at myself in the rearview mirror to make sure it was really me. "What did I do?" I said aloud to the reflection. "What the fuck did I do?"

I was completely stunned. How could I have walked out? I was totally baffled. And suddenly positive I had made a terrible mistake.

I got out of the car and started to walk back into the station. I would apologize. It would be easy. "Mr. Haynes, it was a slip of the tongue. It was actually more than a slip of the tongue, it was whole sentences, but I was wrong. I was definitely wrong. Mr. Haynes I was just excited . . . I was so thrilled. God forgive me, Mr. Haynes. Please forget what I said. I was out of my mind. I was euphoric, that's what it was, Mr. Haynes. I was so euphoric and I said the wrong thing because I . . . because I . . . because I . . ." But I couldn't come up with a good enough explanation. Then I realized that I was still standing outside the front door looking in.

I pushed on the door and opened it, but didn't step into the building. Instead I let the door slowly close and stared blankly into the lobby.

What had I done? What in the fuck had I done?

Walking back to my car, I began to question my own identity as I passed the other cars in the parking lot. "My name is Bobby Shine. Is that correct?" I said out loud to my reflection in the back window of a Ford Galaxy 500.

There was once a television show called *The Invaders* in which extraterrestrials would take over the bodies of humans. I honestly felt as if I had been invaded. Taken over. My mind was racing out of control. *Is this me? Is this really me?*

I wanted to go to the Diner. Run this by the guys, who would make me explain, help me understand. But the Diner was gone and, in a sense, so were the guys. Neil was dead. Ben was a drugged-out mess. Turko hardly ever went outside, he was still so afraid of Cromwell. And Eggy seemed to be working all the time. So instead I made my way to the White Tower coffee shop and sat alone. It was aptly named—everything was sparkling clean and perfectly white as the morning light flooded the shop. There seemed to be no color. The place was empty except for me. As I sipped my coffee at the counter, I did my best to concoct a theory to explain my actions. Perhaps the subconscious brain worked privately and reached conclusions without informing the conscious side of the brain. I kept working on this theory. If that was indeed the case, the subconscious side of my brain hadn't bothered to provide the conscious entity with the slightest bit of information to explain my unusual behavior. So, in effect, I was left out of the decision-making process. I let this sink in for a while and finally decided it was crazy. I couldn't even rationalize correctly. I couldn't come up with one logical reason for what I'd just done. So I gave up thinking about it and actually started to laugh in that empty, white-tiled coffee shop. It must have seemed to the waitress as if I had lost my mind. And maybe I had.

To celebrate the promotion, Annie and I had planned to meet on the steps of the church across from the flower mart in Mount Vernon. The outdoor market was once a very Waspy social activity, but in the last few years it had been changing. Black people were beginning to attend and there were newspaper articles stating that hippies were going to be a strong presence at this year's event, possibly to use it as an antiwar venue. The police force was on alert, nervous about public pot-smoking and worried about a potential demonstration. There was a lot of tension lately between the police and both the hippie and black communities. There had been a recent civil rights march where a number of people had been arrested. Some minor violence had erupted as well.

I was oblivious to the tension in the air, though. All I'd thought about—before my meeting with Mr. Haynes—was how pleasant it would be to stroll through the flower mart with Annie, hand in hand, reveling in our future. Now, all I could think about was how hurt and angry she was going to be when I told her what I'd done.

Nothing prepared me for this year's mart. The crowds were massive, close to sixty thousand people. And it all felt very confrontational. A huge collection of Baltimore's Wasp community was face to face with an equal number of stoned-out hippies, would-be hippies, and the "coloreds," as I heard one Wasp lady say, all dressed up as if she were attending the Easter parade. "So many coloreds," she said to the woman next to her. Her friend, dressed in much the same manner, agreed. "What's the mart coming to?" was her response.

It was nearly impossible to move through the throngs. Everyone stood shoulder to shoulder, inching in and around the myriad booths and stalls selling flowers, used books, fudge, hot dogs, crab cakes, and baked goods. The air was filled with the familiar scent of the popular lemon-and-peppermint-stick confection. This Baltimore tradition consisted of a lemon with a hole cut through the middle. A peppermint stick was poked into the hole the way a straw might be, and when the stick was sucked, the sour juice of the lemon penetrated the peppermint and made an unusually delicious taste. I have no idea why this was a Baltimore tradition, but even today I can smell and taste the combination of lemon and peppermint from that day's fair.

As I did my best to move through the crowd, over a loudspeaker I heard the flower mart song, which sounded as if it came from the turn of the century:

> There's a very gay affair
> In which all the people share
> In the merry, merry month of May
> There are flowers to be bought
> And the lemon sticks are sought
> And the music of the band will play

Flower mart, flower mart
Down in Mount Washington Square
Come with me, come with me . . .

When the song ended, I heard one man say to a hippie who had his shirt open to the waist, "If I had so little hair on *my* chest, I think I'd button up my shirt." To which the hippie replied, "If I had as few brains in my head, *dad*, I'd keep my fucking mouth buttoned."

Bongo drums and guitar music filled the air now. The older people complained to each other, disgusted and angry at the hippie takeover of the city's traditional rite of spring.

I passed more and more policemen working their walkie-talkies. They seemed to be tracking the movements of young black male students at the mart, watching them with particular care and caution.

Although I hadn't yet seen him, Turko was in the crowd with Neddy, who was passing out anti-Vietnam War pamphlets. Turko wasn't making any romantic progress with her, she was still too devastated by Neil's death, but he couldn't quite let her go. Being with her, whenever she would allow it, was good enough for him.

I finally caught up with Annie on the church steps. "God, can you believe this mob? I've never seen anything like it. I'm sorry I'm late. I apologize."

"I just got here myself."

I had to tell her about the John Haynes meeting, but I wanted to get to a place that was slightly less chaotic, so we moved toward the Peabody Conservatory. As we approached it, I noticed a large flag draped over the west wall. It was later reported in the newspaper that it was a thirty-by-forty-two-foot replica of the 1814 fifteen-star flag.

We tried to find a quiet spot, but it was impossible. We were trapped in the crowd. So amidst all the noise and the confusion around us, I told Annie what took place with Mr. Haynes.

Shaking her head, having to yell to be heard, she said, "You did *what*?"

"I just found myself saying 'I quit,' " I yelled back.

She was breathing heavier now, trembling, and I kept trying to explain as best I could. I wanted her to understand, more than I'd ever wanted anything in my life, but *I* didn't understand. So how could she?

The more I talked, the worse it began to sound.

"Bobby, what is wrong with you?" she cried. Then she quickly began to move away from me, disappearing into the crowd.

"Annie, listen to me," I pleaded as I followed her.

She yelled back, "You walked away from law school with a year to go, and now this?"

"I couldn't do it," I screamed, my voice getting hoarse. "I just couldn't. I went down that hall. I was ready. Guys congratulated me. I don't know why. I just couldn't do it."

Then she stopped and turned back toward me, trying to compose herself while people jostled her as they passed. There were tears in her eyes as she spoke. "I can't take all these things happening to me. Neil . . . and now this."

"I know, Annie. I understand. I wish I didn't have to tell you."

"I wish you hadn't *done* it."

She moved away again, heading over to the small park that flanked the Washington Monument. We were near the spot of Neil's circular march. I wished we were anywhere but there, but I followed her. Hippies lay in the grass playing music, singing and dancing, smoking pot. It was festive and lively, but I felt as if I couldn't breathe. When I caught up with Annie, she said, "How can I expect my parents to understand, for God's sake? How do I explain that you walked away from a job you desperately wanted? I don't understand you."

I grabbed her and held her close to me. "I can do that job. I can direct the news. I proved that. I've *done* it. That challenge is over. Money doesn't matter to me. It's what's next. That's what I want. I want the next thing."

Annie pulled back from me, and I felt the chill that came from her, and the anger.

"What is that, Bobby? What is the *next* thing?"

"I'm sorry. I didn't want this to happen. I know the timing stinks," I told her.

Then her anger boiled over and she started shaking and screaming. "It's not about the timing, Bobby! It's you! Don't you understand that? It's *you*!"

I didn't say anything for the longest moment. Around us, the traffic moved slowly. It seemed as if the entire city was bottled up. Then Annie said, no longer yelling, "I can't marry you."

The statement startled me. Life had surprised me plenty. Nothing had turned out the way I'd always thought it would. But the one thing I knew was that Annie and I were permanent. We were forever. We *had* to be. "What are you talking about?"

Now horns were blaring. The traffic jam was turning ugly.

"I can't," she said. Tears ran down her face. "One day you want this, and then you want that. You can't settle on anything."

"Why do I have to *settle* for things now?"

"How do I know that you won't change your mind about *us*? How do I know that? You can't make up your mind about anything. Am I the next thing you want or the next thing you're going to walk away from?"

"Annie, I'll never change my mind about you. I never have. I never will."

She looked at me and wiped the tears off her cheeks. She began to walk up the street against the heavy traffic, but this time I didn't follow.

Everything was so chaotic—the horns blaring, the chatter

from the crowd, the music, all the noise . . . then it was quiet. It all disappeared for me. There was only silence. Except for Annie's voice saying "I can't marry you." I watched her disappear. Then I walked back through the park toward the center of the flower mart. A young hippie was playing a new song by Procol Harum on his guitar—"Whiter Shade of Pale." I didn't know what the song meant, and at that moment I didn't care.

In the distance I saw Turko and Neddy, so I moved toward them. I wasn't the only person who saw them at that moment. John Cromwell was there too, checking out the stalls with his secretary girlfriend. She was sucking on the flower mart favorite, the lemon-and-peppermint-stick treat, when she nudged Cromwell and pointed to Turko. The ex–Baltimore Colt sliced through the crowd as if he was attacking an offensive line, heading for the quarterback. People bounced off him as he moved in on Turko. Turko intuitively knew who it was heading in his direction, but it was too late for him to make a getaway.

It was too late for a lot of things. There's perception and there's reality. All too often the perception of what takes place creates the harsh reality that follows. A lit match by itself is not dangerous, but drop it into a pool of gasoline and you have an explosion.

Local police were prepared for something to go wrong at the flower mart. They were fearful of the new counterculture generation they were confronting. They were fearful, too, of a newly empowered young black community.

The flower mart was a Baltimore institution, and the white and the genteel—the old regulars—were afraid of change, and felt as if they were under siege. Their territory was being taken over by the undesirables, the uninvited, the unwelcome.

Cromwell was under control when he approached Turko.

"Look, it was a big misunderstanding," Turko began. "Believe me, the last thing I want to do is get involved with your girl-friend."

"Why?" Cromwell asked suspiciously. "You don't think she's attractive?"

"No, no, she is. But as soon as I heard you were going with her . . . hey, it's not my style, that's what I'm saying."

They talked for several moments, Turko sincere in his expla-nation, and Cromwell nodded. He believed what he was hearing. "I don't want you talking about her," he warned. "We clear about that? I don't want to hear you boasting about what you did with my lady."

Turko agreed. It seemed as if a peace treaty was in place. Cromwell seemed more than amicable. And then it all happened because of one word.

"Boy," Turko said, "I'm glad that's over."

"What?" Cromwell stiffened. He was suddenly angry.

"What?" Turko responded, confused.

"You call me a fucking *boy*?" Cromwell's anger was ready to burst now.

Turko didn't have any idea what he meant. "What do you mean, 'boy'?"

Taking this for a racial insult, Cromwell pushed Turko in the chest. The Turk lost his balance and toppled into two dowdy middle-aged women festooned with large flowery hats. They all fell to the ground.

A policeman saw Cromwell's action and sprinted toward him.

One of the women on the ground began yelling at Cromwell. "My God! You monster! You monster!"

The policeman grabbed Cromwell by his shirt, but the football player was looking toward the two women, one crying in pain, the other accusing him—he was startled by what had just hap-pened. So he didn't know it was a policeman grabbing at his sleeve. As a reflex, his arm pushed away, recoiling against the body contact, and his hand hit the policeman's face. The policeman immediately pulled out his billy club and swung at the black man, cracking him in the back, dropping the defensive end to the ground. The secretary screamed.

Four young black students began yelling angrily. The policeman waved his billy club threateningly, trying to make them back off. Two of the black youths took up the challenge and jumped him. Then total chaos broke out.

I was caught in a tide of people trying to get away from the violence. Mounted police began to move in when the fighting broke out. Hippies responded to this invasion of force by chanting "Pig! Pig! Pig!" Some took used books from the stalls and threw them at the police.

Turko kept trying to get to his feet but was continually knocked down by panicky people running in every direction. The hoof of one of the mounted police horses stepped on his ankle and he yelled out in pain. It was pandemonium.

Blacks were fighting hippies, cops were swinging nightsticks, and lemons, flowerpots, books, corn on the cob, hot dogs, chunks of ice—items from the flower mart stalls—flew through the air.

Neddy was hurling insults at the police: "Pigs! Pigs! Pigs! Fucking pigs!" I saw her struck on the forehead by a flying book. It sliced a cut across the top of her eyebrow and blood poured down her face.

That was the last time I ever saw Neddy. She became an image frozen in time: a beautiful girl, flowers in her blond hair, wearing a Salvation Army thrift store vintage sundress as gold as the day had begun . . . covered in blood. None of us ever saw her again. Ever.

I finally made my way over to Turko, who was holding on to his ankle and in serious pain. I lifted him up and tried to move through the crowd. We were caught in a war zone; the static sound of police radios filled the air as deployment information was being relayed. Fifteen feet away, Cromwell was struggling to get back on his feet as several uniformed policemen were trying to cuff him.

The secretary was hysterically pleading, "It's all a mistake! It's just a mistake!"

Cromwell tried yet again to break free but the policeman's hard billy club struck him in the face and blood spurted out of his cheek.

A tough-looking white teenage boy, seeing the secretary crying over the limp and bleeding Cromwell, yelled out, "Nigger lover!" and he started kicking at her. Then a billy club cracked against the tough kid and he, too, fell to the ground.

I tried to drag Turko away from the madness all around us. There was so much pent-up resentment and hatred—the ignorance of the ill-informed—and it all exploded on that day Baltimore celebrated the beauty of spring. The last thing I remember was the large replica of the 1814 flag bursting into flames. Above it all, at the top of the monument, stood the father of our country, George Washington, who must have been wondering what had become of his children.

There were various reports on the news. Lieutenant Colonel Frank J. Battaglie, the police department's chief of patrol, intimated that the violence had been organized and was part of a preconceived plan. "I think they were trying to shut the flower mart down," he intoned. He estimated that 250 police took part in the dispersal action. Twenty-seven people were arrested and 16 had to be hospitalized.

As I lay in my room, I watched the images being replayed on

television. They showed two students—one black, one white—perched at the top of a statue of John Eager Howard, whoever the hell he was. The white student was waving the Confederate flag, the black student waving the American flag.

Mrs. Robert C. Ferrara, president of the Civic League, which sponsored the flower mart, was interviewed, and said: "I hope the incidents that occurred will be a onetime thing and will go away, like the seventeen-year locusts." She was referring to the strange phenomenon that took place in Baltimore every seventeen years, when, as if out of nowhere, locusts attacked the city. On the first morning I was alive for their invasion, I remember swatting them as I walked to school. The air was thick with these bugs, almost like falling snow. When I was in my classroom I could hear the constant thumping sounds of locusts thrusting themselves against the school windows. We were under attack. We thought we were going to die, that the world was coming to an end, but then within days the locusts just disappeared and didn't come back for another seventeen years. Once they were gone, it was as if nothing had ever happened. They left no mark, no scars. But the battle at the flower mart was another matter. Mrs. Ferrara's wishful thinking was just that. Things would grow progressively worse before they got better in the city I loved. Within a year, sections of Baltimore would burn down and be torn apart in rage. And when the fires were extinguished, the scars of the city would not fade from mind as quickly as the locusts had.

For over a week I kept mostly to myself in my room at home, traumatized by the violent events at the flower mart and reflecting on my life and how it had suddenly veered off course. I was out of work. I was no longer getting married and no one understood me. By the end of the week, I felt I was beginning to make sense out of all of it.

I decided Eddie Collier was at the heart of it. He was thirty-six years old then, and I had AD'd for him on a number of occasions. I remember on one broadcast, when he had his finger up pointing to a monitor ready to snap his fingers, I saw a slight tremor, a sign of nervousness. I made a quick judgment right then and there. The job of directing was important to him—not creatively but financially. He had a wife and kids and he couldn't afford to make a mistake because he couldn't afford to be fired. That job was his bread and butter.

To me, directing the news was an exercise. There was nothing to be nervous about, there was no thrill to it other than the energy rush that came with doing the show correctly. Once I'd done it a number of times, the rush became old hat, and without even being aware of it, I'd begun looking for new things to stimulate me. The reward at the station was money but I didn't care about that. I wanted creative stimulation. I didn't expect most people to understand. But I had to try to make Annie understand. If she couldn't, then I knew I would lose her, and the idea of that loss was devastating to me.

I was aimlessly driving in my car, formulating what I was going to say to Annie, when the radio newscaster reported that the Pentagon had announced that the United States had lost its five hundredth plane of the war. The newscaster went on to say that the

Vietcong had ambushed a truck convoy, damaging 82 out of 121 trucks. In New York, seventy thousand people marched in support of the Vietnam War.

The next thing I knew, I was driving into the cemetery where Neil was buried. I walked across the peaceful grounds to his gravestone. It was warm and sunny, so different from the day he was buried. I stared at Neil's gravestone: "In Memory, Neil Tilden, 1942–1967." We both quit law school in our final year. We both loved Annie, and we had both let her down. We had both disappointed her in different ways. She had lost a brother and, unless I could change her mind, a husband-to-be. Neil was gone, and nothing could be done about that. I still had a chance, I realized.

Neil was dead, but what was to become of me? Where was I going? I didn't feel confident about making Annie believe in me again because, as near as I could tell, the answers to these questions were:

Nothing.

And nowhere.

Thirty-Two

As the late afternoon light filtered through the windows of Long-fellow's, I leaned against the bar, tearing a dollar bill into four parts. The bar was not officially open and we were the only ones in the place.

Turko, Eggy, and Ben watched as I ripped the money as evenly as possible. Then I said, "I saw this in a movie once."

"Which one?" Turko wanted to know.

"I can't remember, but the four friends agreed to meet in ten years. We all hold on to our piece of the dollar, and we put it back together then." I handed a piece of the dollar to each of the guys.

"Three pieces will be easy to put back together, Bobby," Ben said quietly. "It's your piece I'm worried about."

I had already laid out my plan to the guys. Actually, it wasn't much of a plan; it was just getting in my car and going.

"California's a long way off," said Turko, holding his piece of the dollar.

"Ten years," I responded with as much confidence as I could muster. Then I opened my wallet and slipped the paper behind my driver's license.

Ben popped a pill and chased it with some water. "All those people out there in California, they just jump into convertibles.

Never have to open the doors. I never bought into that . . . never bought into that."

Eggy started laughing, and I asked why. "When I was a kid," he said, "I was with my father out in the Midwest once. My father asked this farmer along the road for directions and the farmer said, 'Well, that'll be four sees from here.' My father said to him, 'What's that?' And the farmer said, 'As far as you can see, four times.' "

We shared his laugh, and I said, "Well, the drive for me will be a lot longer than four sees."

Turko looked at me very seriously and said with some concern, "I remember Neil looking at Ben's postcard of the Golden Gate Bridge and talking about jumping off. Don't get any ideas, Bobby."

"Turko, give me a fucking break. Don't get all maudlin here. That was Neil. This is me."

Turko looked at the piece of the dollar bill, then pulled out his wallet and slipped the bill in. "Okay, I'm holding you to that."

Ben poured a beer for me and slipped it across the counter. I took a sip, then Ben said, "I'm not a great one to give advice, but see Annie before you leave. She might go with you."

Turko added, "She should."

"And she's worth it," Ben added.

"I know she is," I told them.

We talked about California some more, rehashing our dreams from years ago of seeing Sandra Dee and Tuesday Weld. I told them my theory that we were living in black and white and how California was Technicolor.

We lamented the changes that had taken place in the city over the past few years. How the movie district of Lexington Street was torn down for a high-rise.

"The smell of those Planters peanuts," Ben said. "That's what I miss."

"Mr. Peanut," Eggy added.

We talked about all the girls we knew, and the ones we wish we had dated, and the ones we wish we hadn't.

The hours ticked by, and we just kept talking about the past. Maybe we were afraid to talk about the future, but I think that probably we were more afraid that the past would soon fade from our minds, that those images, those feelings, those emotions, would be gone forever.

Four guys having drinks at a bar, and none of us could imagine what the next ten years would bring.

We toasted to a pause in our relationship and we toasted to a reunion, and then we said no more.

On the way over to Annie's, I didn't know if I could convince her to go with me. I couldn't come to grips with the fact that this might be the end of our relationship. The closer I got to her house, the more that possibility began to overwhelm me.

The headlights of my car hit the dark asphalt, and for no reason I remembered driving to Atlantic City some years earlier with Ben, Eggy, Turko, and Neil. Neil was driving, one of the few times we allowed him to get behind the wheel. A hard rain was falling. The Isley Brothers' "Shout" came on the radio, and it was like an explosion of energy. We listened to the song, our bodies bouncing in our seats, caught up in the music. It was infectious, and we were incapable of sitting still. The DJ was so into the record that he played it three times, back to back, and each replay seemed stronger than the first.

We barreled along the dark highway as the rain continued to fall. Five guys dancing in a sitting position. Then Neil lost control of the car. We started sliding sideways and cars swerved to avoid us, but we kept singing along to the song "Shout." Somehow we were not nervous or frightened, even as the car slid across the rain-slicked highway, heading for an embankment.

We were about to go over the edge when suddenly the back tires hit something and the car jolted to a stop. We were on the edge of the precipice, barely hanging on, so close to death, and yet we continued to sing, "Shout . . . kick up your heels, Shout!" For some reason, that moment never made much of an impression on us. We never talked about it. In the countless thousands of hours of Diner talk, we never recounted that story. But we did often talk about the song "Shout."

I pulled up at Annie's house, and before I could beep my horn she was out the front door and down the path to my car. She was wearing the bathrobe I loved so much, the one I found so sexy.

We sat and talked for a long while. I tried to explain everything once again. I spoke with more clarity—told her exactly what I was feeling and how much I loved her. Finally, I told her that I wanted her to come with me.

"I can't," she said sadly. "I just can't."

"All I have to do is hit the gas pedal and we're on our way to California."

Annie didn't even have to think about it. "I'm not made that way," she said. "I can't just go—no idea where I'm going or what's going to happen. It scares me too much."

"I love you, Annie."

She leaned toward me and kissed me lightly on the lips. "I love you, too. More than you'll ever believe." Then she quickly got out of the car and started up the path.

I opened my car door, stepped out, and called out to her, "You know what Neil wanted to do more than anything else? What he wanted to become?"

She turned back to face me, a questioning look on her face.

"He told me once when he was drunk, or stoned. He said he wanted to be an automotive designer."

"He never said anything about that to me."

"He drew these amazing designs—cars of the future."

Annie was surprised. "He never showed them to me."

"He said that when he was about fourteen, he mentioned it to his dad."

"What did my father say?"

"Neil said all he did was laugh. And from that time on Neil just wrote it off as a silly idea, a childish dream."

I waited for a reply, but Annie said nothing.

Once again, I said, "Come with me, Annie." She shook her head, trying to hold her emotions in check. She had lost her brother, and now she was about to lose me. But she turned and walked back into the house. I watched for the longest time, hoping that she would open the door and change her mind. But that hope was not fulfilled. She never came back out.

I got into my car and pulled away.

I passed the sign that read ROUTE 40 WEST. I would take it until it hit Route 66, and then drive until the end of the land—the far side of the continent. *As far as dreamers can go,* as Neil once said.

But I was different from those who had migrated west before me because I had no dream, I didn't know what I wanted. I only knew that I had to run from what I didn't want. Even if it meant saying goodbye to things and people I loved.

I was leaving behind incomplete stories. What would happen to Ben and Janet, Eggy and Turko, and, most importantly, Annie? I didn't know and it saddened me—in some ways terrified me—that I might never find out. I was seized with the realization that what we want to do, what we are capable of doing, and what good fortune will allow are all only variables in some unknown equation.

When we're in our early twenties, some of us are consumed with great ambition. Some of us are content to drift, while others just want to party. But none of that truly determines one's future. There are too many changes; too many accidents. Too many twists of fate. There are too many different realities. In my reality, Freddie Krauss will forever be sailing over the top of the Texaco sign in his red windbreaker. He survived one accident after another, therefore I thought he would *always* be lucky—that luck was part of his destiny. But the Houdini of our time was stabbed to death in a Saigon bar by a waitress because she didn't like the tip he left. The truth is that reality does not acknowledge continuity. And destiny is what we make it. The size of a tip can literally be a matter of life or death.

I remember watching a goose one day and noticing that it could rotate its head to scratch its back. Now, one would assume that geese couldn't do that when the species began. But they never gave up, and over the span of hundreds of thousands of years, maybe more, the head turned a little further and a little further still, until one day one goose was capable of scratching its own back. Then other geese reached that stage. The geese that did not have the fortitude—or a strong enough need to scratch their backs—died off, I presume.

But what was it about the goose that made it *want* to rotate its head? What was it about that itch that made the goose so persistent? How bad could that itch have been, or the need to scratch it, that for so many years it kept trying to reach that spot, so that for a few precious seconds it would feel a tiny bit better? Can it be that that's all we are trying to do? Trying to reach that impossible spot so, for a few brief seconds, we might all feel a little better?

I just threw my hands up in the air—I understood nothing. I only knew that the countryside was becoming less and less familiar to me, and everything in front of me was brand new.

The blue light of the morning was beginning to tint the sky, the sun danced in my side-view mirror, and the rolling hills began to turn a dark green as the black road took me farther away from home. I suddenly felt myself outside of the gravitational pull of Baltimore—my universe, the cradle of my youth—and I thought of the explorers that sailed uncharted oceans in search of land. I wasn't nearly as daring, but I was just as afraid of the unknown. The big trick was not to be fearful, I decided, but to embrace the journey, no matter where it led. I tried to accept that notion, and suddenly I imagined that the tide was at my back, the wind behind me.

I was no longer fighting to get away, I was being taken to a new place, and I turned my rearview mirror away so I couldn't see where I had been.

And then . . . there are gaps.

Director-screenwriter-producer Barry Levinson was awarded the 1988 Best Director Oscar for the multiple-award-winning *Rain Man*, starring Dustin Hoffman and Tom Cruise. In 1987 he directed Robin Williams in the comedy *Good Morning, Vietnam*, which went on to become one of the year's most acclaimed and popular movies. In 1991 *Bugsy*, which was directed and produced by Levinson, was nominated for ten Academy Awards, including Best Picture and Best Director.

Born and raised in Baltimore, Levinson has used his hometown as the setting for four widely praised features: *Diner*, which marked his directorial debut, *Tin Men*, *Avalon*, and *Liberty Heights*.

After attending American University in Washington, D.C., Levinson moved to Los Angeles, where he began acting as well as writing and performing comedy routines. He then went on to write several television variety shows, including *The Marty Feldman Comedy Machine*, which originated in England, *The Tim Conway Show*, and *The Carol Burnett Show*. A meeting with Mel Brooks led Levinson to collaborate with the veteran comedian on the features *Silent Movie* and *High Anxiety*.

As a screenwriter, Levinson has received three Academy Award nominations, for . . . *And Justice for All*, *Diner*, and *Avalon*. Levinson's other directorial credits include *The Natural*, *Disclosure*, *Wag the Dog*, *Bandits*, and, most recently, *Envy*.

He returned to Baltimore to film the television series *Homicide: Life on the Street*. His work on this drama earned him an Emmy for Best Individual Director of a Drama Series, three Peabody Awards, the Quality Television Founders Award, and two TCA Awards for program of the year and drama of the year. Levinson and Baltimore Pictures also received the 1999 Humanitas Award for the series' "Shades of Gray" episode.

Levinson produced such films as *Quiz Show*, *Donnie Brasco*, and *The Second Civil War* (HBO) through his production company Baltimore Pictures, Inc. At the beginning of 1998 he partnered with Paula Weinstein, forming Baltimore/Spring Creek Pictures. Together they produced *The Perfect Storm* and *Analyze This*.

Along with Tom Fontana, Levinson has also executive-produced the HBO television series *Oz*, which just finished its sixth and final season.

Sixty-Six is Levinson's first novel.